Josiah W. Whymper, Louis J. Jennings

Field Paths and Green Lanes

being country walks, chiefly in Surrey and Sussex

Josiah W. Whymper, Louis J. Jennings

Field Paths and Green Lanes
being country walks, chiefly in Surrey and Sussex

ISBN/EAN: 9783337231125

Printed in Europe, USA, Canada, Australia, Japan

Cover: Foto ©Andreas Hilbeck / pixelio.de

More available books at **www.hansebooks.com**

AMONG THE CHALK DOWNS.

ST. MARTHA'S CHAPEL, FROM NEWLANDS CORNER.

Frontispiece.

FIELD PATHS AND GREEN LANES.

BEING

COUNTRY WALKS, CHIEFLY IN SURREY AND SUSSEX.

By LOUIS J. JENNINGS.

ILLUSTRATED WITH SKETCHES BY J W. WHYMPER.

NEW YORK:
D. APPLETON AND COMPANY,
549 AND 551 BROADWAY.
1878.

PREFACE.

I AM not without hope that this little book will prove interesting, and in some degree useful, to those who find an unfailing source of pleasure in wandering over England, deeming nothing unworthy of notice, whether it be an ancient church or homestead, a grand old tree, a wild flower under a hedge, or a stray rustic by the road side. To anyone who has eyes, there is much to see in this small but infinitely varied England, so much that, as Emerson says, to see it well, "needs a hundred years." If a man cannot walk, it is perhaps better to ride or drive through the country than not to see it at all ; but walking is the best of all known means of getting from one place to another ; and take care to go with no other companions than the Handbook and a pocket-compass, for then you can cry halt wherever you please, and have no one's whims or oddities to perplex and harass you. It is not possible to feel solitary amid Nature's works, any more than to be lonely with all your books about you. Moreover, if you are trudging along unfettered by a companion, you may, by proper management, get the country folks whom you meet to talk to you, and from them pick up many a quaint saying or odd scrap of information ; but they are as shy of the tourists who hunt in couples as they are of the wild man who flies past them on a bicycle.

In these little expeditions of mine, I seldom lost an opportunity of having a few minutes' chat with the wayfarers on the road, and what they said to me, or I to them, I have faithfully set down. No attempt has been made to exhaust the attractions of any particular district, unless it be the tract of country for a dozen miles or so round Dorking, to which a tolerably thorough guide will be found in some of the Surrey chapters. All the walks described have been taken during the past year, during every month of which, in spite of all that is said adverse to the English climate, I found it not only possible, but extremely pleasant, to go forth upon my rambles whenever an opportunity offered itself.

I have invariably followed a green lane or a field path, wherever one could be found, and have endeavoured to give directions which will enable others to follow it also, for very seldom is it marked upon the maps. All that can be done is to ascertain the general direction, and jog along without further thought of the matter. Most of my walks were through secluded districts, abounding often with the wildest scenery; yet it would be possible, by an early start and the skilful use of the railroad, for a Londoner to take the best of them, and return to his home to sleep. I trust that the hints to this effect which I have thrown out in the course of these pages, will induce many a jaded townsman to betake himself to the fields and hills, and be of some help, too, to my American friends, who are willing to see far more of this country than they generally do, if they only knew how to set about it. There are few things in life better worth living for than the pleasure of starting out on foot, in fair health, and with no particular anxiety pressing upon the mind, for a long day amid all the beauties which Nature spreads before her true lovers by every hedgerow and brook and hill-side in England.

CONTENTS.

CHAPTER I.

WINCHELSEA AND RYE.

CHAPTER II.

ROUND ABOUT HASTINGS.

CHAPTER III.

TWO OLD CHURCHES.

CHAPTER XII.

TO LEITH HILL BY WOTTON.

CHAPTER XIII.

FROM DORKING TO LEATHERHEAD.

CHAPTER XIV.

TO GUILDFORD OVER THE HILLS.

CHAPTER XV.

FROM CATERHAM TO GODSTONE.

CHAPTER XVI.

NORBURY PARK, ALBURY, AND THE DEEPDENE.

CHAPTER XVII.

REIGATE, GATTON PARK, AND THE PILGRIM'S WAY.

CHAPTER XVIII.

REDHILL TO CROWHURST.

CHAPTER XIX.

EWHURST, ALBURY, AND CHILWORTH.

CHAPTER XX.

FROM EDENBRIDGE TO PENSHURST.

CHAPTER XXI.

THE WYE FROM ROSS TO CHEPSTOW.

LIST OF ILLUSTRATIONS.

FROM SKETCHES BY J. W. WHYMPER, AND PHOTOGRAPHS.

——◆——

FIELD PATHS AND GREEN LANES.

CHAPTER I.

WINCHELSEA AND RYE.

Old "Spithead and Portsmouth."—A Wondrous "Sea Change."—
St. Thomas's Church.—Old and New.—The Friars.—History
of Winchelsea, by a Native.—The Road to Camber Castle and
Rye.—Sheep Farming.—A City of the Past.—Rye Church.—
The Reflections of a Sexton.—The Butcher and the Lamb.—
The "Mermaid."—Peacock's.—The Plague.—Where is the
"Mermaid?"—The Dutch Tiles and Lone Widow.—A Field
Walk to Hastings.—The Hermit of the Beach.

THERE are two hills facing each other in the south-
eastern corner of Sussex, with three miles of marsh
land between them. On the one stands Winchelsea,
on the other, Rye. Both have been maritime towns
of great importance, the "Spithead and Portsmouth
of their day," as someone has said; but when the sea
deserts a maritime town, and sulkily withdraws to a
distance of two or three miles, what is to become of
it? Six hundred years ago Winchelsea could boast
of a very large commerce, but at that time it stood
three miles away from the present town, which is
comparatively modern, although it was founded in the

time of Edward the First. Doubly fatal has old ocean
been to Winchelsea, completely destroying the first
town by its untimely encroachments, and then ruin-
ing the new one by its equally untimely retreat. But
besides the raging of the sea, the inhabitants of these
parts were constantly harried by the French, who came
upon them at all sorts of unexpected times, slaughter-
ing their men, plundering them of their provisions,
and, what was much worse than all, carrying off their
"beautiful women." So quiet and deserted is the
place now that it is difficult to imagine it the scene
of wild excitement and daring deeds. The old church
and the court-hall, the gates, the ruins of the Lady
Chapel in the "Friars," a few old houses here and
there, are all that remain to remind the visitor of the
glories of Winchelsea. The great John Wesley well
called it a "poor skeleton." One feels, indeed, on
entering it almost as if one were wandering about in
another age amid the ruins of another world.

All that is now to be seen of the old church of St.
Thomas is the chancel, but that is spacious and beautiful, far finer even as a fragment than many a complete church which is run up at contract price in the
present days. Some of the monuments are magnificent, and contrast strangely with the modern slabs,
mere dabs of marble, which have been stuck upon the
walls. The old Alards under the exquisitely carved
canopies must wonder what race of men have now got
hold of England, and why they commemorate each
other with flat pieces of stone carved into uncouth

shapes? The ivy grows through the roof here and there, and time has levelled nave and aisles to the dust. Yet enough still stands to shew what a grand old church it must have been when the mothers and daughters of the town went to bed in fear and trembling lest their enemies, the French, should be at the gates.

The "Friars" stands a little way back from the roadside, and the ruins (which the stranger may see any Monday) are in the garden—a very pretty garden, with fine large ash-trees in it, and good sycamores, and a Portugal laurel which must be thirty feet in height. A monastery once stood here, and the shell of the choir of the chapel dedicated to the Virgin Mary still lies embosomed among the trees. On my way from this pleasant spot to the Strand gate, I learned the history of Winchelsea from an old man with whom I had a long talk. "When this town was in its prosperity," he said, "the sea used to wash right up to this 'ere precipice, and there was once a town over theer (pointing to the eastward), but the sea came and took it away. History do tell as a high tide came up upon the *hekinok* (equinox), and what could stand against that? Now sir, supposin' as another high tide came in upon the hekinok, the sea might take its own land again, and mebbe our harbour could be used. Fairlight cliff acts as a breakwater to us, but the sea is washing it away very fast. It costës a good sight of money to keep the sea off these lands now, and I have heern say that the House of Commons wants to let the sea take back its lands rather than pay so much to keep her out." Doubtless this old man is still standing by the roadside, waiting patiently for the sea to come back to Winchelsea.

You pass beneath the Strand gate, near which Edward the First nearly lost his life through his horse shying at a windmill, and pursue the road to the right, from which presently a fine view is to be had of the old town, and of Fairlight downs and church far beyond. This road to the right, *not* crossing the bridge, is the only way to get to Camber Castle— one of the castles which Henry the Eighth built to defend the coast. "There is but little of interest now," says a local historian, "in these crumbling remains," and yet, being here, one is reluctant to pass them by unvisited. It is necessary to keep much to the right, and pass an old farm before striking off towards the grey and frowning old mass of masonry, for the "waterings" are wide and numerous, and it is very easy to lose a good deal of time and trouble on these marshes. The old men in 1624 remembered the time when "400 tall ships of all nations" had been seen anchored in the Camber, "where now sheep and cattle feed." Countless sheep were grazing when I was there, and it was the lambing season, and some of the new-comers into the world looked miserable enough, shivering under a bleak east wind. A hundred or more had crept under the lee of the old castle, and a dead sheep lay not far off. Sometimes as many as ten dead a day are found by the "lookers" on these wide marshes.

All in ruins as the castle is, I found it far from
uninteresting—the massive windows, the strong central
tower, a keep inside, the dark passages leading underground, even the wallflowers growing out of the crevices,
all had a certain charm in my eyes. Many of the lower
blocks of stone on the sea side are quite fresh and good,
and the stones which are partly gone look as if they
had been violently wrenched out. The pickaxe and
the crowbar have done more to dismantle the castle
than time and weather, although during the winter
tremendous gales must sweep from the sea across these
marshes, and strike full upon the old walls.

From the castle we go towards Rye, with its red-
tiled roofs running down the hill, and its noble old
church standing guard over them. The marsh is much
intersected with water-courses, so that it is difficult to
find one's way across them. Strike off from the castle
in a north-easterly direction, and you will see a little
fence or gate, by the side of a ditch. Get over that,
and keep on the embankment beyond, and this will
lead to the swing bridge at the entrance to Rye. The
stranger is at first rather surprised to see some signs of
activity in this town, a town of weird aspect, like to
that of the "bound of Lyonesse:— "

> " A land of old upheaven from the abyss
> By fire, to sink into the abyss again ;
> Where fragments of forgotten peoples dwelt, ·
> And the long mountains ended in a coast
> Of ever shifting sand, and far away
> The phantom circle of a moaning sea."

One walks the streets almost in a dream—mediæval

streets, round which Arthurian or other legends might cluster, but with difficulty to be thought of as an abode of the men of 1877. But the ancient harbour is still of use, and boat-building goes on, and fishermen ply their calling, and the tempest-tossed mariner is occasionally driven here for shelter. Plague, fire, famine, foreign foes, all have ravaged this wonderful relic of ancient England, and it is exactly five hundred years ago (in 1377) that the French came upon it, and put many of its inhabitants to the sword. We breathe the very air of the past in these antique streets. They ramble deviously up and down, hither and thither, roughly paved, with many an old gabled house here and there, and strange ruins, and mouldering gates and towers. The people about the streets seem to be an anachronism in their modern dress. Nothing more recent than the cavalier's cloak and hat and ruffles should be seen at Rye.

While wandering about the churchyard, I saw an old man digging round a few shrubs and plants. His face was in harmony with the scene, so covered with wrinkles that it was quite a masterpiece of Time's handiwork. I asked him where I should find the keys of the church, and he said in his pocket. There could not be a more convenient place.

"That is an old house," said I, pointing to the remains of the Carmelite chapel on the south of the churchyard.

"It was built five hundred years ago," replied the sexton, "and that was before *I* was built."

"Yes," I said, "you must not try to persuade me that you are much more than a hundred and fifty or so. I see your graveyard is nearly full—you will not be able to find room for many more."

"Oh, they've a-done here sometime; we ha' a cemetery up yonder—a tip-top place." "Tip-top" was decidedly a modern phrase, and I tried to imagine what a tip-top cemetery could be like. "Ay, there be a many changes in Rye," continued the sexton, "since I first knew it. The more I thinks on it, whether I be a-lying in bed or a-walking about, the more I be sure as everything is going upside down."

The last thing that occurred to me on looking round about us was that the town had suffered much from the hand of the innovator. Scarcely a tile can have been put upon a roof for a hundred years.

"Can you tell me," I asked, "where is the Mermaid inn of which I read in my book?"

"I never heerd of it," said he, as he opened the door. "But here's a church for you—what do you think of that?"

I thought it was the largest church in a small place I had ever seen—a church, moreover, full of beauties in arches, and mouldings, and windows, though much mutilated by time and rough usage. The woodwork in various places is evidently of great antiquity, and one fine screen particularly may be of almost any age, and seems to be fast mouldering away.

"The church is eight hundred years old," quoth the sexton, "and *that* was before I was built." He chuckled

and laughed at his joke till he shook all over. Presently
we stood over a slab to the memory of a Mr. Lamb who
was slain by a "sanguinary butcher."

"That was a queer thing, sir,—have you *catched*
that in your book yet? A good many comes here to
be a eye-witness to this, because they see it in the book
and don't believe it. When the butcher was tried, he
said he didn't mean to do it—howsomever, they didn't
give him a chance to stab any more. They gibbeted
him! When the French reigned here, they took up all
the brasses out of this church, and in the wall you can
see where their cannon shot did hit. The French have
reigned here several times, but not since I was built."

"It is a pity you were not built before, for then you
could have told us all about it; but now I want you to
tell me what are the changes in Rye which make you
so sad."

"Why, it's *all* changed—all topsy-turvy. They
want to make this church Roman Catholic."

"Who does?"

"Them as has got the money," said the old man
mysteriously. "I never see the rector to speak to
him; or I would tell him, 'why not make half the
church Protestant, and half Roman Catholic for them
as likes it?' It's big enough for all."

"Well," said I, as he let me out, after I had
sufficiently admired the grand old church, and the big
pendulum swinging inside, and the heavy weights of
the clock, "it is a wonderful church, and I hope you
will be showing it for fifty years to come."

A woman who was passing by laughed ; at this
levity the worthy sexton's youthful vanity was fired.

"You may laugh," he cried to her, "but I shall be
worth as much as you are then at any rate."

"How old are you," I asked.

"Nigh upon eighty."

"A mere boy," said I "you will see many more
wonderful changes in Rye yet."

"My Master takes care of me," said the old man,
touching his hat.

The George hotel stands opposite Peacock's school,
which was founded in 1636, and to which Mr. Thackeray
sent his "Denis Duval." At the George I slept that
night, and dreamt that the plague had again broken
out, and that the mark of a cross had been chalked
upon the door, and that men were going with a dead
cart about the streets, crying "bring out your dead."
I had been reading in the evening how that in 1563,
no fewer than 562 men and women were smitten down
with this dire disease in the then ancient town. But
the next morning all was bright and fresh, and a commercial traveller's big parcels in the passage reminded
me that I was living in an improved and enlightened
age. Little boys soon made their appearance at the
door of "Peacock's," and the enterprising tradesmen
of Rye began to take down their shutters. The busy
day had begun.

"I hear there is to be a war, sir," said the old
landlord.

"Indeed—between whom ?"

2

"I can't rightly say, sir; I think it was the French."

Perhaps even now a true Rye man thinks this little
world is peopled by only two nations, the English and
the French.

The Mermaid—still I looked about for the Mermaid
inn. I roamed up and down Mermaid Street, over the
rough cobble stones, loth to give up the search.

> "——— at the helm
> A seeming mermaid steers."

At last I met with an ancient man, who looked as
if with a little effort of memory he might recall the
Mermaid, or perhaps be the Merman who married her.

"Ah, sir," said he, with a sigh, "the inn has long
been closed. How curious you should ask for it. Gone
ever so long ago, sir."

More changes!—the sexton was in the right of it
after all.

"But," said he, "I will show you the house which
was the inn ; a labouring man lives in it now. It
goes up three or four steps—there it is, sir."

I knocked at the door, and a woman opened it—*not*
old for a wonder.

"Can you tell me," I asked, "if this was the Mermaid
inn ?"

"Yes, but now we lives in. it." And she, so far as I
could judge, was not a mermaid. Presently, she offered
to show me the old carvings, for which the house had
a certain sort of celebrity, and I followed her without
fear or trembling down a long and dark passage, and

into a large room, where the broad fireplace was enclosed in a framework of fine carved oak, black with age. There were carved oak panellings near it, and probably they had once gone round the entire room, but the hand of the spoiler has been there.

"Would you like to see the tiles in the old lady's room," asked the young woman.

"I should like it much," said I, "if the old lady would not object."

So I went upstairs, and was shown into a room large enough to hold a hundred people. There was only one old woman in it.

"I am a poor lone widow, sir," said she, "and have only one room."

"But see what a big one it is," said I, by way of keeping up her spirits, "you couldn't very well have two of this size."

"Many gentlefolks come here to see these tiles," said she, pointing to her fireplace; and indeed they were well worth seeing—fine old Dutch tiles, blue and white, going all round the chimney and hearth. Each tile was the subject of a different picture, and most of the pictures represented seafaring scenes, such as must have been constantly before the eyes of the dwellers in Rye, when this old house was new. I stood a long time studying them, and meanwhile the occupant of the apartment impressed upon me that she was old and a widow.

Then they took me up into the attics—large, roomy apartments, with huge oaken timbers running across

them; and from thence into so many rooms and closets
and queer old places that I got lost, and should never
have found my way out without a guide. The old house
had been built to last for ever. How can a modern
builder go into such a house as this without being
crushed by the sense that he is a wretched impostor?
Fit to build? "No, not fit to live."

As I came out, the father of the girl appeared, with
a woman standing behind him, and immediately the
latter began to make signs to me. At this I was much
concerned, not being used to such attentions.

"Do you ever see any ghosts here," said I.

"No," said the man, "but they told us the place
was haunted when we came into it. The only ghosts
we has now are the gentlemen of the Archæological
Society, and some of 'em weigh eighteen stone. But
lor, sir, they can walk over our attics without falling
through—they never seem a bit nervous. They know
how people built in those days."

Meanwhile, the mysterious person in the background
became more extravagant in her signs and gestures,
and I was more and more bewildered at her addresses.

The father cast his eye over his shoulder and saw
what was going on. "Don't mind *her*, sir," said he,
"she was took so at two years old, and now she is
thirty-five, and cannot dress herself. She is what we
calls a *himbecile*."

Poor woman, and poor father! I gave them each a
trifle, not forgetting the lone widow, and left the
Mermaid with good wishes all round.

And now where was the Yprés tower ? How was one to ask for it ? I did ask repeatedly, but no one knew what I meant. It is at the " S.E. angle of the town," said Murray, and thither I wended my way. I found a very old tower, with a very ugly brick building wedged into one side of it, and an inscription over it setting forth that it was a soup-kitchen. Never was a greater barbarism inflicted upon a town in the name of charity.

" What do you call that tower," I asked of a fisherman who stood near, smoking a pipe.

" It used to be called the *High Press* tower," he replied, " but now we generally calls it the jail."

" You ought not to want a jail in Rye with that beautiful old church there."

The fisherman showed that he knew a great deal about the church, and took an honest pride in it, and in his famous old town of Rye. " It has been much neglected," said he, " but it's improving a little now. We have thirty fishing-boats go out from here now, and catch a sight of fish."

" That is the reason they told me at the George Hotel that I could not have any for dinner last night."

" Yes, sir, we take it to Hastings, and it goes to London."

Even this old town, in a deserted region, cannot be allowed to consume the few fish that are caught off it. The great monster of London swallows all.

To Pleyden church, half a mile beyond Rye, is a pleasant walk, and far and wide the views extend. But soon it became time to jog along on the main journey of the day, which was to walk from Rye to Hastings, about twelve miles.

For the turnpike road between Rye and Winchelsea little can be said except that it is useful—pretty it is not. I got over it, and past the Friars at Winchelsea, and far on towards an old gate at a distance from the town towards the sea, in less than an hour. My object was to walk across the marsh till I came to the cliffs, and then mount the cliffs and so to Hastings. It was a fine breezy day ; not yet ten o'clock ; the sea and sky blue as a sapphire ; the air full of the songs of birds ; the whole earth and ocean covered with divinest beauty. They sing of " Jerusalem the Golden "—will it, then, be fairer than this earth which we know already, and which seems to grow more beautiful as the time draws nearer for taking leave of it ?

Through that old gate standing far away from the city in the midst of green fields, the road winds round, but we must leave it, and climb over a gate into the marsh-lands. An embankment is visible a quarter of a mile distant, and upon that I had been told it was possible to work one's way to " Cliff's End." The embankment runs by the side of a canal, half overgrown with rush and grass. Not far beyond is the sea, which has been all over the marsh during the past winter, especially on the 1st of January, when it seemed very much disposed to claim its own again. A mile or more along the embankment, I saw that it was necessary to cross the canal by a wooden plank, put there by way of a bridge ; and still keeping by the

water, I came out at last still closer to the sea, and to
the right a fragment of an old mouldering cliff, and
beyond a coastguard station. A few hundred yards
further I saw a thatched hut, and a man standing at
the door of it with a black duck in his hand, and upon
his head a cap of skins, such as I had seen on a trapper
of the West, and upon that famous hunter, Kit Carson,
whom in 1865 I met in the wilds of Virginia.

I gazed upon this old man with great curiosity; his
hut was a little way up on the shingle, but close to
the sea; and there he stood with his black duck and
skin cap.

"Is your name Carson," said I, "Kit Carson?"

"It is not, sir," replied he; "it is Collins, Thomas
Collins."

"I thought you were a mighty hunter of America—
but he's dead."

"Ameriky? No, sir, I have never been there. But
I have heard our preachers talk of it."

"Do you live here alone?"

"Quite alone, sir."

"And may I ask you how that came about?"

"Well, sir, I lived at Hastings, and was out of work,
and so one day I took down a shrimping net which I
happened to have, and I says to my wife, I may as
well go a-shrimping, says I, as do nothing. So I walked
along the beach, and got very tired, and at last I came
to the ruins of a hut. I found out that it belonged
to Mr. Shadwell, and he let me put a roof on it, and
just as I begun my poor wife died. But I came to

live here all the same, and have lived here ever since. I hope, sir, to go, when the time comes, where my wife has gone."

I said nothing, but walked in with the old man, and sat down. The walls were of bare brick, except that here and there a faded photograph, or a text of Scripture, was hung against them. The shrimping net and another net or two hung near the ceiling, which was merely the thatch of the roof. There was a large chest near the door; a cottage mahogany bedstead; an iron saucepan; a table and two or three chairs; finally, a few books.

" You are a perfect Robinson Crusoe," said I; " no doubt you have read all about him."

" Oh yes, sir, by Daniel De Foe. I read a good deal here. Ever since last November I have never been able to go out a-shrimping, for I was seized in the water with a terrible pain in my head, and it comes back now, and besides I have sciaticy very bad."

" And how do you live ? "

" My daughters help me a little, and I grow a few potatoes, and get bread at the coast-guard station ; but I never fear. If we try to do what is right, sir, there is One above that has promised never to desert us. And he has not deserted me yet—I shall not starve."

" There are plenty of men," said I, " who think themselves very wise, and believe they know everything, who would call you an ignorant old man for talking like this. But I think you are wiser than they are, and you look to me a good deal happier."

"Yes, sir; the nights are very long in winter, and the storms are very violent, but I am happy here. In that chest that you are sitting on, sir, I have good clothes, and under my bed there is a box of linen, and I have a comfortable bed to sleep on, and owe no man a penny."

"Many a great man who lives in a mansion and rides in a carriage would be glad to change with you," said I.

"Perhaps you have heard of Mus'er Gladstone," he said.

"I have, often."

"One of my wife's darters lives with a son of Mus'er Gladstone, as nurse. They think a good deal of me, my darters do, although I am not their father, for my poor wife was a widow. I wish that I could lead as good a life as she did, and be as ready to go when the time comes. I hope that I shall go to meet her, sir."

I promised to lend Thomas Collins some books, and I hope that if any reader happens to be passing that way he will take him an ounce of tobacco, for he likes to smoke a little. He is sixty-eight years of age, and lives directly under the very last of the cliffs, just where they descend into the marsh.

It is a steep climb up the cliff from Collins's hut— an ugly path, especially in wet and slippery weather. My head fairly reeled before I reached the top, but Collins is used to it, and is even obliged to carry all the water he needs up and down it; for there is none to be had nearer than a mile or more from his hut. At the top of the cliff there is another coastguard station, and from thence I could plainly make out the French coast—the vessels in Calais roads were as distinct as the fishing smacks off Hastings. To the left I saw Dover cliffs, and far to the right Beachy Head, with France to the south-eastward. Could any one desire a grander sea-view? Then the path wanders a little from the edge of the cliff, and passes through acres of gorse in full bloom, dazzling the eye with its beautiful shade of yellow, and scenting the air with its faint smell, like that of the cocoa-nut. Soon we come abreast of Fairlight Church, and see its white tombstones shining in the sun; on the one hand, the "resounding" sea, flecked with vessels bound to many a port; on the other, the common port to which all our barks are hastening; and looking at both, and thinking how soon this voyage of ours is over after all, one cannot help hoping and believing that poor Thomas Collins down below there on the beach is right in his simple faith, and the wise men of the present day, and the scientific men, and the philosophers, all wrong.

CHAPTER II.

ROUND ABOUT HASTINGS.

Sunshine and Storms.—A Dark New Year's Day.—The Fishermen of
Hastings.—Getting under Weigh.—To Fairlight by the Beach.
—The Churchyard.—The Sexton's Story.—Bexhill.—Modern
Protestantism.—The Two Bricklayers.—Hove and Catsfield.

ON an afternoon in December or January to look
out of one's window upon a blue sea and sky, two or
three dozen fishing smacks flitting about hither and
thither, and large steamers making towards home after
long voyages—all this is a great contrast to the smoke
and fog of London, or to the damp and chilly atmosphere which hangs over many of our inland towns,
especially after rainy weather. During the winter of
1876-77 the fall of rain was unusually heavy, yet it
was seldom wet underfoot at St. Leonard's or Hastings
—the esplanade in front of the beach was always dry
enough, as soon as the rain ceased, for children to go
there without fear of catching cold. There was as
much rain, I suppose, as at other places—but never
any fog, seldom even a little mist at early morning.
Even in the most cheerless evenings of winter the
scene is not without its charms—when dark masses of
clouds are rolling in from seaward, and the sombre

outline of Beachy Head is still faintly visible, and the "Sovereign" light flashes out three times from the gathering gloom, and a few phantom-like vessels are sailing away into the darkness.

It must be admitted, however, that scenes of a very different kind are occasionally presented at Hastings, as in November 1875, and again on the 1st of January 1877. No one who has seen the place in summer only can imagine in what a formidable shape the sea of even this comparatively sheltered line of coast can present itself. The green waves break upon the esplanade, the houses at each end of the town are flooded, the sea-wall is broken up as if it were made of paper. On New Year's Day last the storm began about seven in the morning —I noticed on looking out of the window that some men just setting to work in the road could scarcely stand upright before the furious wind. Before twelve o'clock, the esplanade all along the town was cut to pieces by the waves, the large slabs at the edge were flung about like pebbles, beach houses were swept off, and the pier-head carried away. In Robertson Street a river had formed, along which boats were rowed to the rescue of persons imprisoned in their houses. The row of dwellings known as "Beach Cottages" had all their windows and doors beaten in, and the furniture in the rooms was knocked into shapeless masses and flung into corners. The kitchens and basements were completely filled up with water and shingle, and all traces of the ordinary road were effaced. Similar havoc was made at the west end of the Marina—the contents of the rooms were literally swept into the back yards, where I saw the furniture floating about, mixed up with books, trinkets, and the toys of the poor little children, who were weeping over the loss of their Christmas presents.

The sea has frequently made dashes of this kind at Hastings, and never failed to leave some trace of its awful power. In 1236, according to the county history, the old church of St. Clement was destroyed; and in 1597, while the pier was being rebuilt, "behold, when men were most secure, and thought the work to be perpetual, appeared the mighty force of God, who, with the finger of his hand, at one great and exceeding high spring-tide, with a south-east wind, overthrew this large work in less than an hour, to the great terror and amazement of all beholders." So runs the account in the books of the Corporation, and it is to be feared that in future years similar records of disaster will have to be chronicled in these volumes. For St. Leonard's, especially at the west end, is built much too near the sea—had its front been on a line with the present assembly rooms, the additional elevation gained would have rendered the town secure even from the highest tides.

St. Leonard's may be the fashionable neighbourhood, but Hastings far surpasses it in picturesqueness. Its ruined castle, and the fine cliff on which it is placed, form a noble background to Robertson Street. Beyond the fish-market, there is a quarter inhabited exclusively by the sailors, and few visitors ever explore it.

This is where the little old-fashioned public-houses are to be found, in which the fishermen spend all the time and money they have to spare, and further on still towards the sea are their cottages, and the sheds where their nets are stored. The fishing boats here, as elsewhere on our coasts, are of the most clumsy, awkward, and dangerous design that the mind of man could have conceived. They are built to take in water easily, to hold it long, to roll heavily in a light sea, and to be as nearly as possible unmanageable. No improvement can have been made for two hundred years. To see one of these big, hulking, unwieldy craft, and then think of the American fishing boat, with its graceful lines and its white sails, easily managed and capable of great speed, excites one's astonishment afresh at the obstinacy with which our countrymen cling to whatever they may have been in the habit of using, no matter at what loss or inconvenience. It takes nearly half-an-hour to launch one of these Hastings boats, and such pulling and hauling as then go on, such shouting, cursing, and swearing, such work with rollers, chains, and ropes! You would think the whole Royal Navy was being launched. When the lumbering craft is afloat, it takes at least a quarter of an hour more to get any sail set—more tugging at ropes, more wild rushing to and fro, more strong language flying about in the air. The sails are as filthy as if they had been stowed away in a coal-hole, and patched all over, and are not worked on rings, but hauled up bodily inch by inch. While they are being set, the ugly old tub rolls about at the mercy of the waves, so that unless wind and tide are both very favourable it is difficult to get it off at all.   At last it waddles away, with its dirty rags helping it along at the rate of a knot or two an hour, and the fishermen who are left behind stare after it as if loth to part with it, and then go and refresh themselves after their exhausting labours at the "Fishermen's Home."   Can anybody wonder that when a great storm suddenly beats on our coasts, so many of these poor fellows go down in their wretched boats—boats which an American fisherman would scarcely condescend to load with mussels or clams for manure on a Long Island farm ?

"There is a little silk weaving carried on at Hastings by one man, but no other manufacture."   So says an account of Hastings, published in 1786.   The silk-weaving trade appears to have declined since the death of the only person who practised it, and now the town has simply its fishing trade to boast of, but that is very considerable, and must be a source of great profit. There are a few old houses and shops here and there in the neighbourhood of High Street, and the churches of St. Clement's and All Saints are worth a visit.   The visitor may find sufficient to amuse him in this part of the town, when the weather is too bad to allow of a longer excursion.

When, however, he is ready for a ramble, he cannot do better than begin by going past the fishmarket, and the houses where the nets are stored, and make his way to Fairlight by the beach.   The road is rough, and should not be attempted by anyone who has reason

to say, with Jack Falstaff, " eight yards of uneven ground
is three score and ten miles afoot with me." The rocks
stretch out far into the sea, so that there is no getting
round them, even at the lowest tide, and between them
and the cliffs there is a tough stretch of shingly beach
covered with large stones and huge boulders. Still, to
one who does not mind such trifles as these, the walk
will be found worth taking, for the cliffs are in many
places lofty and grand, and the look-out seaward is
perpetually changing. "The roaring ocean and the
beetling crags," says the author of Eothen, "owe something of their sublimity to this,—that if they be tempted,
they can take the warm life of a man." It is necessary
to bear in mind the warning contained in these words,
and watch well the tide.

The first glen you come to, with a few cottages above,
is Ecclesbourne, and you have to round the point beyond
that before reaching Fairlight. The bank comes down
tolerably low towards the beach, with the grass to the
very edge of it, and when you see this green place, then
and there it will be well to turn in to the glen. There
is another path further up the beach, but this is the
best, for it winds through a beautiful ravine, bedecked
with wild flowers in the spring, and beautifully wooded
from beginning to end. Nowhere will a search for the
first primrose be more surely rewarded than here, and
I have seen daisies on the grass all through the winter
months. After the path has wound up and down for some
little distance, you come to a brook with a plank thrown
across it by way of a bridge, and on the other side

there is a tree. If you now follow the ravine straight through, it will lead to a road by which you may return to Hastings, but if you want to see Lovers' Seat, and gain some magnificent marine views, the proper way is to turn to the right by a little thatched hut, and climb up the hill. It is a steep climb, especially as you approach the top, but at every step you are rewarded by wide and bold views of the rugged cliffs, and far away over the sea. The Lovers' Seat is a well-known spot—a ledge of rock under the brow of the cliff, much sought after by young men and women out for a holiday, and therefore not to be recommended to the true pedestrian. From the green sward at the top of the cliff just as fine a view is to be obtained, and there you do not meet so many enthusiastic persons with their arms round each other's waists.

There is now a path through and across the fields in a northerly direction to Fairlight Church, which can be distinctly seen from the cliff. This path (keeping on the edge of the fields, past a cottage) will bring you to a gate leading into the main road, not far from the church. After a spell of rain, this will be found a wet and slippery walk, for there is no regular path, and the fields are ploughed close up to the hedges, and every step you take is followed by that "suck, suck," which is so unpleasant a sound to hear, especially if your boots are not water-tight. After gaining the road, we lose sight of the sea for a time, and a scene of another kind opens up northward—a long stretch of undulating meadows and woodland, bounded by the Southdowns,

a welcome change from the sea views which the walk
has thus far affodred. There is a large house just
below, and many farms and homesteads are pleasantly
scattered between us and yonder deep line of hills.
When we reach the churchyard there is the sea again,
with the marshes stretching far into the distance, until
they seem to melt away in the cliffs of Dover. It is
easy to pick out Winchelsea and Rye from this wide
level, and even to discern the lighthouse at Dungeness,
near which the poor souls on board the *Northfleet* were
suddenly sent to their last account.

A beautifully situated churchyard is this of Fairlight, and people have come from far and near, looking
forward from " this bank and shoal of time " to choose a
spot therein for their long home. Although a somewhat
out-of-the-way country churchyard, there are many costly
monuments in it, and several of them can boast of true
beauty in their design. I found the old sexton at the
second cottage beyond the church—a very old man
wearing one of those frocks with much needlework at
the top, back and front, which are now suggestive of
bye-gone days. He was of a singularly mild and gentle
aspect, and although his face was much wrinkled, it was
almost good-looking by reason of his clear grey eye and
honest smile. If this is not a good and worthy man, one
thinks in looking at him, then for once has Nature hung
out the wrong sign upon her work, which she rarely
does.

" You have some grand monuments here," said I,
when we had got into the churchyard.

" Yes, sir, there are many rich folks have been brought
here, and we were obliged to take that piece into the
churchyard" (pointing to the east side of the ground).
"Our church was rebuilt some years ago, but there be
a many old graves in it.   There is a stone here which
they do say is two hundred years old."

" And so strangers come to you as well as your own
people ?"

"Oh, yes.   You see that white marble cross ?   Well,
that, and the two graves next to it, were chosen by a
gentleman from India, as you see his name writ up, and
he had his brother brought here after he had been
buried a many years in London.   Then he had some
others of his family brought here too.   And now you
see, sir, how things go in this world.   This gentleman
was dressing himself one morning, quite well as you
might be, and five minutes after he was dead.   And
there he is.

"Oh, yes, we've had a sight of people buried here,
and money spent on the graves.   Thousands of bricks
have been put in the vaults.   Some people like to do
that, and it makes work, that's all.   You see that grave
over yonder, sir ?   The lady as is there was buried
fourteen year, and when we opened it to *put the gentleman in*, the lid and handles of the coffin were as bright
as they were on the day they were made.   It was a
brick grave, and better nor any vault, for we are very
dry up here.   It's the wet as breaks folks up, sir.

" A year and a half ago I buried my poor missis over
there " (pointing to the south-west corner of the church-

yard). "I have felt lonesome like ever since, although my daughter came to me after her mother died."

We were standing within the porch of the church, the old man bareheaded, and there was that in his face and words which made one silent.

"One day a big boy was trying to prevent some little children going home, just by that gate, and *she* interfered to protect them. The boy up with his fist and struck her on the breast. She was very ill afterwards, and got very thin, and we took her to the doctors, but it was all no use, sir."

"A cancer, I fear?"

"I think that was the name of it, sir. Poor thing! it was only fourteen months afore *she came to the ground.*"

"How old are you?" I asked presently.

"If I live till next month, sir, I shall be seventy-five years, and twenty-four years I have lived here. Yes, sir, it is a lonely place in winter, bein' out of the way like, but I have neighbours, and my daughter lives with me since her mother died."

The old man came and opened the gate for me, and as I walked home there lingered the recollection of his old-fashioned ways, his quaint speech, and the simple pathos of the phrase in which he told of his wife's death: "She came to the ground." With how sharp a stroke it lays bare to the mind the end of this poor little drama in which most of us are playing our parts so ill.

The pleasantest way back to Hastings is to the left of the church, down to the coast-guard station, and

then to the right over the Downs and cliffs, and
through the fields. The sea is once more in sight
nearly all the way, and after passing a good old farm to
the left, we touch the road again, and may either follow
that into the town, or get on to the grass through a
little gate also on the left of the road. This latter
course takes us far above the town on the East Cliff,
and from thence you look down upon Hastings, with its
queer jumble of churches and old-fashioned houses,
and the boats drawn up upon the beach—the most
striking picture of the town which can anywhere be
gained.

Another of the easy walks about here is to Bexhill.
Follow the esplanade to the end of the Marina, then
the road past the railroad station, and under the arch,
and so onward until the roadside inn called the " Bull "
is reached. Near this inn may be noticed a few ruins
in a field. They are all that remain of the parish church
of Bulverhythe (St. Mary), built by the Earls of Eu, or
Ango, and mentioned in a local return of 1372. In the
" Gentleman's Magazine " of October, 1786, I chanced to
find the following interesting reference to this part of the
road :—" Crossing the end of this valley, the road rises
gently to a public-house called Nunhide Haven, near
which are ruins of a chapel. This is a small distance
from the sea, and is said here to have been the place of
the debarkation of William I. A stone under the rocks
between this and Hastings is shown as the table on
which he ate his dinner." This stone is now to be
seen in the subscription gardens at St. Leonard's;

whether William ever ate his dinner off it is another
matter.

A few yards below the "Bull" Inn—formerly, I suppose, the "Nunhide Heven"—a gate opens into a field,
and from this point there is a path into the very village
of Bexhill. The distance from Dorman's Library by this
course is about three-and-a-half miles. Even in winter
this is an interesting little expedition to take. I made
it in the middle of December last, and although in the
bottoms the ground was wet and slippery, and the trees
were of course quite bare, yet the redbreast and the
wren were singing merrily in the barren hedgerows.
The leafless oaks seemed twisted into a hundred strange
and distorted shapes in the naked fields. "It is a
great advantage," says Mr. Hamerton, "of the winter
season for the study of sylvan nature, that it enables us
to see the structure of trunks and branches so much
better than we ever can do when they are laden with
summer foliage."* The stunted and crooked oaks in
the fields and hedges on this road will well reward
patient study. Indeed, it is not necessary to go from
London to put Mr. Hamerton's statement to the test.
In the short and dreary days of winter, many a Londoner would find a new world opened to him if he
wandered among the fine old trees in Kensington
Gardens, and marked their wonderful outlines, even as
presented against the leaden sky of the great city.
Not that the sky of London is always of a sombre
colour—only the man who has been up and out very

* "The Sylvan Year," p. 48.

early in the morning, has seen the metropolis at its best. There are certain wondrous studies of clouds in some of Turner's paintings which may occasionally be seen in London, and nowhere else. Let anyone who has ever chanced to see a stormy sunset from one of the bridges, when it has not been raining for an hour or two previously, and the clouds are not too low, recall that wondrous spectacle, and he will own that there are no " effects " in Turner's skies more strange or fascinating.

Bexhill stands high above the surrounding country, in a situation where it enjoys the freshest of land and sea breezes. " People live here as long as they've a mind to," said a native of the place, and the local records go far to warrant the assertion. When George the Third reached his 81st year, a party met at the Bell Inn, Bexhill, to drink the monarch's health, and although there were forty-six persons present, the youngest was over 75. Their ages ranged between that and 87, and several of the festive party lived to be over 92. Only three of the whole number died under the age of 80. In the churchyard there are several gravestones on which are recorded the deaths of persons over 90, and the majority of the population seem to live to be at least 70. Let us hope they find it worth their while.

The church is rude and primitive in appearance, and has been defaced within by heavy and clumsy galleries, but it still remains a picturesque edifice, not utterly ruined by time, spoliation, or bad taste. All these destructive influences have been at work upon it. Formerly, there was a stained glass window in the church, representing Queen Eleanor and Henry the Third, a drawing of which forms the frontispiece to the first volume of Horace Walpole's *Anecdotes of Painting.* This window was taken away from the church by Lord Ashburnham, and given to Walpole, who put it up in his chapel at Strawberry Hill. When the famous sale took place, after Walpole's death, the stolen property was described as "a very fine ancient stained glass window in seventeen compartments," "brought from the church of Bexhill, in Sussex." It was bought by a Mr. Whitaker for £30 9s. 6d., and what was its fate afterwards, no one has ever been able to find out.

Service was being held in the church on the December day of which I have spoken, and a dozen or two candles were scattered about the old building, serving only to make darkness visible. It was a week-day service, and there were exactly four persons present, three women and a man. Under such circumstances, the attempt made by the clergyman and the congregation to intone the service, in cathedral fashion, seemed slightly out of place. All this district however, is intensely "High Church." There is a church at St. Leonard's, nominally Protestant, but where the service is conducted in a manner which renders it impossible for a stranger to distinguish it from a Roman Catholic service. All the congregation make a low genuflexion, and cross themselves as they enter the building. They say they are Protestants—I wonder, then, what they call the martyrs

of old, who were burnt alive because they would not
comply with the forms and ceremonies which are
practised here ?

The road between St. Leonard's and Bexhill is
always a favourite hunting ground for beggars. I had
not got far on my way back when two men overtook
me, and informed me that they had a "long walk,"
and were "dead beat." "And pray how far have you
walked," said I.

"From Eastbourne. A long road, sir, and a bad
'un. Have you got such a thing as the price of a
night's lodging about you."

"That depends on what hotel you lodge at," said I.
"Pray what are you two men ?"

"I'm a laborer," said the first, who looked a respectable sort of person, "and my mate here, he's a bricklayer. We've been to work at Eastbourne and now
are going to Hastings."

"Just got your money for the job at Eastbourne,
and now begging. Paid on Saturday, I suppose, and
this is Monday, and you are already obliged to beg for
a night's lodging ?"

"We've had nothing to do for a week," said the
bricklayer. "Bricks is scarce, you can't get 'em anywhere, and so work dries up. We have to wait for the
brickmakers."

"Then if I were you I would give up bricklaying, and
turn to brickmaking."

"*Their* work only lasts four months in a year, and
then they has to be idle."

3

"Then I would be a brickmaker those four months and a bricklayer the rest of the year. That would be better than begging."

"Come on mate, the gent ain't a goin' to give us nothing." And, in truth, if the visitor hereabouts intends to give to all the beggars who accost him, and to buy all the shells and flowers that are presented to his notice, he had better go out with a very long purse.

At St. Leonard's there will be found an excellent library and many good shops. The subscription gardens are pleasant in summer, and at the back of them, nearly at the top of the hill, there is a house whose grounds are a favourite resort of starlings. They may be seen there in great flocks all through the winter, and towards night their behaviour is exactly that which Charles St. John describes: "As the dusk of evening comes on they wheel to and fro, sometimes settling on, and again rising from the reeds, till at last having arranged themselves to their satisfaction they remain quiet for the night."* There must often have been at least five hundred birds in some of the flocks I have seen in these gardens. Further on the road, past St. Leonard's Green, the visitor will soon find that he is in a country much loved by birds. The robin's welcome and cheerful note may be heard all through the winter, and the skylark and the thrush begin to sing early in February. The missel-bird is also common at that time, and the hedges begin to bud, and wild flowers peep out from under the grass on the bank, and the old folks and

* "Natural History and Sport in Moray," p. 247.

invalids begin to brighten up and persuade themselves
that the winter is over—whereas the east wind comes
anon, and makes sore all their bones, and fills them
with misery.

· From Bexhill there is a very pleasant walk to
Hove, about four miles. The road through the village
leads by a rather steep hill to Little Common, passing
along a ridge which commands very striking views of
Beachy Head and the South Downs, and landward far
over the weald of Sussex. The "Wheatsheaf" at
Little Common is a comfortable old inn, with a fine
tree on the village green before the door. From hence
the visitor may turn to the right, and make his way
back to St. Leonard's through the picturesque High
Woods and Sidley Green—a long round, but one
which will lead the traveller, whether on horse or foot,
through some of the loveliest country in this part of
Sussex. From the "Wheatsheaf," the road to Hove
goes straight forward, the beginning of the parish being
about two miles from the inn. The village is ten miles
from Hastings, and the best plan is to take the train to
Bexhill and walk from there. The ancient church
contains a curious stained glass window, with figures, as
some say, of Edward III. and Queen Philippe. The
window is said to be of much the same kind as the
one stolen from Bexhill. There is also a long but
lovely walk to Catsfield, where, at a corner of the
churchyard, an old pollarded oak may still be seen,
which was in its gay green youth before the days of the
Conquest.

CHAPTER III.

TWO OLD CHURCHES.

Crowhurst and Etchingham.—The Road to Crowhurst.—The Wild
Flowers of Winter.—Modern Houses and Old Ruins.—The
Famous Yew Tree.—Californian Trees.—Yews in Churchyards.
—Etchingham and its Church.—The Village Graves.—Spring
Time in Sussex.—A Specimen of "Old Sussex."—"Ameri-
canisms."—Burwash, or "Burghersh."—The Parish Clerk and
his Ancestors.—The Iron Slab.—A Request for Information.—
The Use of a Wife.—A Walk to Robertsbridge.

CROWHURST and Etchingham churches are among
the oldest in Sussex, and certainly among the best
worth visiting, as well for the associations connected
with them as for the scenery which surrounds them.
They are far apart, but anyone who can give a day to
each will not call his time misspent.

From either the London road at St. Leonard's, or that
which runs up by the side of the Assembly rooms, the
way to Crowhurst is very simple. A little beyond St.
Leonard's Green, there are some pleasant residences on
the left. This is called Hollington Park, and a short
distance down, a path will be seen running across fields
to the left. Take this, and it will bring you on to the
main road, near an oak tree, by which a road runs to the
left again. If you follow the latter road, it will bring

you by a pleasant walk out upon the Bexhill road, or
by fields back to St. Leonard's. The Crowhurst road
goes straightforward, and will be found to consist chiefly
of hills—not at all a road to be tackled by poor pedestrians. The distance from St. Leonard's is fully six
miles. This road is strewn thickly on both sides with
wild flowers—by the first week in March, I found the
daisy, herb-whort, and wild strawberry in abundance,
primroses were so thick as almost to hide the grass,
and the lesser celandine shone out brilliantly from its
bed of leaves. The views range far over the fields and
hills, or seaward over the headlands, and miles away
towards Beachy Head and the Channel.

The village of Crowhurst makes a fair appearance
from the hill, but when you get down you wonder what
has become of it, for it has almost entirely disappeared.
It lies, however, to the left of the point where the road
forks, while the road to the right takes you to the
church—a delightful old church, neat and pleasant
within, and rendered a true pilgrim's shrine without
by its grand old tower, its amazing yew tree, and the
ruins just below it of an old manor house, said to have
been built in 1230. The effect of these ancient remains
is much marred by an unsightly red and yellow brick
building, a farmhouse, which has been stuck there
without the slightest regard for common decency. For
surely this old church and its surroundings deserved
better treatment than to have these hideous flaring
monstrosities pushed up close against it. A little way
above, at a point to which the visitor naturally goes for

a good view of the church, there are three or four abominable cottages, the models of everything that is unsightly and detestable in "architecture." How can the man who built these have the coolness to look his fellow-creatures in the face again?

If the church tower and the old manor-house could not have kept back the hand of the spoiler, that venerable yew tree in the churchyard ought to have scared him off. Mr. M. A. Lower relates that it "is said to be three thousand years old." I will believe almost anything of a yew tree, but not quite *that*. Mr. Lower gives thirty-three feet as the circumference of the tree. Murray speaks of it as twenty-seven feet at four feet from the ground. I have measured it more than once at five feet from the ground, and find it twenty-six and a half feet to a fraction. But there is a split or cleft in the trunk, causing rather a wide opening, and that, of course, increases the measurement. In the Rev C. A. Johns's work on Forest Trees, there is a view of a "yew tree at Crowhurst," which, doubtless, was intended for this tree. But it never can have been a correct view, for the path is placed on the wrong side of the tree, and neither at Crowhurst in Surrey or Sussex does the great yew stand in any such position as that represented in the engraving, nor is there any resemblance to the tree itself. The top alone is now green, and even that is much broken off and battered by the winds, while below all is a melancholy wreck—the trunk shattered and hollow, and crumbling to pieces with age. A part of the trunk is held to the main body of the tree by an iron band, which looks as if that also needed to be renewed. Mr. Selby in his *Forest Trees* says that this yew "still carries a noble and flourishing head." That description of it could not be given now. There are still green leaves, but there is scarcely a branch or twig which does not look as if it had been snapped off in the middle, and the heavy gales of last winter did it grievous hurt. I stood by it one windy day in January when the groaning and creaking of its branches, as they ground against each other, was a distressing sound to hear.

We often hear much of the "big trees" of California, but are many of them larger in girth than this ancient tree? The South Park Grove is said to boast of a tree, the home of a trapper named Smith, which is thirty feet in diameter. But some of the largest which have been properly measured are no more than eighteen feet round. When we come to *height*, it is another matter, for, according to the old story, the trees in California are so high that it takes two men and a boy to look to the top of one of them.

Now supposing that this yew is 1200 years old, it will be a very difficult thing to make any one believe that it was planted there as "an emblem of immortality." This is the explanation given by Mr. Johns and many other writers of the yew being found so frequently in churchyards. "Generation after generation," he says, "might be gathered to their fathers, the yew tree proclaiming to those who remained, that all, like the ever-green unchanging yew, were yet living, in another world, the life which had been the object of their desire." The idea is, no doubt, an attractive one, but it is far more probable that pagan superstition led to these ancient trees being planted in the spots where we now find them than a belief in the Christian doctrine of immortality. Mr. Bowman supposes that its branches were employed by our "pagan ancestors, on their first arrival here, as the best substitute for the cypress, to deck the graves of the dead and for other sacred purposes." The theory that the yew was planted in churchyards in order that it might protect the sacred edifice, or provide the neighbourhood with wood for bows, seems to me to be exploded in a few words by a writer whose article I happened to come across in the "Gentleman's Magazine" for 1785 (Vol 56, p. 941). He says: "It is difficult to discover what influenced our ancestors to place this tree so generally in churchyards; scarce any could be selected which is so ill adapted to be planted for protection, from the slowness of its growth and the horizontal direction of its branches, both of which circumstances prevent its rising high enough, even in a century, to shelter from storms a building of moderate height; neither would one tree answer the purpose of supplying a whole parish with bows." Many of our churches were doubtless built on spots where our ancestors worshipped before the introduction of Christianity, and the yew, which was regarded with merely superstitious feelings, was suffered to remain.

Instead of returning to Hastings by the same way,

the visitor may continue on past the church, and the hideous cottages before referred to, and so straight forward till he comes to another main road running right and left. He will turn to the right (the left leads to Battle) and go straight down hill through the despicable village of Hollington, with its stuccoed cottages, past Silverhill, and so on either to St. Leonard's or Hastings. About three-quarters of a mile beyond Crowhurst church, there is a fine view of Battle in the distance, and also of Mr. Brassey's house "Norman-hurst." Crowhurst Park skirts the roadside, but the house is not within sight.

The pilgrimage to the fine old church at Etchingham (properly Echyngham) is a more distant one from Hastings—fourteen miles; but it may be made in a pleasant manner by taking the train to Etchingham, and returning from Robertsbridge. The church stands at a short distance from the line, and the keys may be had at the shop in the village. Passengers on the railroad often ask, "Where is the village of Etchingham?" fancying that there must be a respectable sized town near so large a church. But it is not so; all that there is of Etchingham can be seen from the line—a general shop, a public house and stables, and a few scattered cottages beyond. The house on the left of the line was once a fine old mansion known as "Haremare," but it has been entirely altered or rebuilt.

On entering the church one is struck with its height and the beauty of its proportions, and is not surprised to find in Mr. Lower's "Compendious History of Sussex," the opinion that " when complete and undefaced by the barbarous neglect of later times, this grand edifice must have been among the noblest of baronial churches." Some fragments of the stained glass still remain in the windows here and there, and the weather-vane outside is said to have been originally on a still older church than the present, although this one was erected in the fourteenth century. The vane is " banner-shaped," and is said to bear the " fretté coat of the De Echyng-hams," that family which once were lords of the manor, and several of whose members now sleep in the church. In the chancel, in front of the altar rails, is a brass to the memory of Sir William de Echyngham, of the date 1345. The head is gone, but the rest of the figure remains untouched. Just westward of it is a fine brass with three effigies upon it, a lady between two male figures, all in perfect order. The men have a bluff, Henry the Eighth, sort of look about them ; the lady was perhaps intended to have been pretty. This brass is dated 1444. The choir and screen are ancient, and give the church a stately appearance. On the south side of the nave is a very plain brass with two female figures engraved upon it, and near a pillar is a plate from which I copied the following inscription : " Here lies the only sonne of Sr. Gyfford Thornhurst Barronett an Infant by Dame Susan Thornhurst, Now Living, the only daughter of Sr. Alex. Temple, Kt., 1626." The letters are as fresh and clear as if they had been cut but yesterday. There is an old helmet and other relics of a knight hung high upon the wall. The font is of great antiquity, but has the appearance of having been much polished up or "restored." The church, five hundred years ago, was surrounded by a moat, and Mr. Lower says that there is a legend setting forth that a great bell lies at the bottom of this moat, and that it will "never be brought to light until six yoke of white oxen can be found to drag it forth." After a great prevalence of wet weather, such as was experienced in the winter of 1876-77, the visitor will be inclined to think that the moat is by no means a thing of the past, for the meadows near the church are flooded, and the whole "bottom" is under water.

There is a very old yew-tree at the west end of the churchyard, much decayed and weather-beaten, but fighting time gallantly, as its family have a way of doing. When I was last there in March, the simple country graves were covered with homely bunches of primroses and "Lent lilies," and the thrushes and blackbirds were keeping up the sweetest of all choruses in the neighbouring bushes and trees. It was the lambing season, and great was the bleating going on in all directions. At the east end of the churchyard there is a smaller yew, and beyond this point the ancient manor-house once stood, also moated. The great yew, which is the pride of the churchyard, is about eighteen feet in circumference, and has a seat all round it for the convenience of the rustics.

About two and a half miles to the south-west there is an interesting corner of "old Sussex" called Burwash —that being the shape into which the ancient name of

Burghersh has gradually twisted itself. The manor once belonged to the family of De Burghersh, but the race has long since disappeared from this part, and the name is only represented by the local pronunciation of *Burrish.* I was curious to see this old village—the centre, not many years ago, of one of the wildest and most lawless populations in all Sussex,—and started off to find it.

A little way up the road there is the village post-office, and close by is the rectory, a comfortable house surrounded with fine trees, in which a colony of rooks were hard at work amid much noise and darting to and fro. When the top of the road is reached, there is a lovely view for many miles around; a tall pillar stands conspicuously on a hill a few miles off. This is an obelisk on Brightling Down, known hereabouts as "the Brightling needle." The beauty of this neighbourhood is beginning to attract new residents, and one good house stands a little way back from the road, and, as an old man with whom I struck up an acquaintance informed me, belonged to "a harchitect." This old fellow told me that he was born at Etchingham—which he pronounced "aitch-an-ham," each syllable distinctly—and had scarcely been ten miles away from it in his life. He spoke the East Sussex dialect in all its vigour, and it was with difficulty that I made out one half of what he said.

"This harchitect," said he, "bäirt this place and built it all of the best 'terials, begor. It was nowt but a field covered with ammut castees." "Begor," or "begorra,"

I have seen put into the mouths of Irishmen in novels
and on the stage, but here was this old Sussex man using
the word repeatedly. His "ammut castees" bothered
me until, on my return home, I searched in the excellent
"Dictionary of the Sussex Dialect," by the Rev. W. D.
Parish, of Selmeston (a parish, by-the-by, which is
locally called "Simpson"), and there I found the
words properly entered: "Ammut-castès: Emmet-casts;
ant-hills."

"They rooks as you see on bärson's pläce," continued
the old man, "only coom a few year agoo. About
fi' year back, ten or a doozen coom, and the next year
about värty, and now you see as there be a hundreds
of 'em. Queer birds, they be—sometimes coom all of
a sudden, and then go away again same way."

Two rough-looking men were a little way a-head,
and I was surprised to see them in such an out-of-the-
way place, for they were evidently tramps, and very
bad faces they had. "Do you know these men?" I
asked.

"Wait till we cooms up to 'em," said he, "and I'll
tell 'ee." Then when we had passed and he had taken
a sharp glance at them, he said, "Ay, they be
runagates,"—*i.e.*, ne'er-do-wells.

I was delighted to get a present of this good old
Biblical and Shakspearian word, and was almost
equally pleased when my companion presently used
the word *mad* in the sense of *angry*. This is what
some people would call a genuine Americanism—an
" Americanism" being in nine cases out of ten an old

English word preserved in its ancient sense. My Etchingham friend frequently made use of the expression "I reckon," so that, but for his misplaced h's—and he dropped them all over the road in a most reckless and amazing manner,—he might have been a Southern or Western American. He also used the word "Fall," in speaking of the autumn. I am told that most hard-winged insects are commonly called "bugs," as in America,—thus we hear of the lady-bug (lady bird), the May-bug (cockchafer), the June-bug (the green beetle), and so forth. I have heard the word "axey" for ague in the Eastern States, just as it is used to this hour in many parts of Sussex.

The Rectory at Etchingham is an attractive looking place, but it is quite cast into the shade by the "Pärson's" house at Burwash. It is surrounded with stately old trees, and seems to be one of the most charming residences in this part of the county. "He be rich," said the old man; "why the tithes of this parish coom to more'n eleven 'underd poons a-year." The parish is a very large one—between nine and ten miles in length—and there are many good farms in it. It was formerly the "birth-place or sheltering-place of rick-burners, sheep-stealers, and thieves," and now is a quiet agricultural district. As for the church, the steeple or spire is almost the only relic of its former self which the restorer has spared.

I found the clerk in a little cottage—an old man with a bad cold. His wheezings and splutterings, and the perpetual drop which was unfortunately sus-

pended from his nose, made him rather an unsatisfactory
person to be with for any lengthened period.

When we entered the churchyard, he pointed out to
me a row of six or seven graves. "That's the place,"
said he, "where my family lie. My grandfather and
grandmother are theer, and that's my mother, and
that's my first wife, and them be my two children."
He pointed them all out with a kind of pride. "My
mother died sixty year agoo."

The lime trees in the churchyard are tall and well
shaped, and there is a yew, but of no great size.
Inside the church, all has a bran-new appearance,
except the font, on which is the Pelham buckle, and
a forlorn old slab which used to be in the chancel,
but which is now nailed up in an out-of-the-way corner,
like a bat to a barn door. This slab is of iron, and was
cast at a foundry not far off, in the days when iron
foundries still existed in this part of Sussex.

"It was made at Starkmush Farm," said the clerk.
I had half a mind to ask him to spell it, but that would
have been too absurd. I found out that the name of the
place was *Socknursh*, and that the slab (on which the
words "Orate pro annemâ Jhone Colline" are to be
traced) is to the memory of one of the Collins family, who
became extinct here in 1753. The old clerk said the
inscription was "pray for poor John Collins," vaguely
suggestive of a drink invented by a waiter at the now
extinct Limmer's Hotel.

But, not knowing the facts at the time, I kept repeat-
ing the old clerk's name of "Starkmush" in despair.

"I don't know how they spell him," he said, the tear still persistently dripping from the wrong place. "Some spell it some way, some another. It be like people's names—you spell 'em how you like. Surnames might be anything now-a-days. Can you tell me one thing, sir? They do say as we are all sprung from Adam and Eve, yet there be 95,000,000 of different names in the world. How do you account for that, sir?"

I said I would think it over. Then, seeing that I was writing something in a note-book, he asked,

"Be you a mäkin' of a chronology, sir? Because if you be, you might like to know as the clerkship 'as been in my family ever since the year 1738, without e'er a break."

"I will put that in the chronology," I said.

"Ay, do, sir. I am pretty old myself, but—" he stopped short, and his face fell. I looked round, and saw his wife—not his first wife—coming in at the gate after him. Doubtless she scented afar off the shilling I had just handed over, and was on guard to convey it home.

"If I were you," said I to the clerk, "I would lock the old lady up here in the church while I went to get my glass of ale."

"You would really, sir?"

"Indeed I would."

It evidently struck him as a beautiful idea, and he dwelt on it long and lovingly, and gazed at me as a kind of genius for suggesting it. But he had not the strength of mind to act upon it. "I coom to zee arter

my spectacles," said the old woman, "did you take
'em?" Did anybody ever know one of the sex to be at
a loss for an excuse? The old clerk was taken in tow,
and bade me good day with a disconsolate air. That
dreadful drop grew larger than ever, and as we went
out of the gate he motioned once more towards his
little property in the churchyard, and said, "that's my
own mother, and she be dead sixty year. And that
be my first wife," and a look in his face seemed to
say that it was a thousand pities his second was not
there also.

The one street of Burwash runs straight down from
the churchyard gate. The "Bear" Inn looks old and
snug, and there is a fine house, apparently of Queen
Anne's time, with a well-carved doorway. It is the
very picture of a roomy and comfortable home. But
no one could tell me anything about it.

I now walked back to Etchingham, with the inten-
tion of going from there to Robertsbridge over the
fields—little more than two miles. But the fields were
half flooded, and a steady down-pour of rain came on,
and so I determined to stick to the road.

And this undoubtedly commands the finest views,
for the road runs high above the valley, while the
field-path is in a hollow, hugging the river Rother—a
swollen stream just then—nearly the whole way. The
distance to Robertsbridge by road is a long four miles.
Yet it is well worth walking over—the country is
lovely, the views everywhere superb. You leave the
house of *Haremare* just below you, and keep always

to the right. The rain came down without ceasing, the roads were muddy, and the east wind was rather sharp ; but I had barely an hour to do the four miles in, and the birds were singing in the hedgerows and trees, and I had the satisfaction of spying out among some primroses my first " cuckoo-flower " of the season —the lady-smock of Shakspeare. How could the road be dull ? With a light heart and a quick step I soon reached Hurst Green, a village with nothing particular about it, and then through the toll gate to the right, and all down hill to Robertsbridge, where a rich abbey stood in 1176, the remains of which have been used in our own day for the noble purpose of mending the roads. A pleasant little town is Robertsbridge, with some good houses round about it, and most beautiful country at the back. It is only thirteen miles from Hastings, and for a moment I thought I would go on. But I had made a long round already, and enough is as good as a feast, although how can one tell when one has had enough of these charming old country roads and fields and hedges ?

CHAPTER IV.

PEVENSEY is sacred ground to the archæologist. It
was an ancient British settlement, and the Romans built
a castle here of which the remains are still to be seen even
from the railroad. "Fifteen centuries stand between
[the visitor] and the builders," says Mr. Roach Smith,
and he adds that if the said visitor tears "aside the
ivy that clings to the facing of the wall, he will find
the course of the mason's trowel marked as freshly as
if the tool had smoothed the mortar only a few months
since." But Mr. M. A. Lower would take us back to
a still more distant period. "The most remarkable
coins," he says in his "Compendious History of
Sussex," "ever found here are those of some of the
Bactrian kings, Radpluses, Menander, and Apollodotus,
who flourished about 200 years B.C." As to the

accuracy of this statement, it is beyond my province to
speak—the idle tourist will be content to leave such
questions to the learned Thebans. Certain it is that
here a settlement of native Britons was exterminated
by the first South Saxon king, and that here also, but
so long afterwards that the date seems almost recent
by comparison, William the Conqueror landed for the
first time in England. A long, long history is that of
Pevensey, and short work would the antiquaries make
of any simple summer-day's rover who attempted to
deal with it. Far be it from me to venture on such
dangerous territory. As I walked up the quaint
village street of Westham which leads to the castle, I
thought to myself, "Let us first step aside to see this
old church, with its aisle and chancel of the time of
Edward the Fourth, and its memorials to many a
family now gone and forgotten. Here we shall see a
famous carved screen made in the days of Henry the
Sixth, and ancient windows such as no man will
mind walking a dozen miles to look at." While thus
ruminating on the treat before me, the sound of workmen's hammers fell upon my ear. I had crossed the
threshold of the church, and what a spectacle presented
itself! The whole of the inside was literally "gutted"
—the walls had been torn down and were lying in
confused heaps upon the floor, mortar was being mixed
on grave-stones with ancient crosses carved upon them,
the pews, communion-table, windows, all were clean
gone. "What are you doing with the church?" said
I to a man who was hammering away on an old

slab. "We be a restoring of un," replied he without looking up. I fled in horror from the scene.

Within the walls of "Anderida" a few cows were munching the grass, and turned to look lazily at the solitary intruder who had invaded their domain. The walls are low and ivy-clad, and there is little within them to satisfy the seeker after the picturesque. Yet to those who know anything of the history of their country, few places in England will possess greater interest than this, for every inch of it is classic soil.

Through the Norman arch on the other side there is a glimpse of an old grey street, the "High street" of Pevensey. Nearly all the houses in it are weather-worn and ancient, and there is a Town Hall not much larger than a cottage. You pass through this primitive street to reach Hurstmonceux, the road winding round to the left, across a low marsh, over which the sea washed a thousand years ago. "And will again," said an old man whom I saw mending the road, "though maybe not in my time. She will come here again, I tell ye. Look how she washes over Hastings and St. Leonard's now at high tides. She will go up to them hills again some day, though I shan't live to see her."

"And that is my road, straight through the marsh?"

"Ay, that be it—'Orsemonsoo be about five mile and a half. You can't go across the marsh, because you see the water's out." And, in truth, the ditches were like little rivers, and the fields resembled swamps.

"Do you know what flower this is?" I held up the marsh-marigold, which grew in profusion all over the hedges.

"Not I—I know *naun* about flowers."

"Have you heard the cuckoo yet?"

"No, the 15th is cuckoo day, and ye never hear'n afore." Now this was the 9th of April, consequently a week too soon.

"Look out for the finger postës as you go along—there be a plenty of 'em when you pass the second geät."

The blackthorn was in blossom, and the words of the "May Queen" pictured the landscape :

" By the meadow trenches blow the faint sweet cuckoo-flowers,
And the wild marsh-marigold shines like fire in swamps and hollows gray.'

Yet three-miles of the marsh are enough—I tried the fields over and over again, but the wet and mud were nearly knee-deep. At last the road makes a lucky dash out of the marsh, and mounts up to Wartling Hill, where there is a church by the road-side, "restored." Now as I had no curiosity to cross the devastating path of the restorer again that day, I passed on to the left, and presently came to a " geät " which led into the park of Hurstmonceux.

The park has a bare and pillaged look, the fine trees which were formerly its pride having long since been cut down and sold. As you go over the brow of the hill, glancing at Pevensey Castle five miles away, and ships like specks on the distant sea, all at once you see the

AN OLD ENGLISH FEUDAL CASTLE.

HURSTMONCEUX.

old castle just below you in a hollow, grim and solitary, with the little church where Julius Hare preached so long, and of which John Sterling was once the curate, on the rise of the hill beyond. Popular opinion would doubtless confirm Mr. Lower in his statement that the castle is the "most picturesque building in Sussex," yet I should be inclined to award the palm to Bodiam, although it is much smaller than Hurstmonceux. The great entrance to the latter is, indeed, far superior to anything that Bodiam has to show, although it is far less picturesque than the entrance to Raglan Castle, while in extent it is a mere child's toy compared with the vast ruin at Caerphilly, in Glamorganshire. The few trees now remaining near Hurstmonceux have had their tops all cut off by the fierce gales of last winter—even the three yews at the side look ragged and broken down. The castle was once of red brick, now grey with its four hundred years of wear and tear. An old chesnut towards the road was just beginning to show signs of awakening from its winter's sleep. "It is the forwardest tree about here," said the boy at the castle, "and has the biggest nuts upon it." He was munching a huge piece of cake but seemed a little overpowered by the loneliness of the place. "No one has been here for two or three weeks," said he, "and it is terrible dull. A old man who used to keep the castle died in a room up there. He lived here alone, and no one knew anything about it till they broke into his room, and found him dead. I never see anything all day but them rooks and *howls*." The ground in the hollow was saturated, and one had to go splashing and slipping along very cautiously up the hill to the old church—a church which has been restored with reverence and care, and therefore looks the better rather than the worse for the process.

It is towards yonder ancient yew that one is naturally attracted first, partly because it is so ancient, partly because under it sleeps Julius Charles Hare, "twenty-two years rector of this parish," and his wife. Near to it also lie other members of the Hare family. Across the churchyard, in a meadow, there is an enormous old barn, one of the largest in Sussex. It is evidently of great age, "older than the castle," says the clerk of the church, although there may be no satisfactory proof of that. In another part of this quiet churchyard, there are twenty-six gravestones in rows, evidently bearing record to the memory of one family. The name on them was that of Pursglove—"once," said the clerk, "the Pursgloves were well known here; and they are all gone. They were farmers, and all of them were dissenters. We have no Pursgloves in this part of Sussex now." Then he showed me the graves of three other families, once well known in the parish, now extinct there, although members of them may still be found on the sheep farms of Australia, or the ranches of the Great West.

Inside the church, the flowers which had been used for the Easter decorations were still on the walls and pillars,—primroses, daisies, heart's-ease, daffodils, and other simple but beautiful flowers of rural England, all arranged with a delicacy and taste which the most consummate artist might envy. I was so much taken up with them, as to almost forget to look at the monument to old Lord Dacre and his son in the chancel, which was erected here in 1533, or the brass on the floor to "William Ffienles, chevaler." There is no house near the church or castle, except Hurstmonceux Place, the village called Gardner Street being a mile and a half distant. The vicarage is not even in sight. As for the "Place," it was uninhabited when I was there, and I strolled over it, the workmen not objecting. It was built from the materials taken from the old castle below, but the modern builder was not able to "convey" the ideas of his predecessor so easily as the old bricks. Even these bricks are covered with whitewash, and the house is a large, rambling, ungainly place, a wretched mockery of the noble fabric which stands despoiled below. There are no old carvings in the rooms, as some of the local guide books would lead one to suppose.

From this house, not half so interesting as the great barn near the church, I pursued my walk to Gardner Street, and there at the Woolpack Inn, an old posting-house on the Lewes Road, I managed to obtain without difficulty the standing dish in Sussex—eggs and bacon. The village does a thriving trade with the farmers for miles round, and consequently the "general" shop is a small market in itself, and the landlord of the Woolpack was fat and jolly, and there was an air of prosperity all over the place. I hope it was not the landlord's ale

4

which had capsized two brick-makers whom I afterwards passed on the road to Hailsham, lying dead drunk in a ditch. Was there ever a greater curse to any country than drunkenness is to England? Like travelling through a land smitten with some sore disease, wherever one goes its fatal blight rests upon the people. But then, is not the Chancellor of the Exchequer able to report, year after year, that the revenue from the Excise has exceeded his estimates?

Hailsham is a quiet town, with an old and pleasant church in it, and the door being open of course I went in, for how can one pass by an old church unvisited? On the north wall I was struck with a tablet to the memory of "Colonel Philip Van Cortlandt, a retired royalist officer of the American War, died at Hailsham, May, 1814, aged 74." The Van Cortlandts are still a large and widely-spread family in the United States, but doubtless this old royalist officer found the repose of Hailsham more to be preferred, after the stormy period of the Revolution, than the homestead of his kinsfolk across the seas.

And what are the distances of these places one from the other? The best of the local guide books says that Hurstmonceux is 7½ miles from Pevensey station. Murray puts it at 5½. In all such cases, I have invariably found Murray right, and so it proved in this case, for according to my pedometer, which is never far out, the distance is 5½ miles to a yard or two. From Hurstmonceux to Gardner Street, is a mile and a half, and thence to Hailsham four miles—eleven miles altogether, enough and yet not too much for any man, who would rather any day tramp along the road, admiring the fields and flowers, and picking up odd characters, than ride in the finest carriage ever seen in Hyde Park.

Bodiam is decidedly a "prettier" ruin than Hurst-monceux—its moat alone, still as complete as when the castle was built in 1386, would render it more attractive to the sketcher than its grander rival in Sussex. A special journey must of course be made to the ancient seat of the Earls of Eu and the De Bodiams —if from Hastings, there is a long but interesting walk or drive of fourteen miles through Northiam and Brede ; if by a more direct route, from Robertsbridge Station on the South Eastern railroad. The distance by field-path from Robertsbridge, is not more than three and a half miles, following the Rother all the way. By road, it is over five miles, although the mendacious finger-posts say three and a half from the turnpike gate. But after walking a full half mile from the 'pike, the traveller will see another finger-post, stating that the distance is still three and a half miles, which will be sufficient to open his eyes to the untrustworthiness of these false guides by the roadside. The path through the fields is quite impracticable during the winter and spring, if there has been much rain. The Rother soon overflows its banks, and the meadows are covered ; and indeed in April, 1877, the scene which was presented through all this part of the country was most melancholy. Farming operations were out of the question ; rain had fallen ever since the previous

November, with scarcely an intermission of two days together at any one time; and the seed which had been sown was either washed out into the roads and drains, or lay rotting in the water. I do not like to say that the English climate has a fault—but *if* it has, excessive dryness of the atmosphere is not the one.

A little way on the road to Bodiam I came to a church with a grand old tower, commanding all the road. Men must have cared something for their religion, when they built such a church as this in the midst of a small community. The name of the place is Salehurst, and its church alone would amply justify every Salehurst man in holding his head high in the world. If we had to build a church at Salehurst now, what sort of a thing would it be? We all know—let us not dwell too minutely on the painful picture. Here, too, the restorer has been at work, and that work is of the worst kind—even the old tower has been stuccoed all over, and the stucco has peeled off, leaving the stones, which have stood there for centuries, still far better able to defy wind and weather than our odious shoddy work of the present day. A fine spacious church is this within, with Early English arches, and several slabs near the door to the memory of a family named Peckham, varying in date from 1679 to 1805. Just outside is a very quaint thatched roadside inn, with the sign of "The Old Eight Bells,"—bells which I fear are more in favour in these tippling days than those of the parish church.

"Where does the clerk live," I asked one of the

younger inhabitants of Salehurst, who had just been refilling the family jug with bad ale.

"At whöam," said he. This was encouraging, but indefinite.

"And where is his home?"

"Down theer," pointing vaguely all across the horizon.

"Where are the keys of the church?"

"Don't knöaw."

"What will you do with twopence if I give it to you?"

"Don't knöaw." But he manifested a hearty desire to find out.

It is a very charming walk from here to Bodiam—not following the finger-posts in their deceptive directions, but *turning to the right* wherever a turning has to be made. Then the road winds through some of the loveliest lanes in Sussex, deep in ferns and wild flowers. Before going far from that old church of Salehurst, I made up, according to custom, a morning bouquet for the buttonhole, which, when made, I consider worth a dozen of the kind for which they have the conscience to charge me a shilling in Piccadilly. To-day the flowers offering themselves for selection were the primrose, the wild violet, and the cuckoo-flower, the "lady-smock all silver white." Perhaps some people will say that they would have preferred a few azaleas and camelias from the conservatory, and why should they not? Let them have their own way, and welcome, so long as I may continue to have mine.

When the road comes out at the finger-post which says go to the left, then go to the right; do it every time. At last you will come to the "Junction Inn," and a mile beyond that is the school house of Bodiam, at which you must buy for sixpence a ticket to see the castle. Just opposite the school is a stile going into a field— cross it, and go down the field, and you will presently come out pretty much as at Hurstmonceux, with the old castle beneath you, the rooks making a great fuss round about it, and the green leaves of the water- lilies half covering the moat. A veritable castle, as seen a little way off; only when you cross the draw- bridge, and pass under the gateway, do you find that it is roofless and dilapidated, traces of its inner arrange- ments being almost gone. But there it is, a castle still —to enter it we have to cross a real moat, and we almost expect to hear the warder's challenge and the draw- bridge rattling up. A pleasant castle for a picnic, for it is thoroughly secluded, and there are all sorts of turf- covered nooks and corners in it. But the picnic party should not be very large—not larger than two, I think.

At the little red cottage on the slope the keys are kept. Thither I repaired, the first visitor since Easter Monday.

"I will go and open the gate," said the old lady.

"No, let me go," said her daughter, who had just cut me some bread and butter and given me a glass of milk. And very nicely she had cut the bread and butter, for there is an art in that as there is in most other things.

"Be sure you put on the clegs," cried the mother, and no wonder, for all the field was soaking wet.

Forward tripped the girl, and I followed, she with clogs, and I without clogs. She was a buxom lassie with bright rosy cheeks. Her eyes were grey and clear, and a laugh was hiding in the corners of them.

" This must seem a lonely place for one to live in," said I.

" Yes."

" Especially if one happens to be a pretty girl."

" Oh, I get used to that."

" What, to being pretty ? "

" Oh, no, (laughing) that is all nonsense."

" Is it ? I do not think so."

" Dear me," said the damsel, " I've dropped the key."

" So you have—but here it is, and I declare your cheeks are rosier than ever."

" You are a funny gentleman."

" No, I am a serious gentleman. And now which way shall I go ? "

" You can go wherever you please, sir," said the maiden, looking down.

CHAPTER V.

MAYFIELD.

MAYFIELD is one of the haunted places of Sussex. Many are the signs and wonders which have been seen there. Ghosts are still said to appear in some of the old houses in the neighbourhood, and the stranger is half inclined to believe that the ancient forge at the entrance to the village is the very one in or near which St. Dunstan performed his famous miracle. It is well known, and it would be heresy to question it, that the saint was at work beating out hot iron, when he became aware that the Father of Evil was standing by his side. With admirable presence of mind, the saint seized his wily visitor by the nose with a big pair of pincers, but " Auld Nickie Ben " was equally fertile in resources, and flew away with the whole concern — pincers, saint, and all. The saint held fast, and a terrific combat shook the valley. At last the fiend got loose, more's the pity, and cleared the nine miles between himself and Tunbridge Wells at one leap. There he plunged into the waters to cool his nose, and thus imparted to the springs that flavour of iron which the visitor may taste to this very day. That is one proof of the truth of the story, and if you want another, the identical pair of tongs or pincers with which St. Dunstan greeted the demon may still be seen in the "Palace" at Mayfield, now a nunnery. One of the sisters showed them to me only a few weeks ago; how could I doubt any longer? The iron is worn with time, and seems still to bear traces of the desperate struggle of nine hundred years ago, for it is nearly as long as that since St. Dunstan lived at Mayfield.

"These are the tongs with which St. Dunstan worked his miracle," said the worthy sister.

"I have read of the legend in my book," said I, meaning no offence.

"It is not a legend," replied the sister in a tone of slight reproof.

"No, no," said I, "I did not mean to throw any doubt upon the story."

How could one wish to wage a controversy with this good sister, whom I had heard a few minutes before instructing the muddle-headed boys and girls of the village in religious truths? She was teaching them about the soul, and one of the pupils persisted in calling it *so'*, nor could the patient teacher prevail upon him to add the other two letters. If she chooses to believe in the tongs, why not? Certain it is that they are much notched at the end, and how could that be unless a nose, or some other very hard substance, had been held between them?

You could scarcely find a more interesting specimen of ancient Sussex than Mayfield, entirely untouched as it is by that bane of England, the speculative builder, and unintruded upon still by railroads or other devices which lend a charm to modern life. The nearest railroad station is Ticehurst Road, and that is five miles off. From thence there is a walk which those who love the old parts of Old England will do well to take. On leaving the station turn to the left over the railroad bridge, and go up the road till you come to a cottage on the right. Turn in at a gate there, and make your way by a field-path, past a very old farmhouse and a mill-stream, for nearly a mile, when the path will be found to end at the turnpike road. Cross the road, and go over the stile, and continue across the fields for some distance, till at last the turnpike road cuts it off. By this path fully a mile is saved, a long and dusty mile, nearly all up hill. To this field-path I had no clue on my first visit, and only discovered it by mere accident the second time I made the journey. The turnpike road goes doubling round and round in a provoking manner, but in spring-time it is literally lined all the way with wild flowers. The violets, primroses, wild anemones, and forget-me-nots, are so abundant that the journey seems to be merely through

one long garden. Then you come to an ugly red
building (new, of course), and afterwards to a
comfortable farm-house of the old style, and not far
from that you see Mayfield in front of you on a hill.
But although it looks near, it is in reality some distance off, and the more you walk, the further off it
seems to get. It is a long five miles by the road, and
about four by the field-path and road combined.

An old yew-tree stands appropriately at the entrance
to the village, near the blacksmith's forge. Here, you
will think, is your journey's end, but it is not so, for
Mayfield itself still eludes you, and when you turn
the corner it seems to have entirely disappeared, as if
St. Dunstan's visitor had suddenly returned while you
were mounting the last hill, and flown away with the
whole of it. Up a long and steep street you plod
along, more or less tired—and these Sussex roads will
punish the strongest pedestrian—and at last you come
to some houses which time seems to have overlooked,
and then to the inn called the Star, where there is
accommodation to be had far superior to that which
I have found in many a grand hotel. The butcher
below sells good mutton; the landlord has good
bread and butter and excellent ale, and a clean table
cloth, and a comfortable bed-room, if you want a
night's rest withal. What more does any man seek?
When I sit and eat my luncheon in the old kitchen
(a comfortable room in winter or spring) an im-
measurable distance is between me and the troubles
of life. The great wave cannot come foaming and

tumbling into this secure harbour. The old fireplace
has a large armchair in it, quite out of sight, and I
suppose there must be a big cupboard somewhere or
other in the vast recess, for I notice that the landlord's
daughter disappears bodily in the fireplace from time
to time, and comes out again none the worse. It is
a fireplace in which you might almost hold a town-
meeting, notwithstanding the new range and boiler,
and all the rest of the "fixings" without which a
family of the present day cannot roast a leg of mutton
or boil a potato.

The church is a far more interesting building than
the accounts of it which I had consulted led me to
suppose. It is a large and beautiful edifice, with a
noble chancel, in one part of which there is a hagio-
scope, and a recess in the wall for a piscina. Similar
recesses exist in the body of the church. The pulpit is
of carved oak, and there are some high pews near it
also exquisitely carved—fine relics of a byegone age,
when artificers in wood were valued and encouraged
in England. These old pews have thus far escaped
the restorer, who has, however, destroyed the ancient
roof, and put up one of his own design instead. On
the sides of the aisle the ancient free seats still exist,
all of oak black with age. How long they may have
been there it is impossible to say, perhaps from before
the time the original church was burnt down in 1389.
For it is recorded that the tower, and the lower portion
of the church, as well as the central window, escaped the
destruction which overtook the rest of the building. In

the nave and chantry are several slabs of iron, of native make, to the memories of Mayfield folks of the olden time. The earliest of these slabs are rude in shape and lettering—I noticed one bearing record to "Thomas Sands, who was buryed July the 20th, 1668, aged 72 years," the figure 7 being turned the wrong way. But a great advance is made in the workmanship of the slab next to it, which is surmounted by a tremendous coat-of-arms, and ambitiously ornamented with scrolls and borders. This also is to a member of the Sands family, "citizen and wine cooper of London," and is dated 1708. The two slabs nearer the communion-table bear date 1669 and 1671. Mayfield was once the centre of a great iron-making district, and even now, as the woman who showed me the church assured me, the parish boundaries are marked by farms which are named the "Forge," and iron ore of excellent quality is constantly found in the neighbourhood. The pedestal of the font is apparently older than the upper part, although that is dated 1666. Monuments to the Baker family are numerous in the church, but of the Bakers themselves one representative only is said to remain. The Palace of Mayfield belonged to this family from 1617 to 1858. In this as in many other parts of the country, direct descendants of the old families are rarely to be found. The Cades once flourished here, and Jack Cade himself is believed to have come of the stock, but there is no one of the name hereabouts in the present day.

In the churchyard four martyrs were burnt in the

cause of the Protestant religion—that very religion
which now, to all appearance, is falling a little out of
favour in many quarters. "The Roman Catholics come
to see this church very often," said the woman, "and
they say it belonged to them once, and they will have
it again." Perhaps they will, for no one can tell what
may happen in this whirligig world; at any rate they
are making great advances in all this district. The
priests who have their central point at St. Leonard's
are full of activity, energy, and "missionary" enterprise, while their Protestant brethren are too often
engaged in copying their outward forms and ceremonies, and trying to make themselves as much like
them as possible, except in this immense zeal for
adding new members to their church. There is a
convent at St. Leonard's which sends out men and
women far and near, winning over "converts" to the
"old faith." One branch of this convent is now at
Mayfield, in the ancient Palace. A famous place was
this Palace in its day; the primates of England
regarded it as a favourite abode, perhaps for the very
reason that sickly sisters are now sent to it from St.
Leonard's, on account of the bracing quality of the air.
King Edward the First visited it more than once, and
long after him Queen Elizabeth, and long after her
again came a monarch who will perhaps be remembered as long as either of them, Queen Victoria.
Little remains of the building as it formerly stood,
even the great hall (built *circa* 1350) having been
restored, and turned into a chapel for the sisterhood.

It was the banqueting hall of the archbishops, and had fallen into almost complete ruin. The arches still exist, and give a noble appearance to the hall, now fitted up with more than ordinary display and pomp. Numerous figures or images surround the altar, and lights are constantly burning. The sister who showed me the place took me to the relics, and there I saw the tongs by which St. Dunstan once had a firm hold of the Prince of Darkness, but unfortunately, as I have said, let him go again. I asked for the hammer of which Mr. Lower says, "the hammer, with its solid iron handle, may be mediæval," but the sister said that it had disappeared—how and when no one knew. "It was there (pointing to a corner) when we came here, but one-day when we looked for it, it was gone, and since then we have never seen it again." She showed me an old sword and an anvil, and who knows but that the anvil was the very one on which St. Dunstan was at work when the enemy of mankind appeared to him?

Church and Palace are no doubt the lions of May-field, but there is a great curiosity which will strike the visitor with astonishment and admiration as soon as he enters the town, and that is a timbered house with the date of 1575 upon it. "It is one of the most curious timber houses in Sussex," says Mr. Lower, and it is certainly one of the most beautiful houses I have seen anywhere—quite perfect from top to bottom, the carvings and decorations being wonderfully well preserved, although I notice some differences between the front of the house as it now stands and the engraving of it given in the 21st volume of the "Sussex Archæological Collections." The timber work is of a more varied and ornamental character than is represented in the picture. The house is worth going many miles to see, and there is another of stone at the lower end of the town equally curious, although not quite so picturesque. The smaller houses and inns in any other place would be deemed remarkable, so quaint and old-fashioned are they ; but " Middle House " and " Aylwins " eclipse stars of lesser magnitude.

Rotherfield, with its beautiful old church, dating back to the year 792, so says Mr. Lower, is rather less than four miles distant, and a conveyance may be had in the town by which the traveller may visit this ancient parish, or drive round by Heathfield to Etchingham (a lovely drive, over very high ground), or through Frant to Tunbridge Wells, about ten miles. There are roads enough to Mayfield, and although within the memory of many of the inhabitants, these roads were horrible to travel over at the best of seasons, and quite impassable in winter, they are now hard and good, and at almost every step unfold such exquisite pictures of English scenery that it is with sorrow one bids farewell to them.

CHAPTER VI.

RUMOURS of war had reached this quiet corner of the
South Downs when I was there on the last day of
April. I was watching a nightingale, the first of the
year, which had just flown across the road, and was
perched on a hedge within a few yards of me. Presently it began to pour forth its wondrous song, and
although it did not finish it, perhaps because it fancied
it was a little too early in the season, yet the fragment
with which it was pleased to favour its two listeners—
namely, a poor hedge-cutter and myself—fairly put to
shame the thrushes and blackbirds which had been
trying hard to sing each other down. While I was still
waiting in the hope of hearing the rest, the hedge-
cutter said, "Excuse me asking you, sir, but can you
tell me whether there is war?"

"There is, between Turkey and Russia."

" Not yet."

" Ah, sir, they will never come here—England is safe. And if they did come, I reckon they would soon be glad to get away again. We are too much for 'em all."

That was how the great "Eastern Question" presented itself to his mind. Confidence is an excellent thing, especially when it is not pushed too far. "I see you a-listenin' to the nightingale," said the hedge-cutter, "it be a good bird for singin' like. I heard one for the first time three days ago. As you go up the road mebbe you'll hear two or three."

With or without nightingales, one might well be glad at any time to walk a few miles on such a road as this. I had started from Berwick Station and turned my face straight towards the South Downs, that beautiful ridge of hills which, to the eye of Gilbert White, seemed a "majestic chain of mountains," and which, in good earnest, appear much higher than they really are when you are upon them, so vast is the sweep of the view they afford over land and sea. Beneath these noble hills there are still villages to be found which are almost as they were three or four hundred years ago, and towards one of them I was bending my steps—to Alfriston, the "Aluriceston" of Domesday Book, a parish in which there are more British and Roman barrows to be seen to-day than new houses. At every stage of the road there are abundant signs that you are travelling in an old country. The farm houses and barns have never known the hand of the modern builder. And when, about two-and-a-half miles from the station, you come to the village, and see the ancient up-hill street, with the long sloping roofs of the houses, and the remains of the market cross, which may have stood there five hundred years or more, it is difficult to realise that one is living in commercial England, in the midst of a driving and pushing age. About half-way up the street there is an inn which will gladden the heart of any man who takes an interest in the traces which are still allowed to exist of the old times in England. This inn is called the " Star," and it must have been standing here at least three hundred and fifty years, with no great change inside or out. At each side of the door, and along the front of the house, there are carved figures, one of St. Julian the friend of travellers, another of a priest, a St. George waging a gallant fight with the dragon, two animals supporting a staff, and other figures or devices which are more delightful to look upon than all the pictures in the Royal Academy put together. At one corner of the house there is a rude figure of a lion leaning against the wall, but this is only the figure-head of a vessel which was wrecked on the coast some time last century. All the rest is old, from the roof which is half sunken in with age, to the bow windows with their small panes of glass, and the narrow doorway guarded by St. Julian and, as some suppose, St. Giles. Alfriston is believed to have been formerly a much larger place than it now is, and Mr. Lower thinks that the Star Inn was " a house of call for pilgrims and the clergy who were wending their way to the tomb of St. Richard and the

Episcopal See." So the house had a somewhat religious character, and ornaments were adopted which "appear at first sight rather incongruous with the objects of a road-side inn." However this may be, the figures are well worthy the notice of the modern pilgrim, who will find few such ancient hostelries as this left in merry England, although he will come in the way of plenty of abominable "gin palaces" and flaring bar-rooms.

While seated in the little parlour of the "Star," at an enormous distance, as it seemed, from the world of the present day—railroads, telegraphs, newspapers, being all like some dim recollection of a disturbed dream—I noticed a circular upon the wall, with an engraving of the old church above it. In this I read, with great sinking of the heart, that progress to a most alarming extent had been made with the work of "restoring" the church—that wooden seats had been put in, "cut from the old large timbers of the south transept interior roof," a new east window made, and the chancel windows repaired. This was sad news, and when, after diligent search, I found the old woman who had the keys, and we entered the church, my worst anticipations were confirmed. Three parts of the edifice had been made to look spick and span new—the other part remains in its old state, simply because the funds have been exhausted. The famous east window is new; it all looks like a lecture hall just finished. Would it not have answered every good purpose to have mended the roof, so as to keep out the wet, and "repair" rather than "restore" the other parts of the building?

" We liked the old church best, sir," said the woman, who was wheezing away dismally. " This don't seem to us as if it were the same church like. See, yonder is the old house where they say the vicars used to live—I would come and show you, but my chest gives out." " Gives out "—a true Americanism if there ever was one.

The old house, at least, was uninjured—a simple timbered cottage, or, as one may read, " an ancient vicarage of post and panel, a specimen of the lowly abodes with which our pre-Reformation clergy often contented themselves." As I stood looking at this house, and thinking that old as it was I would rather have it than many a new one I had seen, an old woman came to the door and I wished her good morning. Presently she asked me if I would please to step in and sit down.

It was a low ceilinged room, that parlour of hers, with an immense fire-place in it, in which she had got her arm-chair and foot-stool, and other little comforts.

We ha' no minister here now," said she, after we had talked a bit, "and of course we miss 'un a good deal. I wish we had e'er a one to come and sit and read a little to a body. Three have died here the last few years."

" How do you manage to kill them off so fast ? " I asked.

" Oh," said the old lady very seriously, " it aint us as kills 'em off; they are worn out when they do come. That's the reason of it, sir. The last one as was here was a nice old gentleman, but his breath was bad, and so he could not get about much. We want a young man, if so be as we could get one, and I should not care how poor he was."

"The churchwarden told me," she went on, "this very märning that he was goin' to write to the Lord Chancery or something and try to get us a minister, and I hope he will, for it is bad to be without one. A gentleman comes over from Eastbourne, but I can't understand what he do say. Perhaps it is because I am old."

"How old are you?"

"I am seventy-seven, sir."

"And live here all alone?"

"Oh, yes; I have only two children myself, but how many *they* have I really do not know. I have the rheumatism very bad, all down my side. No, sir, it is not this old house as gives it to me, and I could not bear to leave it now. I have lived in it a-many years. I want for nothing, sir, for God is good to me."

"And so this is the house where the minister used to live in old times."

"Yes, sir; I have heard say that the Popes of Rome did use to live here." What on earth could have put that notion in the old lady's head? It fairly took my breath away.

"I do wish, sir," she continued, "that we could get a minister here, but no one seems to want to come. The place be too poor, I suppose. Oh, no, sir, I am not afraid to live here alone. God is good to me, sir, and I am very thankful."

She repeated these words very earnestly. No doubt there are some who would have gone into that room,

and looked round, and seen very little for anybody to
be thankful for; but it is not always those who have all
the good things of this life who are the most grateful
for what they get.

"I am very glad you are comfortable," said I, as I
turned to go away. "From what I can see in this world,
those who believe as you do seldom come to much harm."

"They do not, sir, for if you trust in God he never
deserts you, sir; no never."

The landscape was rather blurred to my eyes when I
left that little room. No doubt some profound philosopher, who has discovered all the secrets of the universe,
could explain to this poor old woman that she was the
victim of an exploded delusion, and that in fact there
is no God but "matter," and therefore nothing for any
human being to trust in. He might also propose
to her several infallible tests—prayer-tests and the like
—by which she could ascertain for herself that matter
was the be-all and the end-all; but what if she took the
test of her own daily experience and life, and found that
conclusive? No doubt the philosopher would have to
give her up as beyond the reach of reason—one of those
besotted "lower classes" for whom nothing can be done.

Through the meadow at the side of the church, and
across the little bridge over the "River Cuckmere"—a
river about as wide as a lady's ribbon—there is a foot-
path to Wilmington, under the very shadow of the Downs.
Or the visitor may turn to the Downs at once, and
mount to Firle's Beacon, and make his way over the
top to Lewes—a distance of nine miles or so; or he

may go over the hills in the opposite direction to Eastbourne. But I went towards Wilmington, after a
glance over the training stables which are at Alfriston, across that ancient street known as "Milton
Street," where there are two or three of the oldest and
quaintest cottages and barns in all Sussex. A stranger
does not often find his way into this solitary, yet
beautiful, region. Wandering on over the path which
looks like a thread amid a vast field of young green
wheat, one's eye is caught by a colossal figure of a man
on the side of the Downs close by—the Father of Giants,
with each hand closing on a huge staff, a strange wild
figure, upwards of 240 feet in length. How came it
there? It is thought that the monks of Wilmington
cut it in the chalk, in the days when a priory existed
here, a priory which was founded in the reign of
William Rufus; but the country folk hold that the
fairies made it. For the fairies are still believed to
have their homes in these Downs, and many a large
"ring" or "hag-track" may be seen in lonely spots, and
strange figures cut out on the grass. I have often stood
before them wondering how they were made, and who
made them : no one knows; but certain it is, that anybody who rambles about these lovely Downs will see
many strange things and hear strange sounds.

A wonderful old place is Wilmington, or "Wineltone"
as it was called before the Normans came over here, in
the days when it was held by the great Earl Godwin,
King Harold's father; a village with part of its old
priory gate still standing, and a farm-house made out of

the monks' former home, and a church so old that one gives up trying to find out the exact date of it. It is primitive enough in construction, for some of the windows and doors are cut out of the chalk. On the west wall, outside, I saw a grotesque figure, with its knees doubled up nearly to its chin, carved in stone; and inside there is a finely carved pulpit with a beautiful canopy over it, and chalk walls and arches, and ancient seats—altogether one of the plainest, oldest, and least "improved" churches in England. In the churchyard there is an enormous yew tree, of great height (for a yew) as well as girth—a tree said to be at least a thousand years old. Its companions are the dead; and how many must have come to it since first it struck its roots in this soil !

As I walked into the churchyard from the fields, I saw a white head appearing every now and then from an open grave, and heard the dull thud of earth falling as it was thrown up by the spade. It was the sexton digging a grave. Just beyond him was that solemn yew now about to be joined by still another companion, and the venerable church, and the solitary ruins, and the weird figure on the hill-side seeming to be watching all. "Ade, Ade"—scarcely any name but this old Sussex one of Ade on the gravestones. A large family, and death has reaped them nearly all.

I wandered over to the open grave. All was silent in this ancient and lonely churchyard, save the beating of the mattock and the dull fall of the earth. The sexton, like all else around, was old; his hair was white,

5

and he had a white beard. He worked very slowly, and as he worked he threw human bones into the hill which was fast rising outside the grave. It did not seem a real scene in any way. I should not hope to persuade anybody that all was as I saw it there that day. Yet there was the old man in the grave, and those were bones, the bones of some man or woman, which he was throwing up in every spadeful of earth. There was a thigh bone, and the smaller bones of the leg, and many more, and the earth near them had a tinge of brown, like iron-rust. It was all very strange. The words of Hamlet rose up, unbidden, to the mind : " Did these bones cost no more the breeding, but to play at loggats with 'em ? Mine ache to think on't."

"These are human bones," said I to the old man.

"Yes, sir, and many a year they must ha' lain here, for you see there is no sign of a coffin. That must ha' rotted away long ago."

"Do you know whose grave it was ? "

"Oh, no, it is too long ago for that. We ha' not used this part of the churchyard much. A very old grave, sir, and bad workin' in it." He struck hard into it with a cruel-looking three-pronged tool, and then began again with his spade, and threw up more bones. I tried to turn a little earth over them with my stick, but they refused to be covered.

"And so no one knows who was buried here."

"Why, no, sir, how should they? It was long ago, for the ground is so dry that it must have taken a long time for a body to get like this ; the grave is very old."

"Some poor person, I suppose?"

"No doubt, sir, but it makes no difference now. This is what we must all come to, sir, and we don't know how soon."

The grave told the tale; it needed no sermon from within it.

"I have not much time to spare," said the sexton, "for the funeral be at half-past four." It was then near three. "I shall not get home before milkin' time."

"And who is to be buried here?"

"Oh, sir, it be a poor 'ooman as lived over yonder, and very sad it be about them. She had three children at a birth a month or so ago, and she was very destitute. Her husband works on the line now, although he was formerly a labourer. The children all died, and the poor mother lingered on till last Friday, shocking destitute as I believe, sir. Poor thing, she was fairly wore out. Very sorry I be for 'em all; for the other five children as they have got are all young, and the father is dazed like. It be a great trouble for him."

"And the mother is to be buried in an hour's time?"

"Yes, sir, and she is better here perhaps; but I be sorry for *him* and the children. They live over there."

He pointed into the beautiful country beyond, more beautiful than usual it seemed as I turned from that mournful earth, and the ghastly relics of some fellow-creature who had once walked over these fields as lightly as the best, now tossed into the sunlight as if in grim irony of existence. To look out from the churchyard upon the endless landscape startles the mind. *That* all

seems so serene and immutable, while we—'tis but a day
we have before us to wander through these fast-vanishing
scenes; a brief day, well-nigh over before we realise that
it has begun, and the end of it is a heedless labourer
digging a hole in the ground, and a few solemn pathetic
words said over deaf ears, and a vacant place left in
perhaps one or two faithful hearts, and a hillock covered
with grass. An end but too familiar to us all, yet never
familiar. Who can but think of that noble passage of
Carlyle, loftiest of all modern teachers :—"This little
life-boat of an Earth, with its noisy crew of a Mankind,
and all their troubled History, will one day have
vanished; faded like a cloud-speck from the azure of
the All! What then is man! What then is man!
He endures but for an hour, and is crushed before the
moth. Yet in the being and in the working of a
faithful man is there already (as all faith, from the beginning, gives assurance) a something that pertains not
to this wild death-element of Time ; that triumphs over
Time, and *is*, and will be, when Time shall be no more."

Past the old church and the ruins of the Priory
there is a narrow cart-track which leads straight to a
chalk pit, and close to that pit the Long Man stretches
himself far up the hill. I walked up to the spot, and
found that the outline was bricked-in, a work of recent
times. In Horsfield's *Sussex* it is stated that the
"indentation is so very slight, as not to be visible on
the spot, although it may occasionally be seen at the
distance of two or three miles." It is to be seen quite
plainly now, the bricks being clear of grass and laid

two deep. Some people in the neighbourhood have taken this precaution to prevent the disappearance of their local giant. There appears to be a large tumulus in the hill just below it. From the Long Man a broad path runs round the brow of the hill, and half England seems to be at your feet. The Downs at this height present as fine a field for walking as any one could desire, but it is evident that few *do* desire it, for a boy who was frightening crows from a newly-sown field told me he had not seen a stranger there for three weeks. He seemed to be having an uneasy time of it. Two or three large crows would alight at a far corner of the field, which was on the hill side, and as soon as he made pretence to go towards them, some old stagers descended upon the ground from the other side, and this game they kept up as long as I watched the scene. It did not seem to be a pleasant way of passing the day. The Downs were in many places literally covered with the cowslip, the "freckled cowslip," as Shakespeare calls it, the bed of the most life-like of all fairies, Ariel.

> " In a cowslip's bell I lie ;
> There I couch when owls do cry."

On this particular day, there were miles of cowslips lighting up the green hills. I kept along the Downs till I found myself nearly opposite Polegate, with its junction, and then struck down towards it, and soon reached the station—thinking much of the yew tree and its silent companions, and of yonder lonely grave, and the sad group of children left motherless in a hard world.

CHAPTER VII.

IN THE SOUTH DOWNS.

AT Pulborough Junction, whither I had come on my
way to Parham, I met with a man who puzzled me.
He had a thin, keen, intellectual looking countenance,
a sharp eye, a somewhat sallow complexion, a tuft of
hair on his chin. An American, thought I, beyond a
doubt—and yet, how comes he here ? This is not the
road to Paris, nor even to Shakespeare's birth-place ;
not a part of any beaten track ; and, moreover, this
man has not a tourist's new suit of clothes on—facts
which tell against my surmise. I felt bound to speak
to him.

He evidently knew a great deal about that part of
the country, and the people who lived in it, but what
he was doing there was still a mystery. He had only
a small black bag in his hand, and could not possibly
be a commercial traveller, neither was he an artisan.

He seemed to be a well-educated and long-headed sort of man. I could make nothing of him.

"These are all rather poor places about here," said he, "Hardham, Greatham, small places not worth seeing."

"But I have come here on purpose to see small places. I don't like big ones."

"Well, if you want pretty scenery, you had better get nearer to the Downs—it is not very good about here."

"So I see;" and indeed the prospect from the railroad station is not very brilliant. "I will go on and sleep at Storrington, and see Parham on my way."

"You have heard of that affair, I suppose, sir? It was——"

"Yes," said I, "I know all about it, and do not want to hear any more, thank you. Is there any business doing about here?"

"Business? No, this is the wrong part of the world for that. We have a great seed merchant living just above there, and what do you think I noticed the other day? All his bags were stamped with some maker's name and the address, 'Ontario, Canada.' I asked about it, and they told me that Canadian-made bags have driven English bags completely out of the market, for they are both better and cheaper. What do you think of that?"

"I think," said I, "that the same sort of thing is going on in many trades just now. American calicos are better and cheaper than English goods of the same description, so they tell me. We shall have to bestir ourselves by and by."

" Yes,—you can get American calicos now in every village. It is all because we let the Americans see our machinery in the Great Exhibition, sir. Of course, they went away and imitated it, and we shall lose our trade. I always thought we did wrong to show our machinery."

That was his explanation of a great change in the current of trade, which is yet destined to make some noise in England when it is properly understood. For some time to come, our supreme confidence in ourselves will prevent our being much troubled about a competition which has already cost us dearly.

" I do not think that is the cause of it," said I, " but never mind. You will not be offended if I ask you what brings you to this dull part ?"

" I walk about all over Sussex, sir."

" Dear me, and so do I."

" But you are not in my trade, sir."

" I do not know that—tell me what you have got in that little black bag, and I shall be better able to judge.'

" My instruments."

" Well, well. You must be a dentist."

" No, sir ; and yet I go to almost every house far and near, at one time or another."

" Surely you are not an undertaker," said I, starting back, for I have no partiality for undertakers.

" I am not, sir ;" said the man ; " I am a *piano-forte tuner*."

I can give a shrewd guess at the trades of most persons at a glance, but what outward sign or token is there to denote a piano tuner? My friend was soon out of sight, black bag and all; and I shaped my course for Parham, that old house which is stored with countless curiosities of art and literature, from Coptic and Syriac manuscripts to a book called the "World of Wonders," containing an autograph of our Shakespeare; one of the very few relics of his handwriting in existence. I thought I had made arrangements to get a sight of these treasures, but I misunderstood them, and consequently I was obliged to content myself with a survey of the building from the carriage drive.

It is a picturesque house, with its gray old face turned towards the South Downs, and standing in the midst of a fine and well-timbered park. The oaks are ancient and wide-spreading; near the house are magnificent elms, and on the way to it, some incomparable hawthorns. The woods are thick; one wanders on through them knee-deep in ferns, turning up rabbits by hundreds. A somewhat melancholy looking park is it, with all its beauty, as many of these old parks are apt to be. The weight of years has settled down upon them. Parham can boast, among many other things, of a heronry. "Formerly," says my beloved Yarrell, "in the palmy days of falconry, the places where they were bred were almost held sacred; the bird was considered royal game, and penal statutes were enacted for its preservation. Now, however, the heron is disregarded, and left to depend on its own sagacity for its safety." But here it is still protected, and Mr. A. E. Knox, in his interesting "Ornithological

Rambles," tells us that Parham "can now boast of possessing one of the finest establishments in the kingdom, of this magnificent and interesting species."

When one has gazed one's fill at the house, there is nothing to do but to pass on, by the road which runs near the mansion and the little old church near it, and then almost touches a farmhouse called Springfield, and comes out at the very foot of the Downs. From thence it is a pleasant walk of a mile and a half to Storrington, where at the "White Horse" Inn I was furnished with a stuffy bed in a stuffy room, and had for dinner the toughest mutton that any man's teeth could cope withal—and this in the very midst of Mutton-land, where the genuine South Down sheep are as common as blackberries on the hedges. If you wish to taste the worst butter, milk, and cream in the world you must go to the country for them ; in Herefordshire you cannot get an apple ; in the South Down region there is no mutton fit to eat ; at the seaside there is no fish until the train comes in from London ; I should not be surprised to find nothing but American cheese sold in Cheshire, just as it is very certain that five butchers out of six are now selling American beef for English. And when good, it is better beef than ours, for it is grass-fed, whereas most of ours is the product of oil-cake and patent cattle-food and similar compounds. But too often the meat sent over here is not good, nor is it possible that the best descriptions could be imported at a profit, seeing that "prime joints" are from 25 cents to 27 cents a pound in New York, or a shilling and over,—

in other words, much about the same price as beef in England.

Storrington is a small old-fashioned place, with dark pine woods and commons in front of it, and the Downs rising somewhat abruptly at the back. In an evening stroll I came to a long, low, antiquated looking building about three-quarters of a mile out of the town, and wondered what it could be, for clearly it was not a gentleman's house, nor a farm, nor could it be a prison. Two tramps at that moment came along, one limping painfully in his stockings, his shoes being slung over his shoulder. "Beg pardon, sir," said the first, "can you tell us where is the Union?" A vile face he had—guilt, not wretchedness, was stamped in glaring characters upon it. There was a boy sitting on a rail over a little stream whittling a stick, like the traditional Yankee. He seemed buried in thought. "What place is that?" I asked, pointing to the long barn-like building. "It be the *workus*," replied he, the destination for the night of the rascally looking tramp and his limping companion—a brace of rascals who, I engage to say, will never do a hard day's work as long as they can get food and lodging for nothing. Why should they?

I started off betimes in the morning for the walk which I had marked out, to wit, from Storrington over the Downs to the Devil's Dyke, near Brighton, a journey the length of which I could not estimate, for the path over the hills is a doubtful and circuitous one. It turned out to be nearly twenty miles, including the descent upon Steyning and Bramber and the climb up the Downs again beyond Beeding. But the morning was so lovely—a perfect summer's day at the beginning of August, with a westerly breeze and a sky of blue, dappled with white fleecy clouds—that the prospect of a long walk was all that any man could need to put him in good spirits. Soon I was on the very crest of the Downs behind Storrington, and could see the sea gleaming like silver some miles away, and vessels seeming no more than small black dots upon it. Landward a column of light smoke marked out the city of Chichester, and nearer still the eye rested on the dark foliage of the thick trees at Parham, while far in the distance was the clear blue line of the Surrey hills. The white clouds, soft and billowy, which occasionally passed over the face of the sun threw wonderful shadows on the grass; a huge giant appeared all across the path, then a turreted castle—one could almost make out the sentinel on the walls—strange and gigantic animals, shapes not to be likened to anything known to us on earth. All this and more were visible on those glorious Downs that August day, for what forms will not the shadows take in the early morning or at eve, especially in wild and lonely places? Nothing could have been changed for the better, not even the weather which people abuse so much, for it was such weather as only the English summer yields, neither hot nor cold, but with a delightful freshness in the air which makes the blood dance again. Nathaniel Hawthorne, decidedly no

lover of England or anything English, could not refrain
from breaking out now and then in praise of these
summer days. "I think," he says in his *English Note
Book*, "that there is never in this English climate
the pervading warmth of an American summer day.
The sunshine may be excessively hot, but an over-
shadowing cloud, or the shade of a tree, or of a
building, at once affords relief; and if the slightest
breeze stirs, you feel the latent freshness of the air."

It was not very long before I came within sight of
the little church of Washington, high up on the hill
side,—a very different place from the other Washington across the Atlantic. This little spot was a Saxon
settlement, as Mr. Lower relates :—" Wasa-inga-tún,
the settlement of the sons of Wasa." It was in this
parish, as the same industrious archæologist tells us,
that three thousand pennies were found, of the reigns
of Edward the Confessor and Harold II. They were
supposed to have been hidden just before the battle of
Hastings; and what is very curious is, that down to
the very day they were found, in 1866, local tradition
had pointed out the spot as that in which a great
treasure was concealed. Local tradition, as I have
more than once pointed out in these pages, is not so
mean an authority as some people would have us
suppose. The vessel which contained these coins,
says Mr. Lower, "was turned up by the plough, and
they were so scattered broadcast, that they were
regarded by the peasantry as pieces of old tin, and
sold, principally to the village innkeeper, for the

purchase of ale. In one instance, half a pint of them was offered for a quart of ' double X.' "

From this point the Downs rise up sharply, and begin to be covered with shrubs and small trees, which get thicker and thicker until a dark belt of wood is reached at the top, like a huge cap on the brow of the hill. This is Chanctonbury Ring, a landmark for many a league round about. I had seen it from distant points so often that I was well pleased to make nearer acquaintance with it. The view from the "Ring" is superb, and the spot has something more than a picturesque interest connected with it, for it is said to be an earthwork of Celtic origin, planted round with trees. To the right of it on the plain, almost under its shade, there stands the beautiful old house known as Wiston Manor. I made my way down to it, not without some scrambling, and found another of those wondrous parks which add so much to the beauty of England. The house looks stately, and even solemn, among the green fields, distinctly the memorial of another age,—an age when the Shirley family flourished here, and when one of the three famous "band of brothers" went into foreign lands and married a Circassian lady, and afterward came back and lived with his wife in this house at Wiston. But the roving spirit was strong in him, and he returned to the East, and died in Persia, and his wife ended her days in a nunnery. The last of the Shirleys died in 1638, and the estate came into possession of the present family, the Gorings, in 1743. " No Shirley relics now exist in the house at Wiston," says Murray's *Handbook*, but nevertheless I much longed to see the grand old hall and dining-room within, and stood a long time admiring the magnificent entrance, the heavy mullioned windows, and the exquisite park with deer moving in stately herds to and fro.

A short walk along the road brings one to Steyning, a clean and comfortable-looking town, with an inn, the " White Horse," which looks as if it might be made a pleasant home for a day or two. Few towns in Sussex have struck me more favourably than this. I was directed to the vicarage for the keys of the church, and the gardener came and showed me the sacred building, the chief features of which are the capitals of some of the pillars, of fine workmanship, and supposed to date back to the time of the Confessor. The vicarage is said to be embellished with some curious wood carvings; but although the maid-servant who opened the door to me was gracious, and the watch-dog did not bark or bite, yet I did not like to ask permission to go in. It is an unlucky day when the traveller is obliged to pass three houses of great interest unseen.

Half a mile through a shady lane, across the line, and we are at Bramber. The lane is narrow, and presently I met an elderly gentleman coming along with a dog. We had a few minutes' chat together, for he seemed to be a good-natured man, and in the mood for a talk.

" You would scarcely believe," said he, " that this is the old coach road we are on now."

"I should not," said I, "for there seems scarcely room for a wheelbarrow. I suppose, however, that these young trees and bushes have encroached upon it of late years."

"Not so much as you might think. The roads about here were proverbially bad, and there were only certain places at which it was possible for one vehicle to pass another. That's why they used to put bells on horses, so that the drivers might get out of each other's way in good time."

"Thank you," said I; "now will you tell me whereabouts is Bramber Castle?"

"There, just above you, hidden by those trees. A mere heap of stones is left now, but it must have been a strong fortress once, for the sea came up here formerly, and the castle was intended to guard the land in this direction."

I wondered who and what the civil gentleman with the dog could be, but he passed on without my finding out, and in a few minutes I made my way to the tall fragment of an old tower and the shattered walls, which are now all that is left of the seat of the once powerful Norman family of De Braose. All ruined and broken as the walls are, they still look as if they would last for ever. There is a mound in the middle, encompassed by thorn trees, from which a splendid view of the Downs and surrounding country is obtained. Just below is the church, with its small ivy-clad tower; but the gate thereto was locked, and I went on my way without seeing it.

In the one street of Bramber, near to a clean and cosy-looking inn, I noticed a signboard pointing "To the Museum." What sort of a museum could it be? It turned out to be a very curious place indeed, prepared and fitted up by one man, whose name is James Potter, a self-trained naturalist. Numerous animals, birds, and insects, all caught and stuffed by Potter himself, and made up into striking or grotesque groups, were round the room. There is a "kittens' croquet party," which must be the delight of children, a "squirrels' carouse," a cricket match played by guinea-pigs, and other scenes, wonderfully life-like, and all sweet and clean and pleasant to look upon, which is quite a new feature in connection with stuffed animals. " I suppose," said I, "many of these creatures are only made up?" "Oh no, sir," said Potter, "they are all real. I was obliged to have them alive, or I could not have given them the *expression.*" There were some capital herons and king-fishers, caught close by. I noticed on the wall a certificate, setting forth that in September, 1839, a premium of £2 had been awarded to James Potter for "fifty-six years' continuous service." And a very liberal reward too for over half a century's faithful service, and I hope James Potter took care of his large fortune, and properly secured it to his descendants in the male line.

" Was that your father?" I asked the naturalist " My grandfather, sir, I *believe.*" What an odd thing that he should be in doubt on such a point. Evidently, however, he is a worthy and an industrious man, and I am quite sure he has not squandered the family inheritance in riotous living.

We now come to Beeding, smallest of small villages, where once stood a priory, long since gone to dust. Here I resolved to recover the crest of the Downs, and with that object in view, I followed the chalky road which may be descried from Beeding, turning round by the " Rising Sun " inn.   It is a long and steep road, and near the top I could distinguish a steam-plough at work, and could hear its noise and fuss while still afar off.   A man was cutting oats in a field which I passed, and "after compliments " I said to him, " So you have got the steam-plough even here."

" Ay, it be steam everywhere now," said he, wiping his forehead, " a poor fellow don't get no chance."

" Well, you see, it saves the farmer money."

" No, it doänt ; it ain't cheaper in the end.   The reaping machine do gather up all the stoäns, and mucks the corn all over the plaäce.   It waästes a sight, I can tell ye."

" But it does the work quickly."

" Not much quicker on these hills than we can. And look how clean it is done ; " he pointed down to his little sheaves with some pride.   They were all tied up carefully, and laid by in rows as if for an agricultural exhibition.   " You can't get ne'er a machine to do that.   I sometimes think I will emigrate."

" You will have to go a long way, if you want to get out of the way of steam."

" Well, it be hard to get a living here, and yet this

be the best way of doing the work, after all," going on with his reaping; "you don't gather up no stoäns with this."

The competitors, man and machine, were both left doing their best, and at last I was on the top of the hills once more, with the ever welcome sea again in sight. To the right was Worthing, while just in front one could see the tops of the vessels lying off Shoreham. A large city, covered with smoke, stood a good way further to the left—and this was the once quiet village of Brighthelmstone. The view of the sea from this point seems almost boundless. After "prospecting" a little at the top, you strike a green lane and cart-track, running past a couple of barns over the brow of the hill. Two valleys have to be crossed, but the green lane need not be lost sight of all the way. Every now and then one comes across patches of purple heath, and the ground beneath one's feet is sprinkled with celandine, and is so thickly covered with wild thyme that every step which crushes the grass sends up a fragrance more delicious and more welcome than all the poor imitations of sweet smells which are vended in Bond Street. Everywhere on the hill-side large flocks of sheep are regaling themselves on this celestial food, and turning it into "saddles" and "haunches" which will cause the mouth of the epicure to water and his heart to leap for joy. Southdown sheep may be found in many parts of the world, but without the Southdown grass their flesh cannot have the true and proper savour. Wandering on amid thousands of these adorable creatures, we at last see the little village of Poynings, with comfortable farm-houses near, and the Devil's Dyke above—smooth, round, and *fat* at the top, "muttony," as some one has said of the South Downs generally. And there my walk came to an end, for the road between the Dyke and Brighton is one of the dustiest in England, and is overrun with holiday makers in various stages of drunkenness—noisy, ill-looking, offensive, much to be avoided by all sober and right-minded persons. But of the Downs themselves no one can ever grow weary, for, as Mr. Lower truly says, " In their sweet undulations there are continually changing curves and indents, which vary as they may —from the precipitous valley down which a confident horseman would scarcely urge his courser, to the gentle declivity where the most delicate lady (in imitation of the fairies which of old haunted it) might dance—are always lines of beauty, such as we confidently believe have nowhere else an existence, except, perhaps, in some graceful island group of the Pacific."

CHAPTER VIII.

HAYWARD'S HEATH TO EAST GRINSTEAD.

Another "Country Inn."—An Uncomfortable Night. —The Rich Man
from London.—Cuckfield.—A Vision at the King's Head.—
The Haunted House. — Lindfield and its Church.—Pax Hill.—
Horsted Keynes.—Arcadian Shepherds Carousing.—Broadhurst.
—East Grinstead.—The "Players."—The "Last Performance."

As I have a fancy for starting out on my walks early
in the morning, I went to Hayward's Heath overnight,
intending to explore some of the country round about
it before the main business of my journey began. I
found an inn there almost adjoining the station; a good
inn for aught I know in ordinary times, but it so
chanced on this occasion that the best rooms were all
engaged, as the waiter informed me, by a "London
gent." These visitors from London, with their piles of
money and unlimited orders for all the best rooms, are
grievously in the way of the honest pedestrian, who can
scarcely find rest for the soles of his feet where they
are. They are worse than the Colorado beetle. You
cannot compete for the favour of "mine host," still less
for the smiles of his dame, with a gentleman who has a
gold mine in the City, or who has just brought out a
foreign loan for the benefit of his poorer countrymen

and their widows and orphans. Thus it turned out that my night at the hotel was passed in the most dismal manner. I had to dine on the crumbs which were brought down to me from Dives' table, and Dives with his friends caroused till a late hour, and I had scarcely sunk off into an uneasy slumber, when a horrible groaning, puffing, and blowing brought me rudely from the land of dreams. I at first thought it was the "London gent" careering about in a fit, or dreaming of his bags of gold, and thinking he was being robbed thereof, but it was only a goods train blowing off or otherwise disposing of its steam, a process which lasted all the night long. I seldom go to the country for quiet; when I want that I come to London. The noises at Hayward's Heath that night would have shamed Piccadilly. I will say nothing of the big dog in the stables which barked all night, because he can be poisoned by the next traveller who passes that way. Take a piece of prepared meat with you, and throw it out of window just before going to bed. The early village cock can be "fixed" in the same manner. But the engine is not amenable to this course of treatment, nor is it to be practised on a London gent without fear of the 'sizes.

Before these troubles overtook me, however, I had enjoyed an interesting walk to Cuckfield, a pleasant old town a couple of miles or so from Hayward's Heath. The two quaint inns in it had a look so inviting that they caused me to regret the risk I had run of crossing the blighting path of a millionaire at a railway hotel.

Moreover, as I passed the "King's Head" I spied a fair damsel setting out clean glasses on a spotless cloth,—how infinitely preferable to the ordinary hotel waiter-man, who has dirty hands, and smells of gin and onions. The hands of that rosy maiden were not dirty, I will engage for it, though to be sure I had no means of judging, much to my loss. Just opposite the tap of this inn are several queer little shops, among them a photographer's, with a sign in his window setting forth that he takes "photographs daily,"—a great boon to the Cuckfieldians, and one of which I hope they make good use. Half a mile or so beyond is one of those old houses, around which many associations of legend or romance have gathered—Cuckfield Place, the "Rookwood Hall" of Harrison Ainsworth. An avenue of limes leads to the house, and one of these trees is believed to have had the magic power of foretelling the approaching death of its owner. As the lord of the estate passed towards his home, a bough from the tree fell upon his path, and full of youth and health as he might be, he then knew that he was about to cross the threshold for the last time. I met in the avenue a woman with two children, probably a gamekeeper's wife, and asked her a question or two about the house, which I could see at a little distance.

"It has all been done up the last few years," said she, "except at the back, and that is just as it used to be. You can walk round if you like."

"And can you show me the tree about which they tell the stories?"

"No, I cannot, sir, for I don't rightly know which it is. But I have heard say that when anybody is going to die in the big house a branch snaps off, and they *do* say that when the last master died a bough was found lying on the path the next morning." In this case the warning tree seems to have been a little late with its sign. As I had read that the tree was carefully preserved I looked about for it, and suppose that I discovered it in a veteran of the avenue which was bound round with iron plates, and seemed to be more decrepit than its fellows, as if the awful responsibility of being an instrument for making known the decrees of the dark Fates had deprived it of some share of its spirit and vigour. On the other side of the house everything wears a strangely wild and romantic aspect. There are gloomy pools of water, over which a thin mist was slowly stealing, half hiding the heavy weeds and grass which choked them. Hard by was a decayed out-building, in the yard of which two huge bones were to be seen, and presently a gaunt dog came out slowly and silently, and began gnawing at them, occasionally casting a searching and wary eye up at me. The back of the house had a time-worn appearance, and little stretch of the romancist's imagination is needed to invest it with those spectral guests which from time immemorial have haunted ancient family mansions such as this. Yet there is nothing so uncanny about the house itself as the fateful tree, the dark pools of water, and the crumbling out-house, with the huge bones before it, like the relics which strewed the cave of Giant Despair, and the strange, solitary dog.

The sombre influences of this spot were soon dispersed under the early morning sun, as I started off for East Grinstead. It is a hot and treeless road to Lindfield, fortunately less than two miles in length, and the suburbs of Hayward's Heath are as little attractive as suburbs generally are. But Lindfield is a pleasant village, with very ancient timbered houses in it, the finest examples thereof being at the back of the churchyard. There is a good common at the entrance to the village, and a pond, and then a long street abounding with old houses, all more or less interesting. "Any one tired of the bustle of this changeful life," says Mr. Lower, "might safely retire to Lindfield as one of the most peaceful spots in Britain," and all that I saw there fully confirmed this impression. The church, with its shingled spire, has a homely look, but, alas! it is but another example of the mischief wrought by those architectural wreckers, the "restorers." Whitewash and plaster have done their worst, and some old fine stained glass has been carried off altogether. I saw traces of paintings on the walls, and a man who was cleaning the clock, told me that there were formerly three, of which his description was vague. "On one there used to be someone or other weighing out soles," said the man, or so I understood him.

"A fishmonger?" I asked.

"No, a *hangel*. On the other was the apostles, or something, and on the other—well, I forget what that was. Some party or other has had 'em all plastered over. They do what they like with this church, for you

G

see it's in Chancery, and nobody takes any interest in
it. The old Vicar, who died lately, came here only on
Sunday mornings, and then he tried to make himself
disagreeable. He stopped all the singing." This
bad account I found afterwards corroborated by Mr.
Lower, who says that "within the nineteenth century,
bodies of deceased parishioners, have remained in the
church for several days, for want of an officiating
priest." A curious "sepulchral effigy on three glazed
tiles," dated 1520, has apparently been taken to rejoin
the stained glass; at any rate I could find no trace of
it, nor had the clock-cleaner any recollection of seeing
or hearing talk of such a thing.

From the churchyard, the road passes over an old
bridge, and just beyond it are the gates of an Elizabethan mansion, known as Pax-hill. I learned that the
house had recently been sold—to a "London broker,"
as a matter of course—and that the new family had not
arrived, so I summoned up courage to go to the door,
and ask permission to see it. After some persuasion,
I prevailed, and found the house a very interesting
building, though bearing ample traces of careless treatment and neglect. It has received some modern addi-
tions, which are in the worst possible style and taste.
But the old rooms are charming, and have exquisite
examples of wood-carving within them. There is a
capital hunting scene round the fireplace of the library,
and in a panel I noticed the date 1612. The dining
room is full of admirable carving. It seemed to me
that in some of the old bedrooms, the oaken panelling

has been covered with a cheap and nasty wall-paper. The modern builder and repairer is capable of greater atrocities than that.

From the house one goes out at the other end of the park, and by a pleasant nutty road—and this has been a great year for hazel nuts—to Horsted Keynes, a small old-fashioned village, with a little church below it. In this church the great and good Archbishop Leighton used to preach, and here he worked among the poor, spending "most of his income in works of charity," not in rich vestments, or in efforts to imitate the rites and ceremonies of the Papal Church. I fear such a man would be lightly esteemed by the Society of the "Holy Cross" and "priests" generally. There is a little inn in the village, at which the pedestrian may obtain modest refreshment should he need it, and there is no other between this and East Grinstead, eight hilly miles away. I halted for a few minutes here, for a biscuit and some cider, and found two rustics smoking long pipes and drinking *hot* gin-and-water at a little after ten on a "muggy" day in August. No wonder the poets laud the simplicity of rural tastes! The landlady seemed to be a worthy and respectable woman, and I saw her go to the kitchen and brew the hot grog for the peaceful and innocent swains. She told me that she had very little business, and, indeed, there did not seem to be two dozen people in the place. After looking at the old church and the quaint little effigy inside, I kept along the narrow road, which runs past the churchyard, in preference to the turnpike

above, and eventually came to the ancient house of
"Broadhurst," where Archbishop Leighton lived.   It
is now a farm-house, with very ancient barns near it ;
all the gate-posts and rails are rotting with age, and
one can take pinches of dust out of them, as out of a
snuff-box.   Past the house, the road leads to a gate
locally called "double-gate," and then the visitor must
cross the road, and go over the stile into a field, and
across a second field, which ends in a small patch of
wood and the public road.   It is necessary then to
turn to the right, and follow the road, which will
occasionally offer some fine views of the South and
North Downs.   While still four miles away, East
Grinstead can very clearly be seen, standing on a hill.
The last part of this road has, to tell the truth, little
to recommend it, and the number of times one has
to go up hill and down again, chiefly up, is past all
counting.   The distance from Hayward's Heath, with
the deviations I have described, is over thirteen miles.

A pleasant old town is East Grinstead, as its name
implies—*grenestede*, or green place, "a clearing in the
great forest of the Weald."   The houses have a venerable appearance, and the college founded by the Earl
of Dorset in 1608 is an imposing building.   The church
is mainly new—almost the only new building which I
observed in the place.   Although it was a hot day, the
room in the inn where I took lunch was quite cold and
chilly, a peculiarity of country inns.   Doubtless they
are generally very damp.   While reading some verses
on a tombstone in the churchyard—verses quite equal

to Crabbe's, and much in the same vein—I heard the sounds of a band, and asked an old woman who was passing what was going on.

"It's the players," said she, "they are over in yonder field."

If there is one form of the drama which pleases me better than another it is that which is played beneath a tent in a field, by a company of ladies and gentlemen who have their own ways of interpreting the works of the great masters, and among whom the older traditions of the stage are preserved, from sheer force of necessity, more closely than in the crack theatres of the day. These rovers, now fast dying out, handed down their "business" one to the other, passed on their favourite "gags," and had little time to study "new readings," or invent a new style of acting. I have sometimes thought in looking at them that one got a fair idea of acting as it used to be in Shakespeare's day, for the stage is a great conservator of tradition, and many an old custom is, or was, preserved by the strolling players which had long before been discarded by the great actors in theatres. One of the best *Hamlets* I ever saw was played by a poor fellow in a field in Derbyshire, on a bitter winter's night, when the snow was falling heavily outside, and a charcoal fire in front of the stage scarcely kept us from freezing, and Ophelia had drunk so much beer that her subsequent tumble into the stream did not surprise any of the audience. Why, by the way, is *Ophelia* treated by the priest at the grave as if she had committed suicide, or as if her death was, as he says, "doubtful?" According to the circumstantial account previously given by the Queen, it was a very clear and undoubted case of accidental death, whether according to Crowner's quest or any other law.

The abolition of fairs has taken the strolling player's occupation from him, and I had little expectation of meeting with any of my old Derbyshire friends in the field at East Grinstead. The company, in fact, turned out to be a travelling circus. A woman was brushing the skirt of her gown at the door of one of the waggons or carts, and another was dressing her child on the grass. Their faces were tanned to a copper colour by the sun. I went up to them and asked them how they had fared in East Grinstead, carefully paving the way by giving the child a sixpence. The woman had a listless and care-worn expression, but this did not prevent her from taking the sixpence.

"We haven't done very well," said the one with the child, for the other had retired, probably to put on her skirt.

"Business is bad at all the theatres in London," said I, in order that she might see she had companions in misfortune.

"It has been hard with us everywhere," she said; "and the old woman grumbles at us all, and says she can't keep it going much longer."

"Is the circus owned by a woman?"

"Yes—there she is at the door taking tickets. This is our last performance here."

"Where do you go next?"

"I don't exactly remember the name of the town, but they say it's twenty-five miles away from here. We shall have to foot it a great part of the way, for the horses are tired out, and can't work in the ring and be on the road too, day and night."

I went over to the tent—the performance was nearly over. The clouds were gathering heavily, wild scud was flying about the sky, and there was a south-west wind blowing. "You will have rain for your packing up," said I to the woman who took the tickets.

"Yes, sir, and that's bad, for we have to put the tent away wet, and everything goes wrong. Rain, rain—there's nothing *but* rain," said she moodily as she locked up the bag containing the money and the tickets, and hurried off to the door. The clown was in the ring making the old, old jokes; a man was riding on the back of the wild untamed steed, which was soon to be put in the shafts once more, and drag the dejected party to some other village green far over the hills of Sussex. The poor horse looked as if he had scarcely a leg left to stand upon, and the fearless rider seemed bored to death. The "ringmaster" was indulging in that species of fun which a British audience is never slow to appreciate, knocking down the clown for being "himperdent," or slashing him across the legs with his whip. There was no sawdust on the ground—merely the green grass, turned up a little all round in a sort of narrow trench. Presently the rain came pattering down upon the tent, the wind howled dismally, and the poor old horse slackened his gentle canter, thinking doubtless that the roads outside would be heavy for his night's journey, and cursing his father and mother for giving him a black and white coat, and thus condemning him to the fate of making sport for rustic children in a circus.

CHAPTER IX.

FROM PETWORTH TO MIDHURST.

IT is occasionally a good plan to make some great park or house the starting-point for a long day's ramble, especially if the region you intend to traverse is a wild one. The effect of the scenery is then heightened by contrast. Petworth is a very suitable house to select for this purpose. Although not beautiful externally, it contains within its walls many rare treasures of art, and the park forms a worthy introduction to the scenes which lie beyond. Anyone who can spend an hour among the portraits which may be found in every room of this house, even without reference to the other pictures, will find his time profitably employed. Take the portrait of the ninth Earl of Northumberland, now in what is called the "square room"—and a very square room it is—close by the fireside. What an example is here of the art of portrait-painting! What dignity and melancholy the great artist, Vandyke, has thrown into the expression of this man's face! We seem to read there the whole story of his long imprisonment in the Tower—of the weary waiting for release, and the gradual extinction of hope and peace. The portrait stands out so vividly, that one stands silently before it almost expecting the man on whom sorrow has left so many ineffaceable marks to move or speak. It is a work which, when once seen, can never be forgotten. On the opposite side of the same room, near the door, is a portrait of a very different kind and of a very different person—Queen Catherine Parr. The face is hard, dull, and heavy, but evidently true to life. The painter is Holbein, and in the famous "carved room," a masterpiece by the same artist may be seen— the portrait of Henry the Eighth. Every detail of this wonderful work is a study, from the face and hands of the subject, to the jewels on the clothes. The picture gives, no doubt, an accurate likeness of the king, and we see in it a large-built, fat, sensual person, with small eyes and rather a high forehead, who would look more like a drayman than a king but for his small hands and rich attire. Here again the living man seems to stand before us. The portrait of Edward the Sixth (painted when he was ten years old) should be com- pared with the likeness of his father—there are the same small eyes, and the same general outline of the features. The five portraits of ladies by Vandyke in the white and gold room, and Rubens' curious picture of two prelates kneeling, are among the other works which will live in the memory. However hurried the

visitor may be, he should on no account fail to see
Vandyke's portrait of himself, or Rembrandt and his
wife painted by the great master, or the striking
portrait of Cardinal Medici, or Hogarth's delightful
picture of Peg Woffington.

The new picture gallery was still unfinished in
October, 1876, and it seemed then a somewhat ill-lit and
unsatisfactory apartment. In the middle of the long
passage or corridor, near the chapel, the light was very
bad, although the day was a remarkably sunny and
cheerful one. The tapestry in the hall has been restored, and the colours look so bright that at first one
is inclined to suspect the antiquity of the work. The
grand staircase is one of the noblest in England, and
the old chapel, said to have been built by Hotspur, but
much disfigured by gold angels and cherubim and
other rubbish, is well worth a visit. The place has
a cold and neglected appearance. The magnificent
carvings by Grinling Gibbons in the large room where
Holbein's Henry the Eighth hangs, can scarcely be
properly looked at during the short time visitors are
allowed to remain. But let not the visitor complain
that he is hurried through the rooms too fast, but
rather recollect that it is extremely liberal on the part
of the owner to open the house to the public at all.
For Petworth is one of the great houses which are still
the homes of the families to which they belong. Lord
Leconfield and his wife and children live here for at
least ten months out of the year, and often as the
party of visitors enter a room at one door, they may

see the ladies of the family retreating from it at the
other.

The various views of the park which attract the eye
in going over the house will not be found to promise
too much. The glimpses from the windows are not,
indeed, so beautiful as those which are the chief glories
of the "Deepdene" in Surrey, but they are very
striking, and bid one to expect a lovely walk through
the noble domain outside. And in this the visitor
will not be disappointed. The South Downs run to
the left of the park, only three miles away, and they
help to give the scenery very much the appearance
of the country in many parts of Wales. From a
grove of limes about three-quarters of a mile away
there is a glorious view. Looking towards the house
—which at this distance shows to some advantage—
the South Downs stretch away to the right, and to the
left there is a charming expanse of woodland and
meadow, with herds of deer grazing in the foreground,
and beyond all, the dark ridge of Blackdown. As you
go on, it is well to strike off from the carriage drive,
just past the little church at Tillington, and make for
the higher parts of the park, keeping the "Prospect
Tower" in front. The ground at the time of the year's
decline is in some places an inch deep in chestnuts,
and the noble trees scatter a fresh supply to the
ground with every puff of wind. From this high
ground the larger part of the immense park may be
seen, and as fair a bit of this beautiful England is
spread before the traveller as he could well desire to

behold.   The Tower is worth climbing ; from the leads
you can see for miles around ; to the north of you
there is a broad valley in a semi-circle of hills, and
far in the distance you can make out Mr. Tennyson's
house, on the edge of Blackdown.   The wild scenery
in this direction comes up to the very edge of the park,
and extends from it far as the eye can reach.   One
wonders why the house at Petworth was not built on
the beautiful spot where Prospect Tower stands, rather
than in a somewhat common-place part of the lower
park.

There is, of course, a more direct way of going to
Midhurst from Petworth than that which is here
described—the turnpike road is easily found, and is not
without merits of its own.   But the route which I
made out, and now recommend to others, is by far the
best for those who travel on foot, and who wish to see
as much as they can of the country.   The walk through
Petworth Park is something gained—for although there
is a carriage drive through it, yet the upper and more
beautiful portion is available only for the pedestrian.
From the Prospect Tower the continuation of the road
may readily be seen.   The woman at the tower will
open the gate close by, and the best path to take is
that which runs across the common in front of you,
nearly due north.   You leave an old white timbered
cottage to the left, after passing a pond, and then the
path turns west, and runs through a mass of high ferns
and furze—a specimen of the wild country through
which one may wander for days together in this part of

Sussex, and the adjoining districts of Surrey and Hampshire. Very soon the narrow track takes us into the midst of a copse, which at first sight does not look very encouraging, but at the top the path trends to the north-west, and a few yards farther there is the road, with several old cottages on each side One of them, on the left, has a yew-tree before it. This place is called River, or River Street, and the common we have just passed over is in part Upperton and in part River Common. We go past three more ancient timbered houses or farms to the right, and open a gate just before coming to a yew hedge, cut into various shapes. All this part is very quaint and old-fashioned, and few strangers ever are seen in it, except perhaps an artist or two now and then in summer. In the autumn and winter it is quite deserted by visitors.

The path by the gate just spoken of leads down through a wood, and if you bear to the right, it will bring you to a wooden bridge over a brook—path and wood and brook, each a delight to the wanderer, and combining to form a charming picture. A cart track now runs up straight in front of you, and it is only necessary to pursue that in order to be taken safely to the village of Lodsworth.

Here is another of the nooks and corners of England which looks as if it might have been untouched for hundreds of years, except the church, on which the hand of the restorer has fallen with great severity. Of the ancient building, nothing but the tower and doorway and part of the timber roof remain. Even an

old yew-tree has been carted off, and pretty coniferæ
planted around, looking like so many Christmas-trees
in a toy-shop. There used to be an open cloister of
timber-work on the south side of the churchyard, but
no trace of it is left. It has fallen before wind, weather,
and "æsthetic influences" combined. I managed to
find the man who had the keys. He was a queer
little tailor, adapted by nature to play the apothecary
in *Romeo and Juliet*, and was at work in a very small
shop, next door to his house. When I interrupted
him, he was busily engaged in flattening out a pair of
corduroys for some young hopeful of Lodsworth who
was just going to be breeched. He came out in his
shirt sleeves and slippers, and went over the church
with me. It turned out that he was the "clerk," and
his seat was close by the wall as we entered. "I used
to sit near the pulpit," said he, "but they have put me
back a smart ways. They alters everything. I suppose
it's the march of intelleck." I asked this ironical tailor
about the "open cloister of timber work." He said it
had been blown down and carted off. "I remember,"
he added, "when there were the remains of a chapel
close by the church. It was afterwards used as a
stable, but is all gone long ago. You can see the
stumps of the trees that used to run along side of it."
I looked over the wall and saw *them* plain enough.
"Where did the money come from in this small place
to make all these alterations in your church?" I asked.
"Ah, there you puzzle me," said the clerk; "I can't
make it out. The rector, he never let anything alone;

but now he's gone somewhere else. I suppose he won't let nothing alone there. Bless me, what a rum world it is." "True," I said, "very true; but pray tell me how it is that you have your workshop away from your house. The women-folks, eh?" My friend of the scissors gave me a sly look, smiled slightly, but evidently thought it best not to commit himself to the expression of any opinion, especially as his wife was listening at the open window. "I call it a *very rum world*," repeated he, "and so would you if you lived here. Dead and alive it is. I makes clothes for all around—it would never do to depend on this village;" and I could quite believe him, for there did not seem to be half-a-dozen persons who wore trousers in the whole place,—at least, not of the male sex.

Round the road to the right we come to the "Hollist Arms," a plain sort of inn, with two or three old cottages and a little green in front. It is now necessary to take the turning which runs to the left of this inn, and to keep to it, not wandering off by a somewhat tempting looking road to the right. Some distance on you reach a farm-house, with a box-tree at the corner of the garden, and an old yew cut and trained to grow in the shape of an umbrella or a gigantic mushroom. The box-tree is also trimmed to suit the fancy of its possessor. In front of this farm, the road turns to the left; but keep straight forward, and you will find yourself led down another copse, to a stile, and there across a field in front is the entrance to Cowdray Park.

A party of chestnut gatherers were standing round this stile, having evidently had a successful morning's work, for two large sacks and some smaller bundles, stuffed as full of chestnuts as a turkey is at Christmas, were lying by their side. They turned out to belong to one family—a big brother, three sisters (one of them rather a pretty girl) and three or four children. One of the latter looked very ill, and I asked what was the matter with him. "He has never been well since he had the measles," replied the elder sister, and the poor little fellow was blinking at the light, and coughing, and evidently had a very slight and precarious hold on what my friend the tailor considers "a rum world." "Come, get on with the bag," said the brother, and the poor boy roused himself and took up his bundle, and stumbled along with blinking eyes and a racking cough. I distributed a few pence among them, and received a handful of chestnuts in exchange—the pretty girl had all the big ones in her pocket, and she was for giving me the entire cargo ; but I had as many as I could carry, and left the party in the little wood, with the light of the setting sun gilding the brown leaves all round them, and they plodding their way heavily along the narrow path.

Cowdray Park is a romantic spot, not only in its present aspect but in its past associations. To the left are the South Downs, now looking very near at hand, and "Chanctonbury Ring," just above Worthing, can be very plainly seen. Some old oak-trees skirt the path, and all around there extends a solitary region,

which seems to speak as plainly as any historian
could do of the decay and extinction of some great
family which once ruled as lords in all this part. The
past history of a place often seems to stamp some
outward mark or characteristic upon it, as the byegone
years leave their traces upon a man's face. As we cross
the public road in Cowdray Park, and go down the path
to the left hand, and mark the ivy-clad ruins in front,
the thick belt of trees still covered with the sad colours
of autumn foliage, the deserted aspect of the country
far away towards the South Downs, it is not possible to
prevent the thoughts wandering to a page of family
history as strange as any which the novelist can conjure
up. In a single month, the beautiful house of the
Montagues, and the last male heir to the line, perished
together. The house was one of the most famous in
the country—its walls were embellished with works
from the hands of Holbein and other masters, its
chapel was renowned for its beauty, and of the glory
of its banqueting hall we may still form a faint idea
from the traces which are left. The paintings on
the walls were preserved from destruction during the
civil wars by a coating of plaster. But everything was
destroyed by fire on the night of September 24th or
25th, 1793, and within a month a strange fatality
befell the eighth Lord Montague, who never heard of
the disaster which had overwhelmed the home of his
fathers. He was travelling in Switzerland, and determined to make an attempt, with a companion, to pass
the water-falls and rapids of Laufenberg. "The magis-

A TUDOR ENGLISH MANSION
RUINS OF COWDRAY—SUSSEX.

[*Page* 122.

trates of the district," says one account, "having heard
of the resolution of these travellers, and knowing that
inevitable destruction would be the consequence of the
attempt, placed guards to prevent the execution of it."
But nothing could shake Lord Montague's purpose—of
old it would have been said that the dark fates were
resistlessly urging him on. As he was stepping into
his boat, his servant seized him by the collar and tried
to pull him out, but "his lordship extricated himself
with the loss of part of his collar and neckcloth, and
pushed off." They passed the first waterfall, waved
their hats and shouted in token of success, reached the
second waterfall, and—were never seen again.

Such is the contemporary account, and it has been
repeated with few variations in the different hand-
books. The falls are there described as those of
Schauffhausen, but in the *Sussex Archæological Collection*, vol. 20, p. 203, there is a paper by Sir S. D. Scott
which contains a letter written by M. Bossart, the
chief priest of the church of Laufenberg. In this
letter it is stated that an old resident of Laufenberg,
Johannes Roller, remembered the two Englishmen
attempting to pass the cataract, saw them upset, and
watched them swim to the spot called Oelberg, "and
there, in the so-called strait, they disappeared in a
vortex or eddy, and were never seen again; nor were
their bodies recovered." The account goes on to say
that "the banks were crowded with spectators, but
nobody could save the Englishmen, who swam together,
endeavouring, as it appeared, to lay hold of the boat

that was overset and floating along the current, but they could not reach it. They sunk exhausted in the whirlpool into the depths, and the dog with them."

Thus perished the last Viscount Montague; and it may well be supposed that the double tragedy which had befallen the family in less than a month was not allowed to pass unimproved by village crones and gossips. It was said that a "venerable monk" had predicted the burning of the house and the drowning of the last male heir, as a judgment for the alienation of certain church lands. It is fortunate for other families that this sort of "judgment" is not of common occurrence.

The true story and the legends which have grown up around it, cannot but be recalled with interest as one stands before the ruins of Cowdray—still covering a great space of ground, and enabling the visitor to form a faint idea of the former splendours of the mansion. The offices and outbuildings escaped the fire, and are now used as workshops or barns. The outlines of the banqueting hall and chapel have not been entirely effaced by time; the windows are still beautiful; and on one of the walls can be discerned faint traces of the pictures which formerly covered them. But the ivy is making sad havoc everywhere—tearing down the stone and brickwork, and growing in such thick masses that in many places it looks almost like a wood. It should be cut away with a free and yet judicious hand. Ivy does not make a building damp, as some people suppose, but it undoubtedly helps to crack it. Sir

Edmund Beckett has a few lines on this point in his "Book on Building." He says :—" It is well known that nothing tends so much to keep walls dry as ivy ; at any rate, west ones, against which the rain beats hardest. I have heard of west rooms, rooms which could never be kept dry, till they were covered with ivy. It is also cool in summer and warm in winter. But you must take care that ivy does not get into holes or cracks in your walls, or it will split them to pieces in time."

In front of the ruin there is a little bridge, and the pathway over that will bring the visitor into the clean and broad old street of Midhurst, which can boast of having had a charter at least as far back as Richard the First, and—what will perhaps be of equal interest to the tired or hungry traveller—of being still able to show one good inn (the " Angel ") where a fair dinner and a comfortable night's lodging may be safely counted on by all who need either.

CHAPTER X.

FROM MIDHURST TO HASLEMERE AND GODALMING.

The Road to Haslemere.—A Town half-spoiled.—"Mine Ease in Mine Inn."—Blackdown.—A Poet's Home.—The "Old Gentleman." —Over Hindhead.—Gibbet Hill and the Murdered Sailor.— The Devil's Punch-Bowl.—Only a "Turnpike Road."—The "Green Lanes" of England.—Thursley Church and Common. —Last Stage to Godalming.

THE road from Midhurst to Haslemere goes almost due north, and for some distance lies embedded between trees, and makes its way up a steep hill. Although the distance is not more than eight miles, the walk will be found a sufficiently long one, for it is all up and down hill from beginning to end. The first view that cheers the traveller on his journey is gained at a little over two miles from Midhurst, where to the right the country suddenly opens and enables you to see as far as Horsham. "You may almost see the trains going in and out of the station," said a man on the road, but I am not prepared to testify that I saw the arrival or departure of any passengers while I stood there. A little farther on you come to Henley Common, and then to Henley Hill, where a magnificent view greets the eye—the weald far below, and the high hills, or "mountains" as they used to be called, in

front. Blackdown here wears a most imposing appearance, and no matter how far, or in how many lands
you may have travelled, you will be compelled to own
that you have witnessed few finer scenes than this.
Resuming the road, we reach a point where the boundaries of three counties are said to meet, and which
was once marked by an inn called the "Blue Bells" or
"Sussex Bell." The inn itself no longer exists. We
must now keep to the right in order to avoid being
carried down to Haslemere *station*, and here another
rather steep hill presents itself. When this is surmounted, the old town of Haslemere lies below us, with
Hindhead on the north, ending in a sort of cape, and
all around us lies the wildest and most romantic regions
of the beautiful county of Surrey.

The appearance of Haslemere has been greatly
marred by the new cottages and small houses which
have been erected in and about it—all of which are
very abominable in look, mere wanton desecrations of
Nature's exquisite work. What conscience or feeling—
let us not talk of taste—can a man have who outrages
his native land with these uncouth and detestable piles
of brick and mortar ? In old times, they built cottages
which were at least an ornament to the country, and
artists still make long journeys in order to sketch them.
The artists of the future are not likely to travel far for
the purpose of copying the homes of the labouring
classes which are now being sprinkled all over the
country. All taste in design, all sense of fitness, and
all regard for the surroundings of the house seem to be

deliberately sacrificed. On the outskirts of Haslemere, towards the railroad, there are repulsive examples of this barbarism. The old part of the town has not been so much touched by the hand of the nineteenth century improver. It is a rambling place, with several inns, in not one of which can you depend upon getting a good clean bed for the night. The "White Horse" is "not what it used to be," the ostler told me, and for the sake of those who have lodged there, I hope he is right, for the bed on which I passed an uneasy night was neither dry nor clean, and the tap-room just below was filled with noisy drovers who had come to the market that day, and who were now quarrelling, swearing, and getting drunk over a game of dominoes. It was with great relief that I turned out at daylight and got into the fresh air once more. How glorious the whole country looked under the beams of the early sun! In one direction the dark heath of Blackdown loomed up like a cloud, while, in the other, Hindhead stood out grandly in the morning light—

> —— "the morn in russet mantle clad,
> Walks o'er the dew of yon high eastern hill."

After a season of hard work, or an uneasy night, haunted perhaps by sad dreams and gloomy presages, what relief is there to be found like the sovereign balm of the country? Who has not felt the heavy load of care lifted from his mind, as the mists are rolled from the earth under the first warm rays of the sun?

On my return into the town I met a man driving

some cows, and asked him whereabouts was Mr. Tennyson's house? "Tennyson," repeated he doubtfully,
"Tennyson? I never heerd tell of that name. There
is a Mr. Hodgson lives up there," pointing to Blackdown. For the credit of the Haslemere folk, I must
add that this man came from Midhurst, and perhaps
a poet's reputation can scarcely be expected to extend
in rural districts so far as that. Nor would local
ignorance of Mr. Tennyson's poems be surprising considering that I with difficulty found anyone in the place
who had ever heard of the "old beech tree," which
Murray's *Handbook* reports to be the "lion" of Haslemere. I found this beech after some search, and to say
the truth it is, though old, not a particularly fine tree.
It stands a little off the London road, to the left, about
half-a-mile from the village, and does not look as large
as it is said to be—20 feet in girth.

No one, of course, would dream of going to Haslemere
without paying a visit to Blackdown—a stretch of moor,
knee-deep in heath and ferns and wild flowers. The
views from the upper part are magnificent, and it is
not easy to realise that this wild spot, with so much
exquisite scenery around it, is only a little over forty
miles from London. In the most solitary part of
the moor or heath, slightly below the crest of the hill,
with all the southern country lying below it, stands
Mr. Tennyson's house. I had driven to Blackdown to
save time; and the coachman told me that he had
no doubt I could go round and look at the house.
I asked if the family were there. "Oh, yes," said the

7

driver, " but never mind. The old gentleman does not like to see strangers about his place, but he won't say anything to you. In fact, he seldom speaks to anybody, but goes walking about with his head down. Writes books, I believe—not that I've read 'em. Something about poetry, ain't they, sir ?" Such is fame. The Laureate's house is lonely enough to suit the tastes of the most confirmed anchorite. On a fine day, it must be a lovely spot—such a view as that which extends southward is worth travelling many a long and weary mile to see. But all days are not fine, and in rain or fog, or when the piercing blasts of winter are sweeping over the snow-clad and frozen heath, even a poet's soul may long for the companionship of his fellow man, and for a row of gaslights along a bustling street. Mr. Tennyson does not, it appears, put his love of Blackdown to quite so severe a trial, for he goes to the Isle of Wight in winter. This close intercourse with nature, this incessant communion with her in the midst of all her beauties, have added, it cannot be doubted, many a gem to the noble writings of our great poet—who would have been justly deemed great if he had never written anything more than Œnone, Tithonus, and Lucretius. Some such morning as this in October, when all the trees and ferns are wearing the signs of quick decay, and some such scene as the half-savage one spread before us here, may have suggested that pathetic complaint :—

" The woods decay, the woods decay and fall,
    The vapours weep their burthen to the ground,

Man comes and tills the field and lies beneath,
And after many a summer dies the swan.
Me only cruel immortality
Consumes : I wither slowly in thine arms
Here at the quiet limit of the world,
A white-haired shadow roaming like a dream
The ever silent spaces of the East,
Far-folded mists, and gleaming halls of morn."

From Haslemere to Godalming is a long walk, yet
for beauty I scarcely know of another which can be
pronounced equal to it.   People who have only seen the
tamer parts of Surrey would be amazed if they could be
persuaded to take this most varied and delightful journey.   The best way to go is to pass Haslemere church,
leaving it on your left, and then follow the road
straight before you.   It leads to a common, from which
you can see Hindhead and Gibbet Hill directly in
front.   The path upwards is a steep and solitary climb,
and as you reach the top of the hill which stands
between Haslemere and Hindhead, a picture reveals
itself which one would not be surprised to find five
hundred miles away, but which is startling when
one thinks that it is actually in the same county with
a large part of London, and comparatively a short
distance off.   The sides of the hill are covered with
heath and ferns, adorned with all the varied colours of
the Fall ; sheep are scattered over it here and there, a
few foot-tracks wander up its side, like thin veins in a
giant's body, and a small farm or cottage stands quite
alone, almost at its foot.   As you halt, and quietly peruse
all the details of this striking scene, you discern a green

lane running up the hill and passing over through the
cleft. That is your road, and it is as well not to try
any "short cuts" with it, but keep to it in a friendly
way. Across the valley it wanders in a rather un-
decided sort of manner, and then fairly settles itself
to its work, and goes straight up Hindhead. At every
step some new beauty bursts upon you. There is
not a human being near—but one house, a solitary
farm far away on the ridge of Hindhead, is to be
seen. To the left hand is Gibbet Hill, where two
sailors were executed for murdering a brother sailor
on the way to Portsmouth—as desolate and bleak a
spot as ever romancist dreamt of. A cross has been
erected here to mark the site where the dead male-
factors hung on the gibbet, and close to it is an older
stone with the remains of an iron staple in it. Can
this be a part of the gibbet? In Macmillan's
edition of Gilbert White's "Natural History of Sel-
borne," among the "new letters" there given, I find
the following passage, written on the 1st of January,
1791 :—" The thunder storm on Dec. 23 in the
morning, before day, was very awful ; but, I thank God,
it did not do us any the least harm. Two millers in a
windmill on the Sussex Downs, near Goodwood, were
struck dead by lightning that morning; and part of
the gibbet on Hindhead, on which two murderers were
suspended, was beaten down." The bit of old stone
and the iron staple are far more suggestive of the story
than the new cross, with its "In luce spes," "Post
tenebras lux," and other affected and incongruous

THE OLD PORTSMOUTH ROAD.

HINDHEAD, BORDERS OF HANTS AND SURREY.

[Page 43.

inscriptions. Cobbett says of Hindhead that it "is certainly the most villainous spot that God ever made." To the north are the frowning hills, and far below the huge hollow known as the "Devil's Punch Bowl," into which the two murderers rolled the dead body of their comrade. It is with surprise that in this lonely waste one sees, between the Devil's Punch Bowl and the top of the hill, a fine, broad, and well-kept road, nor is that surprise diminished when you come upon it, and find that it is as hard and smooth as any road in a private park can possibly be. There are very few marks of wheels to be found upon it, but abundant traces of sheep. This is the main Portsmouth road, and to anyone who knows what the roads are in country places, and even in large towns, throughout the United States, this splendid thoroughfare must seem one of the greatest curiosities in England. For the traffic of London Bridge might be driven along it, and even in this steep and wild country it is kept in the most perfect order. I declare that I stood looking at that road in amazement for pretty nearly a quarter of an hour, and I am inclined to think that if I had stayed there till now I should not have seen anybody or anything coming along it in either direction. Will the tide of English summer travel ever again turn towards England itself?

It was now possible to keep on this road to Godalming; but observing a green lane just across it, apparently a continuation of the one I had come thus far upon, I determined to take it. The country now begins to show more signs of life and cultivation, and a comfortable-looking farm here and there is dotted about the hollows. I had faith in my green lane, although it needed strengthening occasionally by a glance at the compass, for it carried me farther and farther away from houses, fields, and even the sound of a sheep-dog. These "green lanes" are among the most curious features of English scenery—they are still travelled over by drovers and others, but the grass grows thick upon them, and I have wandered along them for days in one part and another without meeting a solitary creature, either two-legged or four-legged. One might easily imagine oneself far away in a land which had been deserted by reason of pestilence, or swept bare by the sword.

The lane branching off from the Portsmouth road ends by bringing you safely out to Thursley, four miles from Haslemere ; and it would be hard to say where another four miles of such scenery can be found anywhere within a hundred miles of London. Thursley makes a very satisfactory termination to this stage of the journey. You first see in front of you a primitive cottage with a porch at the door, and then a good old church. It seems a great place for pigs, for pig-sties line both sides of the road like an avenue ; and as all the dogs in the village came out to salute me, and two young ladies in the churchyard looked at me as if I had dropped suddenly from a balloon, I inferred that strangers are not very common in that part of the world. Among the gravestones there is one to the memory of the poor

sailor who was murdered on Hindhead. At the top of
it there is a rude representation of three men com-
mitting the murder, and below an "appropriate inscription" and a "copy of verses." We learn from the
latter that the sailor was killed on the 24th September,
1786, by "three Villains, after he had liberally treated
them, and promised them his further assistance on the
road to Portsmouth." The doleful history is further
described in the "poem":—

> " On bended knees I mercy strove to obtain,
> Their thirst of blood made all entreaties vain."

The view from this stone across to the Hog's Back
is more attractive than the elegiac stanzas, and with
that one's researches in Thursley may fitly end. The
road now winds round to the left, past the shell of an
old pollarded tree ; and when you get through "the
street," it is necessary to turn to the right, and go on
till you come to the common, where another green
path, though necessarily, from its situation, less picturesque than the one above, makes itself visible near
the public road. This path finds its way round by a
pond, marked on the map as "Hammer Ponds." At a
short distance further on, we come out again upon the
Portsmouth Road which we left up at Hindhead—a
grand road indeed, along which it is easy now to
reconcile oneself to travel the rest of the journey,
especially as there is no other way. Through Milford,
a pleasant village, lying near these wide and attractive
commons, and past the railroad to some more venerable

cottages, a little inn or two, and then a queer old market house and a long narrow street. Here we are at last in Godalming, after a walk such as you could scarcely find in any land save England, even though you searched the wide world round.

CHAPTER XI.

DORKING AND ITS NEIGHBOURHOOD.

A Good Old Surrey Town.—The "Marquis of Granby" and old
Weller.—The Dorking of To-day and a Hundred Years Ago.—
Dorking Fowls.—The Scenery in the vicinity.—"Mag's Well."
—A Quiet Road up Box Hill.—Brockham and Betchworth.—
The Holmwood.—Walton Heath.—The Mickleham Downs.—
Pixholm and Milton Lanes.—Ranmore Common and Church.—
Over the Common by Moonlight.—Pickett's Hole.—Wotton
Church.—"Land Hunger."—Bury Hill and the "Nower."

MOST readers of "Pickwick" will remember that
when poor old Weller made that fatal blunder with the
widow, it was in the ancient town of Dorking, at the
"Marquis of Granby," that he settled down. There the
memorable scenes took place between the "shepherd,"
Sam Weller, the mother-in-law, and "Old Nobs."
There are inns without number in Dorking, but there
is no "Marquis of Granby" among them. It is
generally believed that the "Old King's Head" was
the tavern which Dickens had in mind when he drew
the picture of the comfortable, old-fashioned bar in the
twenty-seventh chapter of "Pickwick." It stood on
the site of the present post-office, and some portions of
the building still remain at the back. There was
formerly a coachman named Weller in Dorking, who

drove the coach, and afterwards the omnibus to the station, for many years. This establishes a sufficiently strong relationship between Dorking and "Pickwick," and a more recent writer, Colonel Chesney, has made the name of the town familiar to thousands who have never seen it. I have an American friend who, relying upon the hazy ideas of history which fill the heads of the common run of people, is in the habit of saying, "Of course you remember the battle of Dorking? Well, this was the very place where it was fought!" It is astonishing how many persons there are who do not feel themselves in a position to throw any doubt on this sanguinary engagement.

That Dorking is an old town is very well known to all who have looked into its history. The relics of former times which still remain in it have been effectually disguised by paint, whitewash, and modern improvements. Some years ago, a very picturesque and venerable house, which originally belonged to a Dutch family, was pulled down, greatly to the regret of Mr. Henry Hope, of the Deepdene, who would have purchased it had he known of its destined fate. The chief attraction of the town now is the beautiful scenery which surrounds it. The whole district for miles around is rich in trees, wild flowers, and ferns, and the most melodious of our songbirds so abound that in spring and early summer there is a perpetual concert going on in the open air from sunrise to dusk. Blackbirds, starlings, thrushes and skylarks are as thick as sparrows in a London park, and from many a wood the song of the nightingale thrills the listener in the stillness of the night. I heard the skylark singing till the 16th of November, when some rough weather set in, with hard frosts at night, and there was silence. In the Redland woods the nightingale may be heard all day as well as all night.

The lover of trees will find plenty of occupation for him in every direction. The yew and the beech flourish marvellously in this chalky soil, and there are many fine oaks, limes, and chesnuts in the neighbourhood. The pine woods of Wotton have long been famous. Those who have seen the hill-side of Deubies, in the full flush of autumn, if only from the railroad, are not likely to forget the splendour with which it is clothed, especially at moments when the sun strikes upon all the varied colours of the foliage. As for the climate of the place, not very much can be said in its praise; it is soft and enervating in summer, while in the autumn and winter the mists hang heavily over the valley.

The town still answers well to a description of it which I happened to turn over in the "Gentleman's Magazine" of May, 1763. In little has it changed, although most of the estates round about have passed into different hands since then. "The town," says the writer, "though not large, is well filled with inhabitants. . . . . Though no manufacture is carried on here, yet a great deal of business is done with regard to many necessary articles of life. The streets are wide and open, and from its natural situation the town is remarkably clean." This is just as applicable to Dorking as if it had been written yesterday. The shops are unusually good, and several of them are kept by men whose range of reading and general information would do honour to any career in life. Brayley's "History of Surrey" was wholly printed in Dorking by Mr. Ede, who was a chemist and "perfumer" as well as printer, and who made more money by his bottles of scent than by his "History." In the latter enterprise, indeed, he is said to have sunk over £10,000. "In the summer season," continues the writer above quoted, "there is a great resort of gentry from London, who come to feast on water sousee ; the mill ponds which are numerous, being well stocked with perch, and there being also exceedingly fine carp and tench." I am sorry to say that I do not know where I can recommend the visitor of the present day to go for "water sousee," although the proprietor of one or other of those excellent old fashioned inns, the "White Horse" or "Red Lion," might find it not unprofitable to revive the reputation of the town for the one dish which it brought to perfection. The Dorking fowls are, beyond doubt, more delicate in flavour than any others, but the casual visitor who orders one is more likely to get a bird from London than a true "Dorking." The old breed is now kept up with some care by the school-master of St. Paul's, Rosehill—most of his fowls are partridge-coloured, and have the proper number of toes, five, which characterise this variety. "I have seen capons about Christmas," says the writer of 1763, "which weighed between seven and eight pounds each

AN ENGLISH COUNTRY INN.

"THE WHITE HORSE," DORKING.

Page 140.

out of their feathers, and were sold at 5s. a-piece." A Christmas capon of that weight would now be very cheap at three times the price. The market is described as appearing "much less considerable than it is, because a custom has long prevailed of selling all the corn in the public-houses of the town where it is lodged." It is just the same now. Thursday is market-day, but no one who looked round the streets would suppose that any market was going on. The cattle market is no longer held, and the corn market, if such it can be called, is chiefly carried on at the "Three Tuns," an old-fashioned inn just opposite the "Red Lion." Perhaps a drunken man or two more than usual may be seen about the streets on Thursday evening; that is the only sign of the flourishing trade of Dorking. A relic of old times still survives in the custom of kicking a football from one end of the town to the other on Shrove Tuesday. The shops are all shut up early in the afternoon, and the ball is started from the passage leading to St. Martin's Church. The game is now, however, chiefly appropriated by "roughs."

Mr. Urban's correspondent is among the very few writers who have made any mention of "Mag's Well," a spot which the compilers of all the local guide books have passed by without a word. It is the charmed spring of the district, and lies not far from the village of Cold-harbour. There is a walk to it from Dorking, over fields all the way, starting from Bury Park, and crossing the road at Milton Lane. It is not possible to give written directions which would enable a stranger to find the well, but some of the older inhabitants may be trusted to point out the way. Two of the fields which you cross are covered in June with the bee orchis (*Ophrys apifera*), but the plant is not to be found beyond or around them. Throughout the walk, however, wild-flowers flourish in profusion. The well itself lies in a wood, and it may be reached by a turning from the Coldharbour road. The supply of water was never known to fail, in winter or summer. It still has a certain repute among the older inhabitants of Dorking for medicinal properties. The writer in the " Gentleman's Magazine " says " that the waters, used outwardly, are found to be very salutary in scorbutic cases, and when taken inwardly are said to purify the blood." So also in Manning's " Antiquities of Surrey," (i. 598) I find similar qualities ascribed to the spring. It is "neither cathartic nor emetic, as Mr. Aubrey had been taught to believe, but of great purity, uncommon coldness, and, outwardly applied, detergent. Dogs from the neighbourhood are frequently sent hither to be washed for the mange, and with good effect; and there are instances of extraordinary cures performed by it in cutaneous and even scrofulous disorders." The only virtue now ascribed to the water is that of being good for sore (or weak) eyes, and I have heard of persons sending long distances for it in bottles to be used for that infirmity. When I made a pilgrimage to the well, I found the water, as Manning says, "of uncommon coldness"—like iced water—and I was told that though boys sometimes go there to bathe in the small reservoir of brick which has been built, they are obliged to jump out almost as soon as they jump in. This discourages the visits of the younger generation to the well, and the path to it is familiar to very few.

There are many other walks round about Dorking which are not generally known, and which any good pedestrian will easily discover for himself. But the beaten track is not to be despised. Box Hill may be taken in the midst of the summer season, when scores of visitors are ascending it from the path near the little hotel at Burford Bridge, in such a way as that the crowd may be entirely avoided. To accomplish this, the carriage-drive must be followed to the point at which it turns for the first time, where a thicket of box will be seen straight in front. Through that thicket the visitor may pass to the top of the hill, by a path completely sheltered from sun or rain, and quite unknown to the ordinary holiday-maker, for no trace of his destructive march can be found—not even a sandwich paper or a broken bottle, whereas those interesting relics are as plentiful in other parts of the hill as bones in a rich barrow.

Turn which way you will on going out of doors, those objects abound which are dear to the heart of the Englishman wherever his lot may be cast, whether in his own land, where he can enjoy them, or under foreign skies, where the recollection of them will at many an unexpected hour sharpen the pang of exile. There are the thick hedges, the green trees, the church tower

grey with age, the cheerful farm or homestead, the old
timbered cottage.   The air is full of the faint scent of
flowers and the songs of innumerable birds.   Even if no
longer journey be undertaken than a walk to Reigate—
six miles—there will be much to interest the traveller.
The way to go is through Betchworth park, which is
entered at a little gate not far beyond the " Punch Bowl."
The magnificent Spanish chesnuts, which were fine
trees even when the park was first enclosed in 1449,
will awaken admiration at any season of the year.   In
summer they afford refreshing shade ; in the autumn
they cover the ground beneath them with chesnuts,
and people come from far and near to gather them.
The path beneath these trees leads to a carriage-drive,
and just on the left hand is another gate, which opens
into a less frequented part of the park.   There, within
sight of the road, is a noble double avenue of limes,
one of the grandest and most beautiful sights in Surrey.
A few hundred yards beyond the end of this avenue
the remains of Betchworth Castle may be found, almost
hidden among shrubs, ivy, trees, and a thick under-
growth of wood.   The scene is quiet and solitary, and
not without its softening influences when the dead
leaves are rustling mournfully in the air, around the
fragments of what was once a stately castle.   Near it
are two ancient yews, which flourished when the castle
was in its pride, and now stand over its wreck.   Still
further on by the river Mole is Brockham, which can
boast of a charming village green, and of many a strange
old turning and winding path near the " sullen " stream.

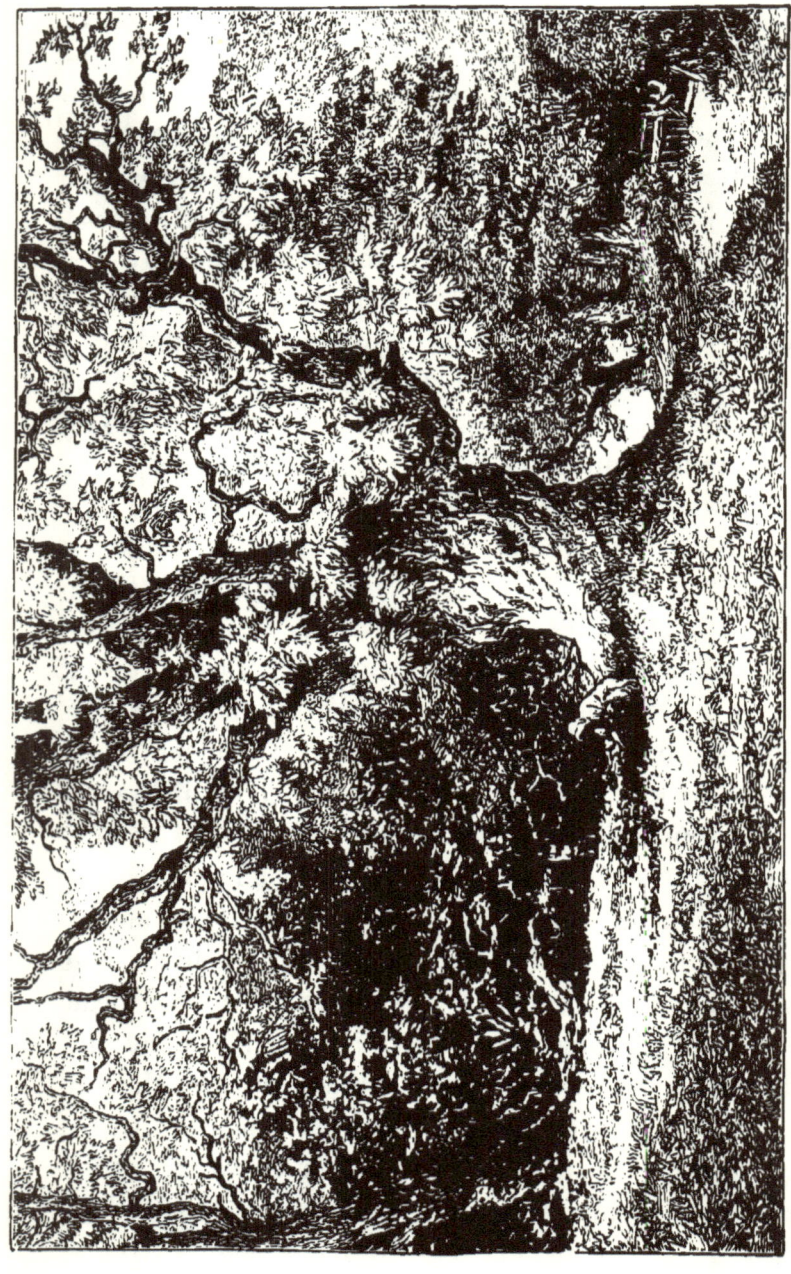

[Page 144

ENGLISH PARK SCENE.
BETCHWORH, SURREY.

Just past the ancient cottage which stands at the corner of Brockham Green, a field-path entices you gently on to Betchworth, a village which strays hither and thither in a desultory fashion, and is chiefly hidden away behind high walls and trees. When you think that you have walked all over it, you turn a corner, and behold, there it is still straggling aimlessly on in another direction—you see an inn such as Moreland used to paint, a group of crumbling cottages, a melancholy church and churchyard, with the weed-covered and neglected grave of Captain Morris, who sung the praises of "the sweet shady side of Pall Mall." Then the road passes pleasantly on to Reigate, where the recollection of ruins and churches vanishes at the sight of a good dinner at the "White Hart," or of a party of pretty girls playing croquet on the lawn.

The Holmwood, formerly a haunt of the red deer, is one of the numerous commons which may be found in this part of the country, and many a good walk may be had upon and around it. An excellent way of reaching it is to go through the wood known as the "Glory," just above Rose Hill, and to continue through the fields at the bottom. The path either to the right or left will lead to the Holmwood Common. The walk to the old church is a very good one, or a longer excursion may be made to Ockley or Capel, both rather pretty villages. There is a delightful walk in another direction which ought on no account to be overlooked. Go past Burford Bridge and along the road till you come to Juniper Hall, which may easily be known by the large and beautiful cedar trees in its grounds. There is a road which turns to the right by the side of "Juniper." If you take this, and keep to the right, it will bring you out upon Headley Heath, a wide space, from which practically one common opens into another for miles—the splendid heaths and downs of Headley, Walton, Banstead, and Epsom, are all to be enjoyed in the course of a long ramble. From Headley Heath the course may be shaped to Epsom, or a return to Dorking may be made by Box Hill—a beautiful walk of nine or ten miles. On another day, the visitor may go again as far as Juniper Hall, take the same road by the house, but at a very little distance up he must turn off sharp to the left. This will bring him out upon the Mickleham Downs, and give him a beautiful walk to Leatherhead. Or he may go to that comfortable old town through Mickleham village and Norbury Park—a very pretty road—or take the longer round over Ranmere Common described in another chapter. It may with truth be said that the beautiful walks within seven or eight miles of Dorking are almost endless in number and variety. But it must be repeated that in this consists the sole attraction of the place. There are few families in the neighbourhood, except those of the large landowners, who visit only with each other. Dorking is not a growing place, and it is not likely to become so while residence there is equivalent to complete isolation in the midst of beautiful scenery. Returned "colonists" and others are apt to think that a town like Dorking is the very place to settle down in, but they make a great mistake. They, of all others, are the least fitted to stand the weary strain of the small and narrow tone and depressing social atmosphere of such a spot. After an active life in the busy world, a man who came to live in Dorking would perish miserably of utter boredom and dry rot.

In Dorking, and yet so much apart from it that the casual visitor scarcely knows of its existence, is a very pretty lane, with two old timbered cottages in it, which must have been standing there for generations. From the Box Hill station of the South Eastern railroad, a path may be seen running across a field, on the left of the station as you come out. This will lead to an old mill and pond—one of the ponds which formerly supplied the material for Dorking's "water sousie." In this pond, and in another on the Betchworth road, there are good jack to be caught at times. The cottages adjoining the mill are ancient, and with the huge mill-wheel close at hand, and the pond just beyond, we have a corner well worthy the attention of the artist. Higher up the lane is another old cottage, picturesque as an object of the roadside, as most of such cottages are, but far from being what house agents call an "eligible place of residence." In the summer they look perfect—but in cold and wet weather they are almost as damp as an "eligible house" which I once went to see at Addlestone, and which I found had two or three feet of water in its lower floors during the winter. It was built over springs, and nothing could keep the water out. On sea or on land,

it is not prudent to begin a long voyage with two or
three feet of water in the hold.   The lane of which I
have just spoken is called Pixholm lane—pronounced
"pixem "—and should the visitor desire to see some
other specimens of ancient cottages, he may find
several in Milton Lane, close by Milton Heath, and
adjoining Bury Park.

Among the chief attractions of this neighbourhood
must be ranked the "Denbies" and all the locality
surrounding it.   A path across the field, seen from
the station, leads into a road close by the lodge gate
of Mr. Cubitt's house.   A little beyond this gate is
another and smaller one, from which a narrow path
ascends straight to the top of the hill, and comes
out just opposite the post-office on Ranmore Common.
The Common at another point may be reached by a
shorter cut.   After entering the path close by the
lodge, open the first gate you come to on the right
hand.   Cross the road, go through the gate opposite
and either follow the road right out upon Ranmore
Common, past the beautiful deep dell or ravine, or take
a path which you will see on your left, a few yards
from the gate.   This winds through a very pretty
wood, with glimpses of the valley here and there on the
way, and eventually brings you out upon the carriage-
drive to the house.   Turn to the right, and you will
soon find yourself upon the common.   A road or path
opens out in front of the upper lodge gate.   Follow
that, and it will take you to a small piece of water,
from whence a green path strikes off to the right, and

this will lead you all across the common in a northerly direction. At the end, a road branches to right and left —by that to the right you may make your way to Great and Little Bookham; by that to the left, to Chapel Farm and West Humble. Chapel Farm derives its name from the ruins of an old chapel, said to have been used by the Canterbury pilgrims. These ruins are now very slight, much of the stone having been carried off by enterprising local builders.

The church whose spire, piercing its way through the trees, forms a landmark for miles around, lies close beside the road on Ranmore Common, and although small—quite large enough for the population hereabouts—it is graceful without and beautiful within, one of the most worthy achievements of Sir Gilbert Scott. It is evidently built to last, and affords another proof that good workmanship may still be had if anybody will take the trouble to insist upon getting it. The interior has been lavishly decorated, and the pulpit and communion-table are alone well worth going to see. In the church-tower there is a fine peal of bells, which send their soft and pathetic strains far and near over the surrounding country. What sound is there which recalls faint memories of the distant years like the chimes heard from afar across the hills and fields? Lucky is the man in whose mind no sad thoughts mingle with the recollections which those echoes awaken! The beauty of the church, and the musical tones of its bells, are in harmony with the green and peaceful graveyard—not yet an overcrowded and gloomy city of the dead, but rather like a garden which is tenderly cared for, with wild flowers and grasses inviting the mother and the child to step aside and renew their recollections of the beloved who sleep below.

Northward from Ranmore on a clear day, the Crystal Palace, and some of the greater towers of London, with the heavy body of smoke resting over the huge city, may easily be descried; and at sunset it is a grand sight to see the wide expanse of hill and vale suffused with a violet light. No one who has the opportunity should fail to start from Ranmore for a walk on a moonlight night. Then the whole country seems to be wondrously transformed. Box Hill looms up in the east, with streaks of silver dashed all athwart its dark summit. The leaves and branches of the trees, especially when autumn has thinned the foliage, are pencilled out in the soft light like the most delicate lace-work. No one who has not paused to gaze at a fine tree, which stands between himself and the moon, can tell how fairy-like is its beauty. It reveals all its outlines in bold relief, like some picture seen in a spectroscope. If, after emerging upon Ranmore Common, you turn to the right, and keep close to the hedge all the way, many a tree will present itself in this bewitching light. The road descends rather sharply, and eventually turns through a gate into a wood—always to the right. This will soon bring you out to some fields, where in summer time the corn and barley are waving in the breeze. With Box Hill to your left, you may now return to

Dorking through acres of ripening grain, and will presently mark a hilly field in which stand four grim old yew-trees, keeping watch over the upland. A weird, unearthly look they have under the moon, like the ghostly sentinels which the poet saw pacing a long-forgotten battle-field. One of them has been struck by lightning, and although dead, yet stands fast, seeming to lift its bare arms in wild remonstrance to the skies. A long line of yews once marked the Pilgrims' way to Canterbury, and on many a lonely slope of these hill-sides, that line may still be traced, as we shall see in other walks.

How many visitors to Dorking have ever been to Pickett's Hole? Even the guide books say little or nothing about it. There is no walk in all this part better worth taking. From the Post Office on Ranmore Common, the road runs due west. Even in July, a fresh and invigorating breeze is most likely to be found sweeping over this fine common. There are few farms or cottages to be seen, and yet the handful of in-habitants look upon Ranmore as a place of some importance, and will scarcely acknowledge that they live in the country. They are like the printer far out West. His office was almost the only house for miles around, but when he hung out a sign on the branch of a tree for an apprentice, he was careful to add the important qualification, "A boy *from the country* preferred." However, if Ranmore is not actually the country, we are certainly near it when we come to a gate which completely shuts off the road to Horsley.

Go through the gate, and take the green path which you will see immediately to your left. A thoroughly rustic path it is, with a border of wild flowers and grasses on each side of it. Presently you will come to a place where two gates stand opposite to each other—pass through the one to your left hand, and bear round to a meadow in which you will observe a foot-track; keep closely to this track, although it has a suspicious appearance of leading to nowhere, and before long a lovely view will burst upon you. Close beside you is a yawning gulf,—the sort of place generally associated in the minds of country folks with a far more depraved and dangerous being than the unknown "Pickett" could ever have been. The gorge is dotted all over with stunted shrubs and bushes, and in front, across the valley, are the dark woods of Wotton, with the old church peeping through the trees—as fair a scene as even the county of Surrey has to offer.

Towards this old church the walk should now be directed, down the hill towards the brick railroad bridge (not the wooden one), with the plantations of "Wood Town" in front. The lover of nature will not be disposed to quarrel with this domain of the Evelyns, although a man whom I once met upon the railroad bridge was apparently not by any means satisfied with it.

"Fine view?" said he, in reply to a remark from me. "Well, I don't call it so. I don't think it at all fine to look over miles of land which is kept up for a selfish purpose, and does no good to man or beast."

Here, thought I, is one of those noisy demagogues who make out their country to be the worst on the face of the earth, without taking the precaution first to see how another would suit them.

" I suppose this man's land is his own," said I.

" I don't know so much about that—very few of these large estates would bear closely looking into, in my opinion. They were got in queer ways, I can tell you that, and are chiefly held by men who look upon the labourer as they would on a dog. What right has any man to hold thousands of acres of land ? "

' The same right that you have to that coat on your back—that is, supposing you have bought and paid for it."

" Excuse me, sir : where do you come from ? "

" Come from ? Oh, all sorts of places. From America last, if it will do you any good to know."

" From America ? Well, now I believe the land is open to anybody there—to one as well as to another ? "

" No doubt, if you have money enough to buy it. I never had any offered to me there for nothing."

" And here, two-thirds of the whole country are in the hands of a few lords and squires—one man owns over 125,000 acres. Do you know that, sir ? "

Yes, I had heard of that. My man seemed to have got the figures pretty pat.

" Now, do you call that right ? "

" Pray, what are you ? " I said.

" I keep a shop at Guildford."

" Indeed ? I wish I did. Shop-keeping is the only

8

thing a man can make money at now-a-days. Well, I dare say there are some people in Guildford who would like to have your shop, and wish much to get you out of it and themselves in. What would you say to them ?"

" Say ? Why I should say they were quite welcome to my shop if they liked to pay for it. Why not ? I am ready to sell it to you or to anybody else; and it ought to be the same with the land. What I say is that if you offer a fair price for the land *you ought to have it*, and that a few hundreds of men ought not to be allowed to monopolise all England. Why should not land be as free here as it is in America ?"

" I have told you before that you cannot get it there without paying for it. And no man would be obliged to sell his land to you unless he liked."

" But it is easy to get it there.'

I could only assure my friend that I had known a good many persons who had not found it at all an easy matter, although they had worked hard for it all their lives. A man may be as well off in a shop in the homely town of Guildford as in a log hut in the backwoods, if he only knew it.

Wotton Rectory is enough to make one forget all the troublesome questions arising out of that " land hunger " which is not confined to Englishmen. It stands half-hidden from the road, and a little way beyond it is the church where John Evelyn lies buried ; a grey old church, deeply embosomed among trees, and defended by a colony of rooks, detachments of

AN ENGLISH COUNTRY CHURCH   [*Page* 155
WOTTON, SURREY

which fly out screaming with anger at the intruder.
It is a dark and damp little church, having within it
some interesting memorials of the Evelyn family, but
not otherwise a tempting place to linger in. The porch
is large and curious, but near it, half blocking up the
park, is a great ugly brick grave—a dismal object.
The high trees outside necessarily give the church a
dark and melancholy aspect; and if the visitor should
chance to attend service there on a wet Sunday, as I
have done, with the rain dropping heavily from the
branches, and the daylight almost shut out, and a
number of sleepy villagers nodding on · the benches
around him, he will find his spirits very much subdued,
and a presentiment will slowly creep over his mind that
some unutterable misfortune is about to overtake him.
Nor is it at all inspiriting to pass into the churchyard,
and behold numbers of long wooden boards stuck up
between two posts, and bearing in large letters the
warning, "Prepare to Die." Thus, in the midst of a
summer's walk, when the thoughts are turned with
thankfulness to Him who made these beautiful hills,
and clothed them with verdure, and has spared us thus
far to delight in them, poor Betsy Stubbs and Giles
Gibbs from below ground must needs wail forth their
ghastly *memento mori.*

> "—— Time driveth onward fast,
> And in a little while our lips are dumb."

Is not the tale told plainly enough in all that we see
going on around us, without the raven note of these
poor rustics who have long been at rest ?

The turnpike road between Dorking and Guildford is hard by the church, and the return to Dorking may either be made through the grounds of the "Rookery," or by Westgate and Bury Park. That park, at least, ought to excite no discontent in any mind, for it is always most generously thrown open to the public by its owner, Mr. Barclay. In front of the house is an artificial lake which contributes to the view the sole feature of beautiful scenery which is lacking throughout the rest of the district—that of water. The river Mole can very rarely be discerned from a distance in this valley, and makes no mark in the landscape. This want has been ingeniously supplied at Bury Hill. In these grounds, also, are many rare and beautiful trees, and vast beds of rhododendron. Then in the park there is the "Nower," a spot which must be dear to the memory of every man or woman whose early life was passed in Dorking. From this gentle eminence, covered with ferns and green turf, there is a striking view of the old town and of Box Hill, and beyond through the Mickleham Valley; while to the south the eye wanders over Holmwood Common, and far away towards the distant haze in the landscape, where the waves beat perpetually against this "precious stone set in the silver sea."

CHAPTER XII.

TO LEITH HILL BY WOTTON.

Two Hundred Miles of Old England.—The Road to take.—A Colony
of Sand Martins.—The "Rookery."—Wotton and John Evelyn.
—The Healing Virtues of Trees.—How to "Corroborate" the
Stomach and make "Hair spring on Bald Heads."—A Carefully
Guarded House.—Friday Street.—The Old Sawyer.—"Age is
Unnecessary."—Through the Pines to Leith Hill.—An Excur-
sion for a Londoner.—Abinger Hatch.—The "British Grum-
bler."—Farming in Colorado.

IT is just possible that a man may go up Leith Hill
for the first time, and find the two hundred miles of
country, which are said to be visible from that point,
spread out like a map before him. But this would be
an unusual stroke of good fortune. The chances are
that a curtain of mist, more or less thick, will be drawn
over a large part of the scene. When the atmosphere
is favourable, ten or eleven counties may be made out,
and the sea is faintly reflected through Shoreham gap.
Even if the distant view is lost, the country near the
hill is so full of charms, that the visitor will never
think his time and trouble thrown away. Let him go
down among the heath, and wander about the hollows
where wild-flowers and ferns make these deserted
places bloom like a garden, and he will not care to

strain his eyes to get a glimpse of the distant sea.
The view from the tower on the top of the hill will
enable him to make out a pathway through even the
wildest part of the heath. For that tower we owe our
thanks to a Mr. Hull who built it for the benefit of a
rather ungrateful public, who have amused themselves
ever since by breaking the windows in it, and scratching
their names upon its walls. Mr. Hull, not anticipating
all this, desired to be buried in his tower, and there
accordingly he was laid to rest above a hundred years
ago. But the "neighbouring gentry," thinking perhaps
that he might get out, took it into their heads to brick
up the tower; and when it was resolved to re-open it
a few years ago, it was found that the "bricking up"
process had been done so effectually, that neither pickaxe nor crow-bar could make the slightest impression
upon it. Another tower was therefore tacked to the
old one, and a woman may generally be found there
in charge of it, able to supply the visitor with such
gently stimulating refreshments as ginger-beer or
lemonade.

About two miles from Dorking, just below the hill
leading from Westgate, there is, at a turn of the road,
a large sand-bank full of martins' nests—many colonies
of martins may be seen in this part of the country, but
this is one of the largest and most conveniently placed
for purposes of observation. A little beyond this bank
there is a gate from which a very pleasant path for
pedestrians, as well as a bridle path, runs through the
grounds of the "Rookery"—a house in which "Parson

Malthus " was born, and which is now occupied by Mr.
Fuller, a banker.   The house itself has nothing to boast
of, but the deep woods and lovely gardens amid which it
is placed make it an interesting spot, and it is always
much pleasanter to walk through this estate than along
the turnpike road.   In point of distance there is not
much difference between the two, but the road is dull
and hilly, whereas the grounds of the " Rookery " are
charming.   The trees, whether seen from far or near,
have all the appearance of forming part of a large and
natural forest, and in early summer the gardens in
front of the house are ablaze with rhododendron—a
favourite plant in Surrey.   The path, at all times open
to the visitor, winds round very close to the house—so
close as to suggest the idea of trespass, with all the
pains and penalties which wait upon that dark crime.
But it is all right—the visitor need fear nothing.
From the house the path goes up a slope and through
a lovely green wood, and then passes across a field into
a carriage drive.   We are now on the Tillingbourne
estate, and the visitor may please himself whether he
will go by Broadmoor to Leith Hill, and see a small
waterfall—a pretty road enough—or by Wotton.   The
latter is by far the best route.   Having, then, come out
at the carriage drive, turn to the right, and go straight
on till you reach the inn known as Wotton Hatch,
on the main road to Guildford.   The lodge gates of
Wotton are a little beyond the " Hatch," but go along
the road till you reach a stile on the left hand, leading
to a meadow.   Get over, and from thence a few

minutes' walk will place you full in front of Wotton House, on the only high ground from which a good view of the whole of it can be obtained—whereas if you turn in at the lodge gates, and follow the carriage drive, the effect is spoiled by your being led to the house on the lowest level, and at the point where it is least worthy of admiration.

Wotton is an irregular red-brick mansion, largely modern, having big patches stuck on it here and there with a sublime disregard of plan, harmony, or effect. It looks somewhat like a gentleman's house turned into an infirmary, and stands on the very lowest part of the estate, so that from every point the water must drain down towards it. The central part alone is connected with the memory of John Evelyn. The author of *Sylva* and the well known *Memoirs* was much attached to the house, as well as to his "own sweet county of Surrey" in general, the beauty of which perhaps struck him all the more because of his long residence at Deptford. There is no country near Deptford which can afford to be looked upon the same day as Wotton. No wonder, therefore, that Evelyn delighted in the home which only became his when he was some distance advanced on the journey of life. "I will say nothing," he writes in his Diary (Vol. I. pp. 2, 3) "of the ayre, because the præeminence is universally given to Surrey, the soil being dry and sandy; but I should speake much of the gardens, fountaines, and groves that adorne it, were they not as generally knowne to be amongst the most natural

and (till this later and universal luxury of the whole
nation, since abounding in rich expenses) the most
magnificent that England afforded, and which indeede
gave one of the first examples to that elegancy since
so much in vogue, and follow'd in the managing of
their waters, and other ornaments of that nature. Let
me add the contiguity of five or six Mannors, the
patronage of the livings about it, and, what is none
of the least advantages, a good neighbourhood."
When this was written the estate seems to have
been worth about £4,000 a year, and Mr. Evelyn was
evidently a good manager. A property was not likely
to deteriorate in his hands. He made an etching of
the house, which is given in the first edition of his
Memoirs—scarcely any resemblance can be traced
between that and the present Wotton.

The gardens are formed in terraces at the back of
the house. There are many fine beeches on the estate
—one particular tree of unusual size—but the pines
lord it all over the rest. In one part there is a pine-
wood almost as deep and dark as the traveller may
find in Maine or New Hampshire. The author of
Sylva was a great admirer of the pine, and once
more proved that he was a shrewd business man, as
well as a great lover of the picturesque, in recom-
mending a more frequent planting of that tree than
was common in his day. He ascribed wonderful
virtues to it, and declared that its bark would heal
ulcers, and that the "distilled water of the green
cones takes away the wrinkles of the face"—a dis-

covery that cannot be generally known. "In sum," he says, "they are plantations which exceedingly improve the air by their odoriferous and balsamical emissions, and for ornament create a perpetual spring where they are plentifully propagated." But the squire of Wotton found wondrous medicinal properties in other varieties of trees. Thus, an oil extracted from the ash tree is good for the tooth-ache and for "rot of the bones." Moreover, he confirms a common superstition which lasted long after his time, and perhaps lingers still in some parts of the country, when he says—"I have heard it affirmed with great confidence, and upon experience, that the rupture to which many children are obnoxious is healed by passing the infant through a wide cleft made in the bole or stem of a growing ash tree; it is then carried a second time round the ash, and caused to repass the same aperture as before." Again, we are assured that the water of the husks of walnuts is "sovereign against all pestilential infections, and that of the leaves to mundify and heal inveterate ulcers." The "distillation of its leaves with honey and urine makes hair spring on bald heads"—a queer remedy for baldness, but doubtless quite as efficacious as the mixtures which importunate hair-dressers try to force upon every unhappy mortal whose head-covering is deserting him. The fruit of the service tree "corroborates the stomach;" the lime tree is "of admirable effect against the epilepsy," and the distilled water thereof is good for apoplexy and gravel. Wine

made from the birch tree cures "consumptions," but
we are to understand that these remedies are only
recommended *en amateur*. "Quacking," says the
worthy man, "is not my trade; I speak only here as
a plain husbandman and a simple forester, out of the
limits whereof I hope I have not unpardonably trans-
gressed." Certain it is that his injunctions as to the
duty of a landowner to plant trees are scrupulously
followed on his own property to this day. There are
no woods in the county finer than those of Wotton, and
the annual sales of timber on the estate must bring in
a very handsome sum of money.

The house contains many interesting relics, among
them the prayer-book said to have been used by
Charles the First on the scaffold. "The leaves are
stained with the king's blood," so I have been told by
one of the very few who have been permitted to see
the book. In the library there are many of Evelyn's
books and manuscripts, but the visitor need not hope
to see this room or any other part of the house. A
written request to be allowed this privilege does not
even receive the scant courtesy of an answer. Yet it
is not unreasonable for the pilgrim to wish to see a few
of the personal memorials of the man who knew
Charles the First, contrived to avoid suspicion during
the Protectorate, was intimate with Charles the Second,
saw James the Second fly from the throne, and was
among the first to kiss the hand of William. But the
door is closed in the face of all, gentle or simple, scholar
or peasant. The stranger, therefore, must make the

most of the road over which the public have a right
of way, and his best plan is to take a path which
runs by the side of the house, and leaves it on the
right hand. This affords an occasional glimpse of the
gardens, and leads out to a quaint and most interesting
spot called Friday Street, for which we may look in
vain on the one-inch ordnance map. Yet it is a
veritable street—a thoroughfare leading from one place
to another, but so primitive in all its "belongings"
that in coming upon it one seems suddenly to have
been put back a couple of hundred years in English
history. It lies in a sort of ravine, with a large pond
at one end of it, and beyond a few ancient and picturesque cottages. It has a totally "untouched look,"
and with its beautiful hills and trees, among which it
lies hidden like a village over which some wizard has
cast a spell, there is no place within the compass of a
day's journey which will more delight the lover of those
half-forgotten nooks and corners of "Old England,"
now fast disappearing before the invincible march of
time and improvement.

"Fish, sir?" said an old man whom I met in this
out-of-the-world street, "oh, yes, there are plenty of
them. Pike? No, trout—big trout, only no one dares
catch 'em. You don't get anything for nothing about
here. *He* (no name mentioned) says that he loses by
this 'ere estate, and that it costs more'n it's worth to
keep it up. Likely, ain't it? But that's when you
want anything done to your cottage. Which road is
the best for you to take? Let me walk with you, sir,

and show you. Oh, it don't matter, I ain't got nothing
to do. I was a sawyer up in them woods for five-and-
forty year, but now I'm losing the sight of my eyes,
and feel shiftless like. I've got one son out in New
York, so he can't do nothing for me. What part of
New York? Well, I can't rightly tell—I think in
Canady. He's a doin' well—they say you can have
your own cottage out there. If you pay for it? Ah,
but here you can't have it whether you could pay for it
or not. Do you suppose *he* would sell one of them
there cottages? Why should he, do you say, sir?
Well, I can't argy it, not being a scholard. I shouldn't
keer if only one of my eyes would last my time, but
I'm obliged to wear a patch over this 'ere left 'un
(pointing to it), because else something would run into
him. He won't shut any more when he goes near anything, and if I didn't cover him up he would run into
a tree or anything that came in his way. Have I any
young children? No, they are all growed up, and what
good am I to them? I can't work any more, but (he
repeated this as if talking to himself) I shouldn't keer
if this 'ere left 'un would do a little while longer, but
he gets darker every day, and he would always be
runnin' into something if I didn't cover him up." Poor
old sawyer! Landor's pathetic lines came into my
mind as I looked on his wrinkled and sorrow-stricken
face :

> " Is it not better at an early hour
>   In its calm cell to rest the weary head,
> While birds are singing, and while blooms the bower,
>   Than sit the fire out, and go starved to bed ? "

From Friday Street I struck up through the pine-woods to the right, confident that they must bring me out somewhere in the direction of Leith Hill. I had taken the "bearings" of my destination before I started, and in such cases as this there is no better plan than to trust to the compass, and go on until you reach the mark you are aiming at. You may wander a little astray here and there, but are sure to come out right in the end. The track in the fir-wood brought me upon a high road, skirted with tall pines on each side; and this I followed until I came to a keeper's lodge on the left, and heathy ground stretching away beyond it. Presently I detected another foot-track, and several old cart-ruts through the heath. I cut into the foot-track, and soon found myself wandering over a sort of moor, with paths straggling away in opposite directions. Into one or two of these I got "switched off," and found that I had arrived at nothing more wonderful than a gravel-pit or a clearing where they had been cutting wood and furze. I made, how-ever, constantly for the rising ground wherever I saw any, and at last the tower came in sight, and I steered for that through thick brushwood and heath. Other hills soon began to make their appearance—the familiar range between Dorking and Guildford, Box Hill, and then an immense landscape was suddenly unrolled far below, with a few farms and churches at long intervals. It was a clear day—only out by the horizon was there a little mist, such as one may notice at sea in the early morning before the sun has risen more

than a few feet above the water. There are many fine
views to be had in the county of Surrey from various
points, but none so grand or majestic as this—it almost
takes away one's breath to look around, and see this
vast expanse of "mellow" English land, green and
beautiful wherever the eye rests upon it. It is a
picture which stamps itself indelibly on the memory,
but a man should no more try to describe it than he
should try his hand on Niagara or the Himalayas.

This wide-spread heath abounds with beautiful
walks, some leading down into deep hollows, others
into woods, and there is one road by which a carriage
may be driven close to the tower itself. No one should
fail to go to the top of the tower—the additional
elevation adds much to the extent of the view. A
glorious path over the hill leads to Coldharbour, a
village able to boast of an almost unrivalled situation.
There is a grocer's shop, a very small place, with a view
from its windows which the owner of the proudest
mansion in England well might envy, and a little farther
on the Coldharbour Road is a plain but comfortable
little inn, where a modest luncheon may be obtained—
a pedestrian's luncheon, not fit for what the people call
"carriage folks." In August and September the whole
of Leith Hill, and the country round about it, is
covered with the purple bloom of the heath, and the
jaded Londoner would find it well worth his while to
spare a morning or an afternoon to run down and see
this beautiful sight. I will suggest to him a plan by
which he can easily manage it. Let him take the train

from Victoria to Holmwood Station, and walk from thence through Tanhurst (Mr. Bosanquet's park) to Leith Hill. There is no possibility of mistaking the road—Coldharbour may be seen from the platform of the Holmwood Station, and the station-master will point out a path across a field which brings you out close to Tanhurst. From thence the road goes, with exquisite views at intervals, to Coldharbour, and close by the church is a path running up the side of Leith Hill. Having spent an hour or so about the tower, a path on the other side—there are two or three, but the woman at the tower will show the right one; it is the *widest*—will lead through the pines down to Abinger Church, opposite to which there is a fine specimen of an old-fashioned country inn, the "Abinger Hatch." The sign-post in front of it is almost worn away by time, and close by are the old stocks and whipping-post, which were never used, because the people of Abinger have always been so good. The church has been restored, but forms a welcome object in the landscape. The inn is just as it was when first built, and when that was I do not know. I asked the landlady, and she said it was very old—older than any of the people about there. As a rule, this is about the utmost idea of antiquity which I have found in the minds of the occupants of old cottages or houses. "It is very old—I have lived here fifty years." The inn at Abinger is more than fifty years old, but very comfortable accommodation may still be found there. We will suppose the Londoner enjoying his luncheon in the little parlour overlooking the pretty garden, and when he is ready, he may take the road over the common to the Gomshall Station on the South Eastern Railroad, the entire distance between the two stations being about seven miles, making ample allowance for a little rambling to and fro on Leith Hill. By properly timing his trains, any man may accomplish this delightful excursion in the course of a summer's afternoon, and how could he spend his time to greater advantage? Not by lounging about London streets, or chattering in a club, or even by perusing the latest infallible disquisition of our dear friend the "able editor."

The return journey to Dorking is best made by the Coldharbour Road, past the "Plough Inn," for it is all down hill, and only about three miles from the village to the town. On this road I fell into conversation with a man who was walking along by the side of his horse and cart, and whom I found boiling over with complaints about everything on the earth and above it —a true British grumbler. The weather was bad—it was a lovely day in June—and the crops were certain to be bad; England was not worth living in. "What was the good of trying to farm in such a country as this, where everything is either scorched up with the sun or drownded with the rain?" And so he went on. I thought of a little account of farming in another land which I had read a little while before, and when I went home I hunted it out, and read it again, and wished I could hear what my discontented friend on the road would have to say to it. It is from the *Golden Tran-*

script, a Colorado paper, and although the account of farming difficulties in that rich state is written in the half-comic vein so dear to the American journalist, yet the difficulties themselves are not in the least exaggerated. Thus it runs: "The farmers in the vicinity are having a pleasant time now. At daylight they get up and examine the holes around the corn-hills for cut-worms; then smash coddling moth larvæ with a hoe handle until breakfast. The forenoon is devoted to watering the potatoe bugs with a solution of Paris green, and after dinner all hands turn out to chase with flail and broom the festive grasshopper. In the evening, a favourite occupation is sitting on the fence figuring how much they would have made had it not been for the bugs, and after a brief season of devotion at the shrine of the night-flying coleoptera, all the folks retire and sleep soundly till Aurora reddens the east, and the grasshoppers tinkle against the window panes, and summon them to the labours of another day." Life in England may have its drawbacks, but has any man yet discovered the country where there are none? If so, I wish he would communicate with me.

CHAPTER XIII.

FROM DORKING TO LEATHERHEAD.

FOR those who want the shortest road between the two towns above named, the walk now to be described will never do. But if anyone desires to ramble for a few hours over commons and hills and fields, with but one or two little touches of a turnpike road here and there, and a village occasionally to enliven the journey, this is a route that he will find in every way satisfactory. The total distance, making allowance for straying out of the way occasionally, is about ten miles.

The first stage from Dorking is over Milton Heath, and through the first lodge gate on the right-hand side after crossing the heath. This leads round close to the Elizabethan house which forms so picturesque an object in the valley from any of the surrounding hills. This house was once in great danger of falling to pieces through neglect and bad usage, but the grand old staircase which it possesses attracted a purchaser who was willing to save it. A narrow cart-road winds close round by the hedge, leaving the house to the right, and passing on to the railroad. It must in common honesty be admitted that mud, much mud of a thick and pasty quality, will be found in this road after wet weather. The path on the other side of the railway goes straight up a rather steep hill, but the best plan is to keep below the plantations, and ascend the slope gradually. From this hill side there is a view of Dorking which will be new even to many who know the district tolerably well. The author of "Forest Scenery" lays it down as a principle that "a landscape of extent and beauty will take the full period of a year to show itself in all the forms it is capable of receiving," and of no district can that remark be more true than of this part of Surrey. Here, for example, is a portion of the valley, the exact position of which must be well known to every one who has visited the locality, and yet there are probably not half-a-dozen strangers a year who traverse it. As you mount the hill, the landscape slowly discloses itself as if a screen were withdrawn from the front of a picture—the whole valley to Reigate is laid bare, and opposite are the beautiful woods of the Rookery. The entire country side is covered with trees, and on the 2nd of last November, when I took this walk, it was tinted with all shades of colour, under the light of the morning sun. The hedges and bushes were covered with red berries,

from which the birds were making a merry meal,
and the song of the skylark was ringing in the air.
The breeze was fresh and invigorating, the sun bright
and clear, most of the trees were still thickly clad with
foliage, and the country was as green as an emerald.
The summer itself had offered no lovelier day. And
yet there are people who will tell you without a blush
that the English climate is a bad one.

I have said that it is best not to go straight up the
hill from the railroad, but to keep on the slope till you
descry two or three cottages above you. This involves
a few yards of rough walking in places, but nothing to
make a fuss about. When you see the cottages, strike
upwards, for you will then be beyond Mr. Cubitt's
grounds. There is a track which will bring you out
at the little public-house on Ranmore Common, and
nearly opposite to that are three or four new cottages.

By the side of the last of these, westward, you will
see three green lanes or paths. The middle one is the
most direct, but who cares for that? Who minds
being carried a little out of his way when the devious
path has anything to show which is worth seeing? If
the visitor here will do as I did, he will take the last of
the three paths—the one which runs nearest to the
road, and starts off nearly west. A little way up this
green lane, there is a curiosity which will detain the
tree-lover a few moments on his road. It is a yew tree
growing out of an oak, and it may be found on the
left-hand side of the path, in a sort of circle formed by
smaller trees. Where the branches of the oak begin to

spread out from the trunk, the top of the yew also
sends forth its branches, and pokes its way through the
oak in all directions. The trunk of the yew—only a
few inches in diameter—grows, to all appearance, out
of the very roots of the oak, and at the ground the two
trees cannot be distinguished apart, except by the
different appearance of the bark. You could not, for
instance, put a sheet of paper between them. The yew
then grows straight up the trunk of the oak, and forces
its branches through those of its companion, making
substantially one tree. The contrast in colour alone
attracted my attention to these twins. A man whom
I met close by said he had never noticed the tree,
although he had lived on Ranmore Common many
years. But how many country people are there who
ever *do* notice the trees, or can tell you the names of
any of them, except perhaps the oak and the elm ?

"You are pretty sure to lose yourself on this
Common," said the man with a grin ; "you will come
out at a very different place from what you expect.
Everybody does." Lose myself? Well, I once managed
to do that, but in a very different sort of place to this.
I was up among the mountains in New Hampshire,
and had strolled off into one of the huge forests there
to see a waterfall, to which there was a narrow track,
covered over in many places with leaves and bushes.
I found the waterfall, and was on my way back as I
thought, when suddenly I looked about me, and saw
at once that I had wandered from the path. Probably
I had not gone many yards, but in the "forest

primeval," with bears known to be about (one had been seen close to the hotel only the night before) this was quite enough. In less than five minutes I had tumbled down a hole three or four feet deep, which had been hidden by the thick brushwood, had scratched myself severely with thorns, and straggled into an almost impenetrable mass of underbrush and large trees. I could not see the sky for the dense foliage, and realised the unpleasant fact that I was lost. The heat was stifling. The mosquitoes and other insects set upon me in myriads. I shouted out to see if anyone was within ear-shot, but no answer came. The forest was in one of the wildest parts of the mountains, and I knew very well that assistance of any kind was out of the question. An hour passed away, and I had only wandered into thicker woods than ever. I must say that I have been in many places which I liked the look of very much better than this; but wherever one may find oneself, on sea or land, there is nothing like taking things quietly, and making the best of them. Still, the fatigue of scrambling through thorns and brambles nearly waist high, had produced a violent thirst, and the heat had left not a dry thread on me. After all, it seemed just as well to wait where I was until it should occur to me to do something, better than go tumbling from one hole to another, and bruising myself against trees. Presently, I heard faintly the sound of water. I began to push and fight my way as well as I could in that direction, but there was nothing to guide me, and no one who has not been in a similar predicament can judge how difficult it is to tell whether you are going forward or merely doubling back on your path. It was evident by the increasing darkness that the day was closing in. But I kept listening for the water, determined if I found it to follow it down hill, and after what seemed an age, I reached the waterfall itself, but at some point above the place where I had left it a few hours before. I now followed the water down, and in less than a quarter of an hour struck the right trail again, kept on it with rather more care than I had shown before, and at last found myself on the mountain road once more, half dead with heat, thirst, and weariness. All this came of getting off the right track ; and thus this proves to be a little story with a moral thrown in.

Beyond my twin trees, the path takes a dip into a hollow, crosses a small ravine, and goes up the other side in a north-westerly direction. A stray partridge rises with a whirr, or a blackbird rustles out with his foolish scream as you approach the bush where he is digesting his ample breakfast of "hips-and-haws." No other sounds will disturb you on this rather lonely part of the common. A distracting number of paths here open themselves up, to the perplexity of the traveller—some of them leading to clearings where chopped wood is piled, and some to gravel pits. In this case, as in many others, the path on which you started is the safest, and although it will land you plump against a fence, yet there is a cart road running to the right and left of that fence, and if you turn to the right you will find yourself ere long near a black shed on the side of the road. From this point there is a good view of Polesden, a house once occupied by Sheridan, and often besieged by his duns. Since those days it has been much improved. It stands in an isolated position, but overlooks a noble expanse of hill, dale, and moorland. Opposite the black shed, a path may be seen winding round a tree, and running diagonally across two fields. That is now our road. When you come to the second field, you will be rewarded with a fine and entirely new view of Box-Hill. Ranmore Common, uneven and covered with trees and ferns, lies to the right, to the left is the ridge with Polesden adorning its side, and between is a deep and well wooded gorge, while beyond all is Box Hill, with its scarred face turned towards the spectator. The whole scene is full of wild and rugged beauty. And within ten minutes' walk there is a total change—a change as great as if you had been transported a hundred miles away on the magic carpet of the Arabian wizard. The path which we have been following comes out upon the main road to Horsley, near two cottages known as "High Barn," and there the wide and open country lies extended before us, stretching far away into Berkshire to the front and left, and to the right over Epsom and Banstead Downs. In the foreground are the villages of Effingham and Bookham. The hills have entirely disappeared, and the whole country has changed suddenly into smiling fields, dotted with old church towers.

9

We now turn to the right, past the cottages. The
cries of a sheep were here so loud and plaintive that I
could not help asking a man in the garden what was
the matter. "Why Sir," said he, "we be a goin' to kill
him directly after dinner for the great house." "He
seems to know all about it." "Oh, no," said the man
laughing, "he don't know what's a comin', and it's best
he shouldn't." The doleful bleatings of the poor animal
proved that if he didn't know exactly what was "a
comin'" he had some very gloomy forebodings on the
subject. Presently Effingham came in sight, first intro-
ducing the "Prince Blucher" inn to one's notice, and
then a little further on, a shop which was enough to
take one's breath away—a truly astounding shop, built
in a style of architecture for which they ought to take
out a patent, and crammed with everything that the
housekeeper could wish for, from mops and brooms to
huge flitches of bacon. But the woman who was serving
behind the counter did not seem at all proud, and
condescended to answer my question as to where I
should find the keys of the church. She gave me a
direction which, as near as I could guess, would have
taken me somewhere in the neighbourhood of Brighton.
There was an old yew tree before the door, the lower
part of it cut to resemble a cannon ball, or it may be,
as more suitable to the place, a large Dutch cheese.
"You have a fine old tree, here," said I. "Yes," said
the woman, "very old; it has been here ever since we
have been in the house." I quite believed her. The
church turned out to be the most dismally restored

building conceivable—the tower has been made to look like the stuccoed front of a new villa on the outskirts of London, and a gang of common bricklayers and plasterers seem to have been let loose in every direction. Never was a poor church more abominably ill-used. There are two or three old seats inside near the porch, with the *fleur de lys* carved at the top—perhaps relics of the days when Walter de Jeddynges was lord of Effingham in the fourteenth century. What would be his feelings if he could see the church they have put up on his former domains ?

Through the churchyard there is a path turning down by the side of a wall, and then running pleasantly across meadows, due east, until it brings you very unexpectedly upon Little Bookham churchyard. You see nothing of that or the church until you have actually opened the gate which leads into them. By the side, separated by a wall, is what is called the Manor House, an ugly, but possibly very comfortable, edifice. In the churchyard is a large old yew, protected by an iron railing ten or twelve feet in height. The traces of Norman arches and capitals outside are very clear and good, and were only brought to light in 1864. The path still goes on straight through this very small and retired old churchyard, and across more fields to Great Bookham —three quarters of a mile from its neighbour. The visitor will notice fine fat barns and good big stacks hereabouts, and other evidences of a land of plenty.

At Great Bookham there is an inn called the " Crown." Here with some difficulty I succeeded in getting the homely refreshment of bread and cheese and ale—each bad of its kind. A damsel who wore spectacles, and who had a voice like a man's, and whose hair was hanging down her back, brought in the repast, and proceeded to pick a few hairs, which bore a striking resemblance to her own, out of the butter. Meanwhile, I examined the works of art upon the walls. The first that struck me was a small engraving of the " Piazza, Congress Hall, Saratoga Springs," evidently some thirty or forty years old, for the fashions of the ladies depicted in the engraving were not by any means like those which I have seen exhibited by the young beauties at Saratoga. "Pray how did this picture come here?" I asked. The beautiful creature with the spectacles suspended for a moment her employment of picking samples of her back hair out of the butter, and said, "It was there when we came here"—identically the answer that one gets everywhere about everything, from a tree to a picture. I next admired a spirited lithograph representing the "Attempt of John Francis to assassinate the Queen, May 30, 1842." We are here shown John Francis attired in a fashionable frock coat, buttoned round the waist within an inch of his life, and the queen and the prince seated in a "shay," pointing out the landscape to each other, in utter disregard of John Francis, who is calmly blazing away at them with a pistol. The "shay" is drawn by four horses, all on their hind legs. I was anxious to buy this sweet picture, but the young woman sternly refused to sell it. I now requested her to remove the butter to some distant apartment, munched my dry bread, and speedily found my way into the street again, without the lock of hair which my fair friend had clandestinely tried to thrust upon me.

I discovered that Mr. Ragge, a saddler up the street, had the keys of the church, and although Mr. Ragge was a somewhat austere man in aspect, as a saddler is very apt to be, he at once handed me the keys. The church is an interesting one, and contains some curious brasses and monuments. An inscription in the wall near the communion-table, which looks as if the letters had been recently cut, sets forth that the chancel was built by "Johanne de Rutherwyka," Abbot of Chertsey, in 1341. Near this is a monument evidently designed to perpetuate the memory of some Roman gladiator, although the name of "Colonel Thomas More" is by mistake inscribed upon it. Then there is a long epitaph on a brass plate inserted in the south wall, descriptive of the virtues of Edmund Slyfield :—

" A iustice of ye Peace he was from ye Syxt Kynge Edward's dayes,
And worthely for vertves vse dyd wyn deserved prayse."

This excellent person died in 1590, and the plate bears witness that—

" Thaire Eldyst sonne Henry this cavsde to be made,
In Faythfull performans of the will of the Dedd."

While I was copying these lines, raps, cracks, and bangs were going on thick and fast all round me, and at last I came to the conclusion that Mr. Slyfield had some message to communicate to me. Once the organ gave a loud thud as if a stop or two had been pulled out, and it was about to perform a " voluntary." Then a pew just behind me went off with a crack, and was instantly answered in an overbearing manner from the pulpit. As I closed my book, a general chorus of crackings and creakings broke out all over the church, and many mysterious shapes appeared. Some people may think that these shapes were only the monuments, but as honest Izaak Walton says when he is relating the story of the ghost which appeared to Dr. Donne, " I am well pleased that every reader do enjoy his own opinion."

From Great Bookham there is a tolerably direct road to Dorking, by Ranmore—5 miles ; a road by the " Crown " to Leatherhead, by Fetcham—$2\frac{1}{2}$ miles ; and a road above the village (the old Portsmouth road) also to Leatherhead, the same distance. I chose the latter, because it affords the best views. The farm labourers were getting the fields ready for the winter's wheat, the birds were singing in the bushes and trees, and the only objectionable thing to be seen was a being of my own species in the shape of a tramp. He staggered up as well as much strong drink would permit him, and begged for " assistance." " What for," I asked—" to enable you to get more drunk than you are now ? " " I haven't tasted a drop for a fortnight, guvner," replied the man, who could scarcely stand upright. " I can't get anything to do." His way of looking for work reminded me of the " loafer " in Vermont who was

hired by a farmer to dig some potatoes. Presently the
farmer went out, and finding him lying down smoking,
began to reproach him. "All right," mumbled the
man, "if you want your potatoes dug, just fetch 'em
on! I ain't going to run all over the lot after them."
Followed by a tempest of curses from the industrious
tramp for refusing to give him more drink-money, I
once more had the old Portsmouth road all to myself,
and presently saw Leatherhead a little below me, with
its church looking like the tower of some old fortress
flanking the hill, and two red houses beneath it, and a
group of miserable "Building Society" cottages at the
back—and the homely meadows closing in around it
on every side.

CHAPTER XIV.

TO GUILDFORD OVER THE HILLS.

THERE are many things to be said in favour of this walk, and a few to be set down against it. In the first place it runs almost entirely along the top of the hill, and that in itself is a great attraction. But anyone who stands in the valley, and looks along the range of hills leading to Guildford, would naturally suppose that the prospect must be extensive and varied almost through the entire distance, whereas you get very few views unless you make long and perplexing sweeps from the proper track, and if you do that, the twelve mile walk will very easily be turned into one of sixteen. For the greater part of the journey, the lovely scenery which stretches far away on each side of the hill is as completely shut out from eye-sight as though the traveller were not within a thousand leagues of it. You have the "green road," with hedges and woods on each side, but it runs far back from the brow of the hill, and there is only the great prize of Newland's Corner to lure you on. But many who start on this trip fail to come out at that famous spot, and so they miss the chief glory of the walk, and thenceforward are fain to hide their heads when Newland's Corner is mentioned. Some travellers might think it an objection that the path is very solitary, although I have nothing to say against it on that score. But there are persons who would dislike being four or five hours on a road much shut in by trees, without the chance of meeting a single human being, or of coming upon a house of any kind where even a glass of water may be obtained. If a man gets thirsty on this journey, especially on a hot day, he will wish that he had never been born, or had been " changed at nurse." Yet to the true lover of the country, or to anyone who wants to get out of the way of the world, and have an uninterrupted talk with himself, this green lane, twelve miles long, may be very safely commended.

The best way is to start from Dorking, and to make for Ranmore Common by the narrow path, already described, just beyond the lodge gates. Having come out opposite to the Post-office, the people about—if you meet with any—will tell you that it is a " straight line " to Guildford, but before you have reached your journey's end you will be of a different opinion. I started off betimes on a fine morning towards the end of July to do this walk, in the hope that the day would turn out cool and pleasant, since there had been a stiff north wind blowing all night. But long before ten the sun burst out in a great hurry, and made up for a little lost time that day by producing a temperature which would have done no discredit to Calcutta. By that time, however, I was a couple of miles on the journey; and, as I hate to turn back when once I have started off, I determined to push on and take my roasting. And a pretty thorough roasting it proved to be—most people may remember that the summer of 1876 was rather hot, and this happened to be one of the very hottest days of that summer. More than once in the course of that tramp I would have given a good price for a bottle of soda-water, but between Dorking and Guildford there is nothing whatever to be had except fresh air and plenty of trees, and one cannot drink them.

The road over Ranmore Common must be followed as far as the point described in the walk to "Pickett's Hole," and then the next turning to the left must be taken—a broad green lane, on the main road to East Horsley, a little below the gate which shuts off the Common. The green road cannot well be missed, for at this part it is nearly as wide as Fleet Street. "Keep on that and you can't go wrong," said a man who was tying up faggots on the Common. But like most other right roads in life, it is far easier to get off it than to keep on it. Sometimes one strays away without knowing it—sometimes you stand looking at two or three paths exactly alike, and wondering which is the right one? For although the "course" is west, yet sharp bends have sometimes to be made to the north, and any man who tries to find his way without a compass will most certainly go wildly wrong. Even with it, the traveller must be on his guard lest he is tempted by promising-looking roads down to Horsley on one side, or Shere on the other, or get all adrift on the Downs. Yes, yes—the " right road " is a puzzle here as elsewhere, whereas the wrong one is provokingly easy to find; so easy that no one who looked for it was ever yet known to miss it.

Very soon the green lane—it is thickly overgrown with grass, like a field, although marked with some deep old cart-ruts—leads into thick woods, where you see rabbits scuttling off by hundreds, and squirrels climbing nimbly from branch to branch. The birds are almost as thick as flies—chiefly blackbirds and thrushes. There is a grove of beeches to the right, wonderfully green and beautiful, and throwing so deep a shade that it seems twilight underneath them. The local tradition is that there are many ravens in this beech grove, but I made several visits to it and never saw any. The trees are among the finest I have anywhere found. Why should not the leaves of this tree be restored to their ancient use ? Evelyn's testimony to their excellence as a stuffing for beds has been confirmed by other writers. The author of *Sylva* says :—" But there is yet another benefit which this tree presents us; its very leaves, which make a natural and most agreeable canopy all the summer, being gathered about the fall, and somewhat before they are much frost-bitten, afford the best and easiest mattresses in the world to lay under

our quilts instead of straw, because, besides their tender-
ness and loose lying together, they continue sweet for
seven or eight years long, before which time straw
becomes musty and hard." He adds, " In Switzerland
I have sometimes lain on them to my great refreshment." It would be interesting to know if beech-
leaves are still used in this manner in any part of
rural England, or whether it is simply one of the old-
fashioned customs which have given way to new ones
not half so good. All through this part of Surrey the
beech flourishes in all its glory, and a more beautiful
object than a fine beech it would surely be hard to find.
I hope there are not many who share the opinion expressed by Mr. Gilpin in his " Forest Scenery" (i. 45),
that "upon the whole the massy full-grown luxuriant
beech is rather a displeasing tree."

As the road passes between belts of beeches or oak,
the traveller will meet with no one, and hear no sound
save the twittering of birds, or the sharp crash of the
woodman's axe in the distance. At about five miles
from Dorking, there is an opening from which a beautiful view to the southward is to be obtained, and it
is not unwelcome after a longish stretch of country
bounded by trees and hedges on each side. Here, too,
the road becomes as broad as any turnpike road, quite
green, and very wild and picturesque. Presently, however, it narrows again, and several paths of pretty much
the same general appearance go bearing away from it
in various directions. It is easy to avoid those which
break abruptly off to the south or north, but it requires

some firmness to resist the allurements of the paths
which sidle a little away, and seem to have as good a
claim to your confidence as any other. In my case,
however, I determined to obey the compass, and I still
kept my face to the west, and considered myself rewarded presently when I reached a finger-post which
pointed straight on " to Guildford." But finger-posts
are not always to be trusted by the pedestrian, for they
naturally direct to the turnpike road, which .it may be
his very object to avoid, and indeed a bad case of the
sort occurs in the course of this very journey, as will
shortly appear.

Beyond this point some cultivated fields came in
sight, and the road began to look more like a common
turnpike. Perhaps the finger-post misled me! At
any rate, the road was running due west. But, alas!
at a distance of seven miles, it took a sudden sweep
downhill to the south, and downhill I was determined
not to go until I reached Guildford, come what might.
What was to be done? There went the road to the
left—to the right was a farm track ; directly in front
was a grove of tall pines, and a wood beyond. I hesitated
a few moments, compass in hand, but as the needle
plainly indicated that if I took to the wood I should be
on my proper course, I resolved to push into it and
take my chance of finding my way out again. Steer-
ing once more for the west, I passed through some
hick trees and underbrush, and in a short time came
out upon a broad green road again—the very same to
all appearance as that which I had left behind me

where the view had been so welcome. Had I then wandered from it, and now recovered it? I had, and have still, my suspicions on the subject. At any rate, I made up my mind not to lose sight of it again ; and, indeed, from this point there is no difficulty in keeping a close grip of it. For at no great distance the traveller will have the satisfaction of coming out at Newland's Corner, and from thence he remains in the "open" until his ramble is over, and has more than one landmark to show him which way his face should beset.

The view from Newland's Corner is inferior in extent to the wide range commanded from Leith Hill, but it has a winning character of its own, which tempts one to linger long over it, to sit down and enjoy it slowly and peacefully, and make a feast of it. At Leith Hill, one has a sort of restless desire to find out places—to look for this or the other well-known hill or clump of trees or church, and to get a glimpse of the far-off sea. But at Newland's Corner the desire is simply to rest awhile, and take it all in little by little—to let this fair handiwork of Nature exercise its own spell over the mind. "The whole scene," says Murray's *Handbook* for Surrey, "recalls some wide-sweeping landscape by Rubens or by Turner;" and the comparison is a happy one. If the visitor to this spot will look around him, he will see something beside the view worthy of his attention—a few ancient yew trees, still marking the line of the path which was taken by the pilgrims to the shrine of St. Thomas A'Becket at Canterbury when they came from Southampton. This most interesting path we

shall cross many times yet in the course of our rambles.
The yew trees, which still define its outlines, are not
less curious in their way than the torn and broken
stones in Canterbury Cathedral, which point out the
spot where the great shrine stood three centuries and a
half ago. From the sides of the hill, other and younger
yews may be traced, down towards the Duke of Northumberland's gardens at Albury, becoming thin and
faint in the distance, like a dark green thread.

Still keeping on the high ground, the view will
presently be found to open to the northward, disclosing
Windsor Castle in the distance. St. Martha's Chapel
is now not far off—a "chapel" which stands in an
isolated and even a melancholy spot, cut off from all
human habitations, and only to be reached from this
side by some rough up-hill work. Service is still held
in it once a month, but very few persons attend it. It
may be doubted whether it was ever used as a place of
general public worship. Manning thinks that it was
originally designed to serve as a chantry, and that it
was erected "over the graves of some Christians who
suffered on this spot." He truly adds that this supposi-
tion is the more reasonable since "it is not likely that
a place originally intended for the ordinary services of
religion should have been erected on a spot so difficult
of access." There seems to be little doubt that the
church was one of the three mentioned in Domesday
Book as belonging to the manor of Bramley. In 1463
an appeal was made for funds towards its repair, but it
fell into ruins, and the present building is compara-

tively modern. It forms a striking object in the landscape, from whatever point it may be seen, and doubtless
has often attracted the attention of travellers on the
railroad, who may have wondered what could have
induced anybody to build a church, which only a
climbing animal could reach with comfort.

As soon as I had passed the chapel, the road began
to descend, and for the first time I submitted to its
guidance, and descended with it. And here the ability
of the pedestrian to steer a good course will be tested
for the last time. The road winds due north, and a
finger-post astounds the traveller by pointing to *that*
as the proper path to take for " Guildford and Stoke."
But I still had my doubts about the trustworthiness of
that other finger-post up above, and hence I surveyed
this one with mingled distrust and aversion. I did not
like its bullying way of pointing me down a road I did
not want to go. The map said, go west; the post said,
go north. Which should it be? It is almost as serious a
thing to fly full in the face of a finger-post as it would be
to contradict an editor in his own room, or a parson in
a church. " To the west," however, I determined once
more to go, and I struck out boldly for it across a field,
leaving the swaggering finger-post at my back. It was
a very good thing to do, for I saved myself a long pull
along a dusty turnpike road. At no great distance the
path clearly made towards the town, and I came out
under the borough police station, near the " Angel "
Inn—a queer old inn, in which there are all sorts of
rambling passages and staircases, and a cosy bar in

front of a clock dated "1688," and low-ceilinged old bedrooms up-stairs, among which you are pretty sure to lose yourself. It is one of the relics of the England of a past age—that England which the wise men think so poorly of, but which was quite as good a place to live in as the England of to-day, all things considered, and perhaps a little better.

A pleasant and comfortable town is Guildford, much sought after as a place of residence by half-pay officers and ladies with a "little in the funds,"—a respectable, though dull, community, "We have five admirals, three generals, and I don't know how many colonels and captains waiting here now for houses." Thus proudly spake a house agent there, and the slight air of contempt with which he referred to such common-place persons as captains served to show what an important place Guildford is. Such a town as this in the United States would have three or four newspapers published in it—here, I believe, there is but one. Perhaps the English provincial journalist is more fastidious than his American cousin, who sometimes finds a newspaper anything but a source of wealth. "We are out of meat, money, and other things. We are out at elbow. We are out of patience." This was the doleful complaint of an Arkansas editor, poor man, not long ago. Another aspiring intellect in Ohio boasted of having received one hundred and fifty new subscribers, but added, "We want about two hundred more subscribers; we need a new pair of socks." It was a more fortunate journalist who published the following triumphant leading article in a Tennessee paper: "Halleluyer! we've got a new shirt." Let us hope that the craft drive a more flourishing trade in this excellent town of Guildford.

While endeavouring to slake a raging thirst at the "Angel," with sparkling hock and seltzer water, two sunburnt and awkward-looking men entered the room. They sat down at the table, and one said to the other, "I have ordered a thick soup, some salmon, some corned beef, and a claret cup." And a very strange mixture it is too, thought I, at three o'clock in the afternoon on a broiling hot day. Perhaps they are going to use the claret cup as a sauce for the salmon.

No, they did not do that, but they drank it copiously with the soup—a strong, dark-coloured soup, an old-fashioned commercial traveller's soup, in which the spoon will almost stand upright. It was passed round three times—an awful thing to witness on a hot day. Then these wonderful men began to exchange notes of foreign travel, and the following conversation took place:—

"How did you like Bolong?"

"Pretty well, but what an ignorant set they are there! I went to the Station Hotel and asked what we could 'eve to eat. They said, 'Anything you like to order.' So I said, 'Soup and cutlets.' They brought me about half as many cutlets as I could have eat myself, and there were three of us! 'What will you like afterwards?' says the waiter. Says I, 'A meat tea, and cook half a sheep for us.'" Here the two epicures nearly choked themselves under the combined influences of laughter and huge masses of food.

"Them French," said the other, "don't know what good eatin' means.   When I was theer, they told me I could have twenty-five courses, but I 'ud rather 'eve 'ed a bit of salmon than 'em all.   (Putting half a pound or so in his mouth).   They know nothing about cookin' or eatin'."

"The women are all ugly," the salmon-devourer went on, "and did you ever see such guys as the men?"

That is your opinion of the Frenchmen, thought I. I would now give a great deal to hear their opinion of *you*.

What were these men, I wondered — farmers? Farmers sitting here drinking claret cup, and gorging themselves with soup and salmon at three in the afternoon of a hot day?   That was scarcely likely.   So when I paid my bill, I said to the host, "Pray what are those two gentlemen in there—bagmen?"

"Auctioneers," said he in a solemn whisper.

"Ah, good morning, Mr. Michaux."

"Good morning, sir."

Whew!   What a relief it is to get into the blessed fields and fresh air once more after sitting in the same room for an hour with some of our dear fellow creatures.

CHAPTER XV.

FROM CATERHAM TO GODSTONE.

A Country of Hill and Vale.—More "Land-Grabbers."—A Cluster of
Villages.—Warlingham and Tatsfield.—Cross Country to Titsey.
—The Poor Church and its Rich Brother.—The "Bull" at
Limpsfield. — A Native Critic of Manners and Customs. —
Emigration.—" Everybody Well Off Abroad."—A Little Ad-
venture in a Church.—Tandridge Church.—The Old Yew.—A
Station Two Miles from Anywhere.—A Dull End to a Day's
Journey.

THE country all round Caterham is so broken up by
hills and valleys that the well-known "bicyclist" who
lives in the neighbourhood must find it no easy matter
to make his way about. The roads go a long way
round, and there are some places not actually more
than four or five miles from Caterham, which cannot
be reached by less than ten miles of travelling by any
kind of conveyance, not excepting that ugly, bewildering,
and offensive machine, the bicycle. Thus, to Tatsfield
the walk over the hill does not exceed five miles, while
by road it is not less than nine. Anybody who wishes
to see the pretty village of Warlingham, and one or two
other places on the way, must do as I did—drive over
to Tatsfield, and perform the remainder of the journey
to Godstone on foot.

In this manner the nature of the country in the neighbourhood of Caterham may be seen to advantage, the total distance traversed being between sixteen and seventeen miles. The roads are all up and down-hill, and the valleys run off in various contrary directions in a most confusing manner. The man who drove me to Tatsfield had lived in Caterham many years, and had very little to say in favour of it. Was it a growing place? I asked him.

"No, leastways not so much as it ought to be. You see they bought up the land about here some time ago, for perhaps £3 or £4 an acre, and now they charge anything they like for it. I suppose you could not get an acre under £300, perhaps more. That keeps people away."

"And who has done this?"

"The tradespeople and others in Caterham."

"So there are other people who are 'land-grabbers' besides the large landowners," said I.

"Oh, yes—we are not much troubled about here with the landlords. That gentleman I was telling of you about (the bicyclist) has only a small place. Isn't it odd, Sir, as a near-sighted gent should fly around like that on one of them queer things? Wonder he don't meet with an accident? Why he does—with lots on 'em. I've seen him come off myself, and then he run agin a man at the bottom of the road here," and he went on to tell me a doleful story which lasted until we reached Warlingham, a very pleasant and quaint old village, with a pretty inn called the "Leather

Bottle" standing in front of the village green. A little way further along the road the church spire of Chelsham shows itself among the trees, and we can see the wooded grounds in which one of the large houses of this part, the "Ledgers," lies concealed.

The road winds round past a public house to Worms Heath, as pleasant a spot as any man need wish to see on a summer's day. The views are far reaching and delightful in every direction—the Crystal Palace shines brightly in the distance, and on the other side of the road you have miles upon miles of downs spread before you, and Leith Hill can be made out beyond the Reigate range. Then we come to a clump of beeches known as "Coldharbour," and presently the road takes another long swing round, and we are at Tatsfield Church. There I dismiss my friend the driver, not sorry to be alone on the good road once more. "I hope you will not meet Mr. Blank with his bicycle," said I.

"Thank you, Sir," said he, "he would never see me if I did no more nor if I wasn't theer."

Tatsfield Church stands on the top of a hill, and is evidently not one of the new fashionable and gim-crack places of worship. I did not observe the traces of many carriage wheels on the road, and the bare cold walls and rough seats inside spoke of a small rustic congregation. The chancel has been restored, but the whole place has a cheerless and barn-like aspect, and cold shivers gradually steal down one's back after standing in it a few minutes. There is a stone tablet on the

wall to the memory of John Corbett, who died in 1711,
and on the clerk's small reading desk below the pulpit
I noticed the letters "R H E. 1661." No other sign of
monument or record is there in this primitive old
church. "Over the communion table," says Manning,
"the Decalogue, Lord's Prayer, and Creed are written
in a most curious but very small hand, and behind
them is a beautiful painting in perspective, representing
the inside of a Gothic church." There are no traces of
these curiosities left now, and the woman who showed
me the arch had never heard of them, neither had an
elderly workman, who was repairing the gate outside.
If the building has little to boast of in point of architectural beauty, there is a view from the churchyard
which might well draw pilgrims hither, and which is
worth going half-a-day's journey to see. Nothing
can rob the neglected old church of this great attraction. In the churchyard, moreover, there is a very
large yew tree, apparently suffering somewhat from
time and weather, but still putting on a good thick
green coat and making believe to think nothing of
its age.

No old stager would have the patience to follow
the roads hereabouts,—instinct, if nothing else, would
compel him to take to the fields and woods, and trust
to luck for finding his way out. But as you can see
the spire of Titsey church from a corner of Tatsfield
churchyard, there can be no danger of wandering far
astray. The field which adjoins the churchyard must
be taken, and that will bring you, at the farther end,

upon the turnpike road. Cross that, and go through a
gate into another field, and keep along the upper side
till you see a third field, in which the characteristics of
this region are pleasantly brought together into a small
space—for in the middle it suddenly dips down and
forms a miniature valley, with hills beyond, so that you
almost begin to feel mystified, and fancy that if you
look over your left shoulder you will see Caterham
again. A more *unhandy* field it would be hard to
find, for the pitch is so sudden and so deep, that even
the sheep graze along its sides with difficulty. Beyond
this field, however, there is a lovely view over towards
East Grinstead in one direction, and towards Sevenoaks
and Tunbridge down the valley—the tops of the hills
being all wild common land, or "chart" as a man on
the road called it. The whole scene is a bold and
striking one, and it is not without many a backward
look that one leaves the field with the big hole in it,
and turns into a narrow lane, which brings us out
on the turnpike road a little above Titsey church. A
very different building this from the church we have
just left behind us! It has been built by Mr. Leveson-
Gower, who has a house close by, and everything about
it is neat, clean, and comfortable. The church has
been completed, inside and out, with great care and
liberality, and the churchyard is as trim and well-kept
as a garden. Just below it are two or three good old
cottages, and the parsonage at a little distance looks a
homely as well as a picturesque place. The "turnpike"
is like the finest park road. The whole place has a

Sunday-like aspect—so well swept and brushed up that one is almost afraid to walk about for fear of dirtying something.

Limpsfield is rather less than a mile and half away —the outlying houses can be seen from Titsey. After following the road a short distance, the visitor can strike into the fields on the left, and make his way to the church. This, again, is totally unlike the other churches we have passed—evidently the church of a large parish, with the graveyard covered with tombstones, among them a stone near the wall of the church with a staring coat of arms engraved upon it. There are few places in which the mummery of heraldry could seem more absurd. An old manor house nearly opposite the church south, was once, according to Murray's Guide, "occupied by the widow of Philip Stanhope, the natural son of Lord Chesterfield, whose well-known letters to her husband were published by Mrs. Stanhope after his death." In the upper part of the village street are one or two small shops and the "Bull Inn," whither I made haste to go for a frugal lunch. I found a notice inside the little bar (which is only about half as large again as the painted Bull on the sign-post outside) making public the important fact that "parriffen oil" could be obtained there at 2*s.* per gallon; but this, although tempting, was not quite what I was in search of. You cannot make a really good lunch on "parriffen oil." Ultimately I succeeded in getting some bread and cheese, and while I was working my way through a "hunch" of dry bread, an old

10

man came in and called for a glass of stout. He was
one of the cross-grained scandal-mongering persons
who seem so common in rural villages—full of little
ill-natured gossip and sour remarks. Presently I
managed to get into conversation with him by asking
him if that was not a very old house just opposite
the inn ?

" Hold ? " said he. " Yes, and it might do well enough
for a hofficer's widow or a hold parson as ain't no use,
but it ain't fit for a human being to live in as is of any
account."

Not being quite prepared for this outburst against
an inoffensive looking house, I said nothing. But the
landlady, who was wiping a glass, interposed : " Account, indeed ? you are letting your tongue wag pretty
free to-day, I think."

" Well, this is a free country, ain't it ? Ain't it, Sir ? "
turning to me.

" I have always understood so," said I, not wishing
to commit myself too far before so slashing a critic.

" May I make bold to ask what brings you out in
this here out-o'-the way place, Sir ? "

" I want to see some churches."

" Well, well ! " looking at me curiously, as if I were
an escaped lunatic. " We has artists down here sometimes—I *know* they are poor, and I don't *believe* they
are over honest. But I never seed a gent as wasn't an
artist going about looking at churches. As for being
poor, I don't mind that. Gi' me a poor man anytime
of day rather than a rich one."

"Then you live in a world where you can be very easily accommodated."

" I tell you what it is," said this old man, thumping his fist on the bar, " the rich are too stuck up, and I want to see 'em took down. They throw a word to you when they do speak as if they throwed a bone to a dog. Look at Mr. —— (mentioning a name). Why you'd think he was made of some better kind of stuff than you are."

"I don't know that he is not," said I; "perhaps he is."

" I know what I'd do if I were young enough—I'd get away from 'em all, and emigrate to Canady or Horsetralia, where one man is as good as another. Everybody is rich over there, or leastways it's their own fault if they ain't."

" But," said I, " I thought you did not like the rich ? You don't mean to tell me you want to belong to them yourself ? "

" You are getting into a mess," said the landlady.

" That's my business if I am," growled the man. "I'm not rambling around pretending to look at churches. I can pay for what I have, *I* can."

Evidently I was becoming a prey to the local satirist, and therefore I went on munching my bread and cheese in silence. "Would I stand some beer ? " said my acquaintance, presently. No, I would not do that, but I offered to treat him to a yeoman's draught of "pariffen oil," for of all other liquors he had evidently had enough and to spare. But he did not care for that, and soon I went on my way in peace.

Beyond the cottage on the left hand side of the road, after leaving the "Bull" at Limpsfield, there is a lane, which presently leads across a little wooden bridge, and then into fields. This is the shortest road to the next village on this little circuit—the village of Oxtead, distant about a mile and a half from Limpsfield. The path across the fields is a beaten track, but rather rough when ploughing operations are going on. I nearly stuck fast in the soft wet earth two or three times. At last, however, I came out upon the hard road, and passed through a farmyard, and so to the old church of Oxtead, with its great heavy square tower, and a substantial farm-house near its gates. This church has suffered much in its time from fire or lightning; it is recorded that in or about the year 1637 it received its first heavy blow, and that in 1719 "it was burnt by a great tempest of lightning." All the five bells were melted by that fire, but ten years later a new peal was placed in the old tower, and on one of them there is an inscription which says :—

> " Good folks, with one accord
> We call to hear God's word
> We honour to the king
> Joy to brides do sing
> We triumphs loudly tell
> And Ring your last Farewell."

The church door was open, and a woman was sweeping in the gallery—an accident which very nearly led to awkward results. For while I was looking round the church, and wondering at its size and reading the

inscriptions on the monuments, the woman went out.
I heard her shut the door, but presuming she had seen
me enter, I thought nothing of it.   The inscription to
the wife of one of the old lords of the manor, Charles
Hoskyns (1651), seemed to indicate that the worthy
lady did not have a "good time" of it in this world.
"Let this Patterne of Piety, Mapp of Misery, Mirrour of
Patience, here Rest." So ran the writing.   Pews had
been put in the chancel without much regard for the
brasses and old monuments, some of which have been
cut clean in half.   Can it be that this large church is so
crowded with worshippers as to need those pews nearly
up to the railing of the communion-table ?   The whole
church has the appearance of being built like a fortress,
to resist an assault.   As I thought this I tried to open
the door, but found it locked. I listened for some sound,
but could hear none.   It seemed to me that there was
likely to be another "Mapp of Misery and Mirrour of
Patience" in the church before the day was over.   It
was then Friday, and the opportunity of studying the
old monuments till Sunday morning was not so attractive as I am sure it would have been to a well-trained
mind.   The windows were high ; the door was thick.   I
began thumping on the latter, but for some time there
was no sign of any answer.   At last, however, I heard a
hesitating step, and saw a dark shadow on the slit of
light under the door.   Evidently there was some un-
certainty about opening the door, but after I had made
several little reassuring speeches, the woman unlocked
it, and stood with a very white face on the threshold.

I saw in a moment that she had the strongest doubts about my belonging to this earth, and as I had no time to argue the matter over with her, I bade her good afternoon in a sepulchral tone and "glided" out of sight.

Beyond the strong tower of the church there is a path going by a small pond across a field. From that field the fine old church, and the red farm-house in front of it, show to great advantage, and to the right the village of Oxtead, about a quarter of a mile off, may be seen straggling up the hill. It is a curious looking place, not quite so dirty as a mining village in South Wales, but still recalling those districts in a general way. It is very much like Blaenavon for instance, and the smoke of the brewery hanging over the houses, and a sort of "dolly-shop" at one end of the mean street, increased the resemblance. The road from here runs direct to Tandridge, but there is a short and pleasant path by the fields. After passing through Oxtead, keep on the main road till you come to a gate on the left about half a mile up. This leads through a field by a lime kiln to a narrow lane, and from the end of that lane there is a charming view over the country through which we have been walking. Across some meadows, which look like a part of a park, we descend upon Tandridge Church—a place, like the others, with many historical associations connected with it. In old days, the Priory of Tandridge must have been a house of some little importance in the village, but there are no remains of it left to-day. I was not aware of this when I visited the spot, and I asked an old man on the

road if he could tell me where the priory used to be ?
" Why, there it is," said he, pointing towards a modern
house which I had noticed. "I mean the *old* priory,"
said I. "Well," said he crossly, "this *is* the hold
priory—the only one as we've ever 'eard tell on in
these parts." "So, then, the old priory," I began.
"I knows nowt about *him*—that theer's the priory, and
good enough for us." Nevertheless, "that theer" could
not have been the priory of which one Walter was
appointed prior in 1306. The church has a very
pleasant and homely aspect, and is evidently properly
cared for by the people round about.

In this churchyard of Tandridge there are at least
two things which will arrest the traveller's attention—
the enormous yew tree, and the elaborately carved
monument to the wife of Sir Gilbert Scott, the
architect. They are both within a few feet of each
other, so that the yew shades the grave. The monument looks far too beautiful to stand out of doors in a
climate where rain is not at all unfrequent. The
immense yew which almost touches it is said to be
decaying, but it looks perfectly green and vigorous.
Just below the church are some old cottages, and some
" carriage-folks' houses " are in or near the village.
But what interested me most were the venerable yew,
that tree for which it is difficult to avoid feeling
an almost superstitious reverence, the beautiful monument of the artist to his wife, and the sweet, country
churchyard, " strewed thick in early spring," says my
companion, Murray's *Handbook*, " with violets and

primroses." It was in November that I stood there, and "God's acre" was strewed thick with dead leaves, and from the trees they came down silently in showers all around—an emblem of our poor human life which at such a time and place sunk deeply into the heart.

From Tandridge to Godstone station it is a long, roundabout, tedious road, which may be shortened here and there by a cut across fields, but in the main has to be taken at its best and worst. There is one old cottage or small farm on the road, and a muddy wood to cross—but Godstone Station is at least two miles and a half from Tandridge. It is about the same distance from everywhere else—a ridiculous station, put down in the middle of a country road, bearing a name to which it has no right whatever, and serving simply as a trap to catch unwary travellers. Here I was doomed to wait three hours for the next train, hungry, cold, tired. I tried the inn near the station—it was a cheerless hole, full of tramps. The evening was closing in ; the mists and fog were coming on heavily ; the tramps were drunk. I should not like to spend those three hours at Godstone Station over again.

CHAPTER XVI.

THESE three estates are not without historical interest, although the houses now standing upon them bear
no outward traces of a long past. Of the families
which first founded homes on these beautiful sites, or
enrolled them among their possessions, some have
entirely disappeared. The Clares, Earls of Gloucester,
to whom Norbury belonged, are remembered as part of
the nobility of England in days when no Disraeli could
have said of it, that it consisted of "families who, in
one century, plundered the church to gain the property
of the people, and in another century changed the
dynasty to gain the power of the Crown." Albury and
the Deepdene have both been in their day the homes

of the Howards, but the Deepdene can trace back its history from long before the time when the brave old Earl Warrenne, who married the daughter of William the Conqueror, held it with the rest of the manor of Dorking. " You ask me for my title deeds," said he, according to the well-known story, " there they are," and he threw down his sword upon the table. Doubtless there have been ere now estates which were held on title-deeds with less claim to respect.

The man who longs for solitude need not " fly to a lodge in some vast wilderness," for he may find what he seeks at Norbury, or within a mile or two of Albury. He may wander about alone for days together, and lose himself in a forsaken region which might be somewhere amid the wildernesses of the Far West—a region without farm or shed to be seen, without even the bark of a dog or the crowing of a cock to be heard for miles around. England is, as we have often been told, a "densely overcrowded country," but several places could be pointed out on the map in which room for a few more families could still be found.

Norbury Park abounds with splendid trees, sheltered woodland paths, and broad views over the loveliest parts of Surrey. It is not a place to be seen at one visit, but to be wandered over at leisure, sometimes in the lower parts in company with the river Mole, sometimes among the woods through which even a July sun scarcely has the power to pierce, and where the ground is covered with cool green moss on the hottest summer's day. Armed with a pencil or a book, or wishing merely to pursue his own thoughts in peace, the wanderer here need fear no interruption. He will rarely hear any footfall but his own. He may enter the park at Mickleham, and stroll quietly on by the Mole, through meadows which are in themselves objects of perfect beauty—English fields such as many a traveller in foreign lands would give a year of his life to see again. Or he may turn towards the house, and soon find himself half lost amidst noble oaks and beeches which are here still contending for the mastery. But, better than all, he may penetrate to that secluded spot still known as the Druids' Grove. If the visitor who desires to see that shrine of tree-lovers will place himself upon the bridge across the railroad in Westhumble Lane, and look before him to the north, he will see a narrower lane winding past a cottage. Let this be followed almost to the end, an up-hill road though it will prove, and then at the right hand there will be seen a five-barred gate. Pass through that, and neither heat of sun, nor sight or sound of your fellow mortal will disturb you. It will be strange if you meet man, woman, or child throughout these delightful groves, where the dead leaves lie a whole year upon the ground, and in the thickest parts of which it is not much more than twilight at noon in midsummer.

Presently the path opens upon a patch of green sward, with a belt of ferns in the background, and here and there an isolated yew—a sort of forerunner of the venerable army which is drawn up in solemn grandeur below. Everywhere the noise of a footstep will cause myriads of rabbits to start up from the grass or ferns, and make for their warrens in all directions. The wilder parts of the park are alive with rabbits, and the surface of the ground is rotten with their holes. There is a certain path between woods, on the Mickleham side, which is rapidly being undermined by these vermin, and when you begin to intrude on their territory, a large army rises up and flies down the hillside from before you, scuttling among the dry leaves with a sound like the rush of rain. The owners of such estates as this would gain rather than lose by allowing the poor to make a dinner occasionally off the rabbits which infest their grounds. There is no danger that the animal would ever become scarce— nature has made ample provision against that. When one sees the havoc made by rabbits in a garden or park, it scarcely seems worth while to send a poor man to prison for catching one without leave. "A young oak," says the author of " Forest Scenery," "just vegetating from the acorn, is esteemed by these pernicious inmates the most delicious food. Thus it may be said, the glory of England may be nipped in the bud by a paltry rabbit." Is it absolutely necessary to fence this creature round with penal laws ?

The open patch of sward is not far from the house, from the windows of which there are some of the loveliest views in Surrey. A carpenter with whom I once had a chat on the road said to me, "I have worked in every large house in this county, and in my opinion the house at Norbury is the best situated of all." I have no doubt he is right, and most people who survey the surrounding country from the lawn will think so too. The house contains some paintings supposed to be a "continuation of the landscape without," but in this instance art has been left far behind by nature. The building is not worthy of the spot in which it is placed —it may almost be said that it is common-looking and unsightly when you are close to it, although it makes a good appearance from a distance. In Evelyn's day, the estate belonged to Sir F. Stidolph (or Stydolf), and since then it has passed through several hands. The whole property, consisting of the mansion and about 527 acres, was sold in 1819 for £19,000—to-day I suppose that £150,000 would not buy it. In Evelyn's "Diary," (Vol. II., p. 295) he speaks of it as a "seate environ'd with elme-trees and walnuts innumerable. * * Here are such goodly walkes and hills shaded with yew and box as render the place extreamely agreeable, it seeming from these ever-greens to be summer all the winter." It is wonderful that so great a tree-lover as Evelyn should have made no other reference but this to the yew-trees of Norbury, and that even Mr. Selby, in his excellent work on "Forest Trees," should pass them over unnoticed.

A private path southward of the house leads straight down to the Druids' Walk. It is best to approach it from the upper end, and to go in summer when the oaks and beeches are in full foliage, for then the shade they cast adds much to the mysterious appearance of the grove. I believe that permission to go over the

grounds, and downwards through the path marked
"private," is seldom refused if asked for at the house.
The Druids' walk is long and narrow, with a declivity,
in some places rather steep, to the left hand, and rising
ground to the right, all densely covered with trees.
The yew begins to make its appearance soon after the
little gate is passed, like the advance guard of an army.
In certain spots it seems to have successfully driven out
all other trees. As the path descends, the shadows
deepen, and you arrive at a spot where a mass of yews
of great size and vast age stretch up the hill, and beyond
to the left as far as the eye can penetrate through the
obscurity. The trees in their long and slow growth
have assumed many wild forms, and the visitor who
stands there towards evening, and peers into that sombre
grove, will sometimes yield to the spell which the scene
is sure to exercise on imaginative natures—he will half
fancy that these ghostly trees are conscious creatures,
and that they have marked with mingled pity and
scorn the long processions of mankind come and go
like the insects of a day, through the centuries during
which they have been stretching out their distorted
limbs nearer and nearer to each other. Thick fibrous
shoots spring out from their trunks, awakening in the
memory long-forgotten stories of huge hairy giants,
enemies of mankind, even as the "double-fatal yew"
itself was supposed to be in other days. The bark
stands in distinct layers, the outer ridges mouldering
away, like the fragments of a wall of some ruined
castle. The tops are fresh and green, but all below in

that sunless recess seems dead. At the foot of the
deepest part of the grove there is a seat beneath a
stern old king of the wood, but the *genius loci* seems
to warn the intruder to depart—ancient superstitions
are rekindled, and the haggard trees themselves seem
to threaten that from a sleep beneath the " baleful
yew," the weary mortal will wake no more.

Beyond this grove the yews lead the way down hill,
and on the right hand, in an opening, there grows a
majestic beech, full twenty-four feet in girth at five
feet from the ground. It throws out its roots more than
fifty feet, and they are all gnarled and interlaced, and
covered with moss. The lower branches reach to the
ground, and run far along it, while the trunk looks like
the body of some huge elephant, bearing many a deep
scar which time and weather have left as traces of their
heavy blows. Here and there the wounds have been
covered with iron bands, and huge props have been
placed under the drooping branches. A nobler tree, far
stricken in age as it is, it would be hard to find. Just
below it, a worthy companion, there is a grisly yew,
standing all across the path, as if to forbid further progress. The branches touch the ground all about it, and
cover a circumference of 230 feet. I measured it with
care. There is another yew hard by which is twenty-
three feet in circumference, but this measurement is
partly caused by a cleft in the trunk. The dark colour
of the yew is beautifully relieved in summer by the
tender green of the ash. " Where the oak decays in
this park," says Brayley, in his " History of Surrey,"

" the beech succeeds; and where the beech decays, the ash springs up spontaneously." The Rev. C. A. Johns, in his interesting work on the "Forest Trees of Britain," quotes a letter from Evelyn, in Aubrey's "Surrey," which refers to this supplanting of the oak by the beech. " That which I would observe to you from the wood of Wootton is, that where goodly Oaks grew, and were cut down by my grandfather almost a hundred years since, is now altogether Beech ; and where my brother has extirpated the Beech, there rises Birch." This process may easily be traced in the Druids' Walk, but there the ash succeeds the beech. In Brayley there is also a note which may be of interest to some visitors here, for it states that the "rare moth, the dotted chestnut (*ylea rubiginea*), of which the locality is said to be unknown," frequents the yews in the Druids' Grove when "the berries are ripe, and becoming intoxicated with the juice is easily caught about the midnight hour in October." Perhaps there are not many persons who being suddenly set down in the Druids' Grove at the midnight hour, would be much inclined to go off in pursuit of moths.

Beyond the yew which stands all across the path, there is another little gate, and from that a path bearing to the right will lead out into Westhumble lane. Just above the railroad station (the Boxhill station of the Brighton line) there is a road leading to Chapel Farm and Ranmore Common, or by a short cut across the fields and Mr. Cubitt's carriage drive, to Dorking. The latter road will take the visitor past

"Camilla Lacey," the house (now enlarged) in which
Madame D'Arblay wrote "Camilla," and in which she
lived for many years.

Albury Park is very unlike Norbury, but it has
many charms of its own, not the least among them
being an old yew hedge and some noble trees. If the
visitor will go past Mr. Drummond's "cathedral"—
which is more frequented than any other place of worship
for miles round—and will make his way over the hills
to East Horsley (a road only to be found by making
enquiries on the spot), he will see what may well be
described as the most desolate region of Surrey. In all
my wanderings, never have I seen in a civilised land
such a deserted tract as this. You go for miles through
a totally uninhabited country, nor does any sign of the
hand of man appear until you reach the Earl of Love-
lace's estate, far beyond the Downs. The land is all
overgrown with large ferns which seem to strangle the
very trees, and drag them to the ground. The oaks
and beeches are stunted in growth, and begin to push
out their short branches directly they come above the
soil. The thick rank weeds and coarse ferns encroach
even upon the narrow roadway, and far as the eye can
reach nothing can be seen except this barren and
melancholy expanse. Not even game is preserved here
—the land, hundreds of acres of it, is simply allowed to
run wild, unfenced and untilled. There are noble sites
for residences in the district, one scarcely inferior to
the site of the Deepdene, and ample space for scores of
farms. But nothing is grown upon it—not even good

trees. A man who once drove me through this part said that he had never seen anybody about here at work, and that in certain places, roads which were formerly used, were now all covered with grass and weeds. "I have tried some of them," he said, "and after a few hundred yards you come to a dead stop." "Do you see much game here?" I asked. "None at all. I don't know how it is, but the birds do not seem to come here—not but what if they did the poachers would not soon have them, for you see there is nobody to prevent them."

All this land is, of course, beyond the limits of the village of Albury, which is one of the most pleasant places in Surrey. The church or "cathedral" before referred to stands very near Albury Park. It is called the "Holy Catholic Apostolic Church," and was originally built for the followers of Irving, of whom the late Mr. Drummond, the banker, was among the foremost. His daughter, the present Duchess of Northumberland, still takes the deepest interest in the welfare of the sect, but the worshippers in the church deny with some warmth that they are "Irvingites," or that Mr. Irving was the founder of their church.

"It is a great mistake to call us Irvingites," said a member of the church to me. "But suppose anyone wishes to mention your church, what is it to be called?" "The Catholic Apostolic Church," he answered. "But I think I have heard of other churches which claim that title?" "No matter—we are the true Apostolic Church, believing in a fourfold ministry, as the Apostles did." "I see—but what particular doctrines do you hold?" "We follow strictly the Catholic Apostolic precepts and the fourfold ministry." Thus, continually travelling in the same circle, I left off my questionings, not much wiser than when I began them.

The services in the Cathedral at Albury are at times conducted with much pomp, and the "priests" are clad in gorgeous vestments. Near the altar there are stalls for the priests, of whom about twelve have their head-quarters at Albury. This is the central church, and from it missionaries or ministers are drawn for service elsewhere. At the door of the church there is a basin containing holy water, incense is constantly burnt, and a lamp is always kept alight before the altar. The sacrament is also kept upon the altar from Sunday to Sunday, and is thus ready, as was explained to me, "for the use of the sick, day and night." There are various texts of scripture on the walls, and a special liturgy is used.

The gardens of Albury Park are close to the church, and although their natural situation is most beautiful, yet they are not properly cared for, and are too thickly covered with trees to thrive well. Evelyn took a great interest in this estate, and was anxious to purchase it, and with that end in view wrote to Sir Edward Thurland, a Baron of the Exchequer, soliciting his interest in the matter. He dwells upon the "favour which (I am assured) you may do y' servant in promoting his singular inclynations for Albury, in case (as I am confident it will) that seate be exposed for sale." He

vows that this service will bind him to the Baron for
ever, and adds, " I suppose the place will invite many
candidates, but my money is good, and it will be the
sole and greatest obligation that it shall ever be in y^r
power to doe for" * the thrifty and long-headed squire,
who afterwards so successfully carried out the astute
line of policy which was ascribed to the "Vicar of Bray."
The great curiosity of the gardens at Albury is the yew
hedge before referred to, now more flourishing than
ever. It is a quarter of a mile in length, and is largely
formed by yew trees, which grow at regular distances,
and form a sort of canopy with their branches on each
side of the green sward beneath. The lower branches
are cut and trimmed every few years in order to pre-
serve uniformity. Under the trees there grows the
hedge proper—it is, in fact, a thick hedge with an over-
hanging roof of yew trees, carefully kept in shape. It
is probably the finest and most remarkable hedge to be
seen in England, and running at right angles with it
there is a holly hedge, to which it would be hard to find
an equal. The shelter given by the upper branches of
the yew trees is now so thick that the visitor will
scarcely need any other protection from sun or rain.
This long dark line gives the entire garden a somewhat
heavy and sombre appearance. The mistletoe seems to
flourish here, and may be seen in great branches on the
false acacia and apple trees. The woods at the back
are bold and striking, but the house is totally without
interest.

* Memoirs and Correspondence of John Evelyn (ed. 1819), vol. ii. p. 96.

The best way to visit all this part is to go to the Chilworth station, and take the road (which cannot be missed) to Albury. Having seen the "Cathedral," a path through a meadow at the back will lead to the greenhouse and the gardener's cottage, where application may be made for permission to see the grounds. The gardener will let the visitor out at the other end, and a meadow must then be crossed into a lane. Turn to the right, and pass over the little wooden bridge which spans the Tillingbourne. Follow this stream by a pretty path to the left, until it ends in the interesting village of Shere, which with its old cottages and barns and church will afford many a subject for the sketcher and artist. There are few more picturesque villages to be found in this part of England than Shere. From thence the road is an easy one to the Gomshall station, or there is a field-path to it through the churchyard— the entire distance between the two stations by this route being five miles.

Among all the fine estates which are to be found in Surrey, we may look in vain for one which can surpass the "Deepdene," long the residence of "Anastasius" Hope, and still in the possession of his family. It is a noble domain, more than twelve miles in circumference, full of magnificent trees and long sweeps of forest glade, deep dells covered with fox-glove and ferns, and solitary paths so clothed with thick moss that the ground is as soft as if it were covered with a velvet carpet. Two large parks have been added to this ancient estate since it fell into the hands of the Hope

family, and one of them—Betchworth—is freely thrown
open to the public at all times, while the house itself,
with its many choice collections, is liberally shown on
Tuesdays and Fridays. Few houses in the county will
better reward a visit. In the entrance-hall, a striking
chamber, are several famous works by Thorwaldsen, and
some fine statues which have come to us from the
hands of Roman artists. In the gallery above there are
some great paintings by Rubens, Domenichino, and
other renowned masters, and a bust of a " cardinal"
(unknown) which I, for my part, can never look at too
often or too long. What shrewdness, penetration, and
intellectual power are expressed in that face ! Who
can fail to be charmed with the large dining-room, so
perfectly proportioned, or with the splendid examples
of Paul Veronese, Correggio, and Raffaelle which cover
its walls? The Etruscan room, with its valuable collection of vases, is both curious and interesting, and no
one who has seen the statue of Minerva in the small
Pompeian room beyond will ever be likely to forget
that wondrous work. It was found in 1797 at the
mouth of the Tiber, and so instinct is the figure with
fire and vigour that it absolutely seems alive. Where
is the sculptor of modern days who could throw all this
wealth of regal beauty into a block of marble ? Even
Canova's " Venus leaving the Bath " at the other end
of the room looks feeble after that divine Minerva.
Then there is the library, which no scholar can regard
without admiration and envy. The calm which reigns
within this stately room, the shelves lined with the

noblest legacies of the "mighty dead," the views without over the sweet fields and rolling hills of Surrey, must ever exercise a potent fascination over those who are well content to pass their lives chiefly amid the unwearying companionship of books. A work planned by an imaginative man *patulæ sub tegmine fagi*, or wandering amid the sequestered glades of the Deepdene, and chiefly written in this delightful library, could scarcely fail to find an enduring place in literature—and such was the history of *Coningsby*.

Above the deep dell, or "Dene," which is the gem of these grounds, there is a splendid avenue of beeches, and to the southward a vast landscape unfolds itself far into the weald of Sussex. The valley towards Reigate is disclosed at the end of the avenue, scarred by deep cuttings in the chalk hills and disfigured by lime-works. In the hollows below are "unwedgeable and gnarled" oaks, lofty beeches, and luxuriant holly trees. In the month of June all the grounds are clad in gorgeous hues, for then the rhododendrons are in bloom, and their brilliant colours stand out in dazzling relief against the dark firs which fill the background. In the spring, the hawthorn and the lilac perfume the air; in the winter the walks are gay with the red berry of the holly. Noble oriental planes, and two venerable cedars, still remain in Chart Park, now but an exquisite fringe on the skirt of the Deepdene, but once the site of an ancient house. This solitary park, with dim associations of the past still clinging to it, and the ruins at Betchworth with their monumental yews, impart a poetic interest to the more radiant beauties which adorn the Deepdene—the enamelled lawn, the tulip-tree near the garden terrace, the dark and spreading cedar beyond, the flowers which sparkle like stars in the leafy paths, and the blue ridge of hills which encircles the magic scene.

CHAPTER XVII.

REIGATE, GATTON PARK, AND THE PILGRIM'S WAY.

Some Points of Difference between Reigate and Dorking.—Drainage
and Comfort.—Reigate Park.—Gatton and the "Marble Hall."
—The Two Members of Parliament.—Merstham.—On the Track
of the Canterbury Pilgrims.—A Scramble among the Yew Trees.
—Walton Heath.—The Yews near Box Hill.

OF all the towns in this part of Surrey, Reigate is
the most popular, and not without very good reasons.
The shops are excellent, the neighbourhood is full of
good houses, and the scenery for miles around is over-
flowing with attractions. The speculative builder has
not been allowed to sprinkle too many of his "shoddy"
and detestable villas over this pleasant retreat, although
examples of his style are not entirely wanting. The
neighbourhood has been chosen as a place of residence
by a larger proportion of active professional men and
merchants than any other town in the valley. At
Dorking, the tone of "society" must be rather weari-
some, for the landowners will not recognise the general
residents, unless, indeed, it be in that condescending
manner which does not add much to the geniality of
social intercourse. The town is therefore, at all seasons,
one of the dullest in England —and for young people it

11

must be intolerable, for there is scarcely anybody of their own age to associate with them, there are no amusements, no one gives any parties, there are the usual narrow influences at work which always grow up in small gossipy places, and altogether life is stagnant there. Everything is different at Reigate. The city men and the professional men infuse some of their own energy and vigour into the social atmosphere of the town, and as young folks abound, there are plenty of parties for croquet or lawn tennis in the summer, and for music and dancing in the winter. Another fact must be mentioned which is not without its importance—Reigate is better drained than Dorking. In the latter town, there is no drainage at all, the only attempt to get rid of the sewage consisting in a partial diversion of it into the Mole at the east end. What happens afterwards may easily be imagined.

No wonder, therefore, that Reigate has left Dorking all behind—has, indeed, more than doubled its population within a very few years. It has an old-fashioned and interesting appearance, its castle vaults are curious, and its church is worth going to see. But it is hard for the visitor to go grubbing about underground, or poking among old monuments, with such attractions outside to call him away. Reigate Park offers far greater temptations to the lover of the beautiful than all the castle vaults. It can boast of some lovely dells, where the children play at hide-and-seek among the ferns, or wander up the hill sides knee-deep in bluebells. Such another place for wild-flowers is scarcely to be found even in the county of Surrey. All the outskirts of the town are intensely "countrified" and rural in their character—it is really the country, not the town. It was after attending the sale of a farm-house hereabouts, that Cobbett burst into one of the most amusing of his denunciations against modern "progress." "When the old farm-houses," he says, "are down, and down they must come in time, what a miserable thing the country will be ! Those that are now erected are mere painted shells, with a mistress within, who is stuck up in a place she calls the *parlour*, with, if she have children, the 'young ladies and gentle-men' about her: Some showy chairs and a sofa (a *sofa* by all means) ; half-a-dozen prints in gilt frames hang-ing up; some swinging book-shelves with novels and tracts upon them ; a dinner brought in by a girl that is perhaps better educated than she ; two or three knick-knacks to eat instead of a piece of bacon and a pudding ; the house too neat for a dirty-shoed carter to come into ; and everything proclaiming to every sensible beholder that there is here a constant anxiety to make a show not warranted by the reality. The children (which is the worst part of it) are all too clever to work : they are all to be gentlefolks. Go to plough ! Good God ! What, 'young gentlemen' go to plough ! They become *clerks* or some skimmy-dish thing or other. They flee from the dirty work as cunning horses do from the bridle." This "Rural Ride" was written, or at any rate is dated, at Reigate, and the old farm-houses whose decline Cobbett lamented are not yet entirely swept away from the district.

The walk to Gatton Park, and onwards to Merstham, is one of the best in all this part of Surrey. Having reached the road outside the railroad station, you turn to the right, and go on up-hill till you come to the suspension bridge. From that bridge a bird's-eye-view of the town and surrounding country may be obtained, and a most fascinating view it is. In many respects it is preferable to the scene which is presented from the point of Box Hill just above Dorking. Beyond the bridge there is a road, with a finger-post at the corner, going off to the right. Follow that—a shady road, with many fine beeches towering up on the right hand— and you will shortly come to a lodge gate, and although there is a board up warning " trespassers " to " beware," yet the road is freely open to all inoffensive strangers, and you may wander about the charming park beyond without fear. This is the place of which Cobbett wrote : " Before you descend the hill to go into Reigate, you pass Gatton, which is a very rascally spot of earth "— but it can no longer boast of its two members of Parliament, which made it " rascally."

Gatton House is generally called a " stately structure," but an impartial observer would probably describe it as a rather ugly building with a great fungus growing out of the middle. The architect seems to have built the house without providing the usual means for getting into it, since the only entrance is by that side door which is commonly set apart for tradespeople and servants. The first impression that strikes one on seeing the place is, " Something or other has gone

wrong with this strange looking house—perhaps some-
body begun it and never lived to finish it." And, in
truth, that is very nearly the state of the case. The
fifth Lord Monson determined to produce on this spot
an exact copy of the Corsini chapel at Rome, and he
went so far as to spend £10,000 on marbles for the
pavement alone. But like many another man, Lord
Monson began to build a house in which he was not
destined to live, and of course no one else cared to
carry on his fanciful and extravagant design. The hall
(to which strangers are readily admitted) was begun on
a grand scale, and finished on a paltry one. The walls
were intended to be magnificent, but before they had
got up very far, a common roof was prematurely clapped
down upon them, and now this ambitious structure has
a pinched up and squat appearance. The frescoes cannot be said to improve matters very much. The hall,
flattery apart, can only be regarded as a rich man's
freak—the sort of thing which country people generally
christen a "folly." The other rooms of the house
dispel the gloomy impression which this unfinished hall
produces. The view from the drawing-room windows
is delicious, and the pictures on the walls, fine in themselves, are displayed to great advantage.

In front of the house is a mausoleum in which Lord
Monson was buried, and close by, on the mound shaded
by trees, is the place where that interesting and important ceremony used to be performed of "electing"
two members of Parliament for Gatton. The con-
stituency consisted for many years of one person—the

lord of the manor for the time being. It cannot be denied that this man at least was very fully represented in the councils of his country. Sometimes he managed for appearance sake to bring up a score or so of "dummies" to the polls, but they voted as their master or employer, the lord of the manor, told them. It was this privilege which always made the property fetch a high price in the market—you bought an estate with two seats in the House of Commons tacked on to it. A very much disgusted man Lord Monson must have been when, after paying £100,000 for the property, the first Reform Bill cut off the Members of Parliament, only two years afterwards. Reigate also returned two members once upon a time, and the Reform Bill of 1832 left it with one, and then in 1867 it was disfranchised altogether for "bribery and treating"—a subject which it does not do to bring up too suddenly in social circles at Reigate.

From this house there is a pleasant walk to Merstham station—through the park, to the right after leaving the house, then across fields—the distance being about a mile and a half. There is not much to see at Merstham, but it is a pleasant little village, with some old timbered cottages here and there, and a blacksmith's forge which recalls some of Dickens's sketches. The church might easily be passed by unseen, for it is a little out of the way of the village, and in summer is sheltered by the foliage of the trees.

Most people know that Reigate was a very busy place in the days when thousands of our countrymen made that pilgrimage to Canterbury which Chaucer would have rendered immortal, even if history had been careless of it. It was here that the pilgrims generally found a pleasant halting stage, and a chapel was built for them which stood until the beginning of last century. The present Town Hall and market stand upon its site. Above Reigate to the north, it is easy to see a line of yew trees going along the slope of the hill, sometimes far apart, sometimes close together. The traveller on the Reading branch of the South Eastern railroad may frequently trace this line of yews between Reigate and Guildford, if he looks from the windows on the right-hand side. Two miles from Reigate there is a long procession of yews going up the hill from Buckland, and in some places thick clumps of them may be made out from the valley below. All these are relics of the Pilgrim's Way. It is by no means a simple matter to get upon the track itself, or to follow it for any distance. There is no regular road. Sometimes the path is effaced by modern cultivation of the land— sometimes it is all overgrown with trees, shrubs, and bushes. To get at any part of it westward of Reigate you must scramble over hedges and fences, and run the risk of tumbling down ugly holes, or of being ordered off some field for trespassing—the last inconvenience being much the worst of the three. Where was the road which the pilgrims who went to Canterbury from Southampton followed for so many years, and in such great numbers? In endeavouring to find it, one is often obliged to fall back upon local tradition for

guidance, but in such matters local tradition is not to
be despised. There is nothing which lingers so long in
popular recollection as an old road or an old name.
In Surrey, instances of men and women living to the
age of ninety are far indeed from being uncommon, and
it takes very few such lives to carry us back to the days
when the long trains of pilgrims were plodding on their
way to the shrine of À Becket. Local tradition, then,
must be allowed some weight, and in Surrey it
undoubtedly asserts that the old road was marked by a
line of yew trees, and in many places that line is still
perfectly well known.

Mr. Albert Way, in a note to Dean Stanley's most
interesting " Memorials of Canterbury," points out that
from Southampton the foreign visitors "would probably
take the most secure and direct line of communication
towards Farnham, crossing the Itchen at Stoneham,
and thence in the direction of Bishop's Waltham,
Alton, and Froyle." At Alton it has been traced, from
Farnham it probably ran along the Hog's Back, and
beyond Guildford it passed by St. Martha's chapel and
over the "green road" still existing, and still marked,
as at Newland's corner, by many yew trees. "The
line," says Mr. Way, "for the most part, it would seem,
took its course about mid-way down the hill-side, and
on the northern verge of the older cultivation of these
chalk downs. . . . . Under the picturesque height of
Box Hill several yews of large size remain in ploughed
land, relics, no doubt, of this ancient way, and a row
more or less continuous marks its progress as it leads

towards Reigate, passing to the north of Brockham and Betchworth." Near Dorking, in Westhumble Lane, there are ruins, as I have already mentioned, which are still known as the "Pilgrim's Chapel." And local names, here and elsewhere, plainly point to the track which was unquestionably followed by the pilgrims, and which is still far from being obliterated, although the explorer must be once more fairly cautioned that nowhere can it be followed without considerable inconvenience.

Between Reigate and Dorking the yews which mark the road are more regular in their course than between Dorking and Guildford, but the road itself is almost closed or overgrown with trees and bramble. A chalk path leads up the hill north of Reigate, and if the visitor finds nothing else to attract him, he will at least admire the noble view from the summit of the hill, extending to the weald of Kent on one side, and to the southdowns on the other. If you go to the top of this hill, you will come to a patch of wood, ankle-deep in mud in wet weather, and leading out upon a common. By the hedge there is no path, but it is necessary to keep close beside it, and presently a gate is reached which opens into a path leading downwards to Buckland, where a post warns all persons against "injuring the yew trees." The line of yews runs all the way down the hill, and goes on westward, but without any visible track to guide the explorer. Keep on, however, till the hill takes a dip, and then go up a field to the right, where the yews become very thick—almost as

deep a wood as the grove at Norbury Park, the trees
growing, as it were, into each other, while the ground
is all dark and bare beneath them. They form an
impassable barrier at this point, and it is necessary to
keep still higher up the hill until another wood is
reached, through which there is a very slight track
made by the country people. If this is followed, it will
be found to lead out to Walton Heath, with a church
and windmill and a few cottages scattered on its outer
edge. The common must be avoided, or it would lead
one too far astray, but some rough scrambling has to
be done before the yews come in sight again. There
they are, however, about half-way up the hill, in a
perfectly straight line, with a steep pitch below and
cultivated fields above. A small valley opens here,
which can only be crossed either by making your way
down to the bottom, or by taking it above. In the
latter case, you will come out upon a green lane, which
leads to private grounds, belonging to the house at the
head of the gorge, and which is called "Pibblecombe."
Here one is compelled to skirt Walton Heath once more,
and to join the main roadway until some woods on the
left (the late Sir B. Brodie's) are reached. A gateway
opens into them, and the track guides you to the brow of
the hill once more, where a backward view of the yew
trees may be seen, and the dip of the hills which inter-
rupts them. There is a path down to Betchworth, but
the hill-side must be followed, through Sir B. Brodie's
woods, and out upon his carriage drive. Immediately
below that a row of yew trees, still running in a

straight line, may be seen, and beyond that again they are occasionally found until you reach Box Hill, and from thence they continue across the valley, below Mr. Cubitt's grounds, and so to the hills again and on to Guildford. By the circuitous road I have endeavoured to indicate, it is fully twelve miles to Dorking, but they are twelve miles of lovely country. It is necessary to be vigilant in many places, for great excavations have been made for lime-works, and the grass grows green to the very edge, and sometimes there is little to denote the vicinity of a huge declivity down which it will not be advisable for the traveller to pursue his researches, for he would be compelled to do so head-foremost. There are few walks in Surrey, however, which present greater attractions than this, either for the geologist or the naturalist or the simple lover of nature.

CHAPTER XVIII.

REDHILL TO CROWHURST.

REDHILL, like most other "junctions," is a scattered, bewildering, unsatisfactory place. It lies sprawling vaguely over a large extent of ground, and after you have walked round and about it for an hour or so, you feel as if you were getting tied up in a hopeless knot with railroad lines. The town has no plan—the streets have grown up by accident, and all kinds of houses have been dropped down upon them at random. There is a good common on the outskirts, but even this is disfigured by large sand pits, which it is advisable to approach with caution. While standing up above one of them, I saw a large mass dislodge itself and come crashing to the ground. "That's nothing," said a man who noticed my astonishment, "I was up here the other day when eight or ten tons fell. Plenty of men have been killed down there." There are some good views towards Reigate on the one side and Horley on the other, from a clump of trees in the middle of the common, and a stirring walk may be taken as far as Reigate. There are also some attractive specimens of Surrey lanes in the neighbourhood, deep and shady, covered with wild flowers in spring, and in the summer almost dark with the foliage of the trees above.

The moment, in fact, you get outside the town of Redhill you come upon a very pretty country. It is impossible to go in a better direction than towards Nutfield, even if the walk now to be described should prove too long for the chance visitor. It is altogether about thirteen miles, making allowance for going a little out of the way occasionally; but Nutfield is close to Redhill. Between the two places there are some unusually comfortable looking residences, commanding wide and beautiful views to the southward. I asked a mason who was at work on a wall who owned most of these houses? He said, London men. "What, merchants?" "Sometimes, and stockbrokers and them sort of people. They buy up all the land now-a-days. The old families are going out, you see, and these people from the city are taking their places everywhere you go."

"You speak as if you were sorry for it," I said.

"And I am—the gentleman makes a better master than the shopkeeper. I've had to work for them both, and I know."

"Then you are not one of the people who complain of the bloated landowner?"

"Not I, sir. What harm do they do anyone? I think everything's pretty well as it is."

"Did you ever see Reynolds's Newspaper?"

"Sometimes I do, down there at the public (pointing towards Redhill), but I don't pin my faith to any newspaper. None of them are to be trusted."

"You are an uncommonly sensible man," said I. "Now can you tell me how far it is to Nutfield?"

"Why this is part of it, and there is the rest of it just below you."

There sure enough it was, within ten minutes' walk, a small forgotten-looking place, with a large old-fashioned inn standing back from the road, a good porch at the door, and a green before it. "Evidently an old posting house," thought I, and in I went, for such antiquated inns are far more interesting than all your grand new hotels, managed by "limited liability" young ladies and waiters. There are many traces of its former prosperity still clinging to this decayed old inn at Nutfield—the remains of large stables without, and marks of good rooms and a thriving business within. I sat talking nearly half an hour with the landlord, in a parlour which must at one time have been an imposing apartment. I noticed two cupboards opening into the wall on each side of the fire-place. "They have been made there, sir," said the landlord, "in my time. You would never guess what they used to be. They were large and comfortable corners in the old fireplace, where people used to sit down and talk and smoke on winter's nights. But what use would such a fire-place be now?"

"I suppose," said I, "that you have very little custom here."

"Very little indeed, sir, and if it were not for the workmen who are employed about here in getting fuller's earth, we should have none at all. That is the only thing that keeps everybody at Nutfield from going to the workhouse."

A very respectable and quiet sort of man he seemed, though a little down-hearted in his manner, as a man has reason to be when he lives in such a little place as Nutfield, on fuller's earth. He pointed out to me the "clerk's" house, where he said I could get the keys of the church. The clerk turned out to be a woman with about half a dozen children hanging round her feet, and another one in her arms—all in one small room, which, however, was clean and comfortable. She handed me the keys, and I walked down to the church, and with some little difficulty opened the door. Before going in I saw the inscription on the south wall which is mentioned in Murray's Guide :

> "He Liv'd alone, He Lyes alone,
> To Dust He's gone, both Flesh and Bone."

Would he have "gone" to anything else if he had not lived alone? If poor Thomas Steer, over whom the women-folks have set up this kind of war-whoop, had flown to the protecting arms of one of the ladies of Nutfield, he would have escaped the fate of being held up after death as an "awful warning"—although he might not have had so easy a time of it while alive. Inside the church there are two or three old grave-stones and a brass, but the inscription which one is most surprised to find in such an out-of-the-way place is to the memory of an American—Augustus Longstreet Branham, who "lived two years in this parish." Below the church there is the Rectory, a charming house, standing in the midst of pretty lawn and gardens, and overlooking a fertile and varied country.

After passing through Nutfield, you come plump upon a windmill, standing close by the roadside. It is certain that Don Quixote never could have passed that without a desperate encounter. I was almost inclined to break a lance with it myself. A few yards beyond, a beautiful view opens to the right, and at this point the visitor is as nearly as possible in a line with Rottingdean, near Brighton. A wide expanse of lovely country, well-wooded and yet well-cultivated, spreads itself to the very foot of the South Downs, and just on the other side of yonder hill is the once pleasant and cheerful "Doctor Brighton," now a huge, over-grown, crowded, noisy city. Doctor Brighton has too many patients in these days for a quiet man. Less than a mile further along the road brings us to Bletchingley, the population of which seems at first sight to be made up of butchers and beagle dogs. While I am waiting for the old clerk to find the keys of the church, I enquire into this phenomenon, and it turns out that the butcher breeds beagle dogs, and gets as much as £5 or £10 a-piece for them. I went down to his shop, and there found an exceedingly cheery and comely dame, who proved to be the butcher's wife. Decidedly Bletchingley is a more interesting place than Nutfield.

I made particular enquiries from the " butcheress " about beagle dogs, and was receiving much information in a most agreeable manner, when the clerk, a volatile young gentleman of eighty-five summers, hove in sight with the keys, and we went into the church. Bletchingley has but one church now, although formerly it could boast of seven ; and it used to return two members to Parliament. " A little way to the right (of Godstone), cries out Cobbett, " lies the vile, rotten borough of Bletchingley; but, happily for Godstone, out of sight." When Members of Parliament were thus plentiful at Bletchingley, what a price the butchers must have got for their beagle dogs—just before election.

The one church of Bletchingley is now far too large for the village, and it has a monument inside it far too large for the church—a monument which absolutely covers up the whole side of a wall in the south chancel. The person whom it commemorates is Sir Robert Clayton, who died in 1707. He never could have done anything bad enough to deserve this terrific monument. The figures, the " angels," the inscription, everything about it is like a fearful nightmare. I tried to turn my attention to a brass near the altar, to a priest—no inscription. Thereupon the clerk, who had a very melancholy manner—as how could a man fail to have who was doomed to live within a few yards of that fearful monument ?—told me a curious little story :—

" You see that brass ? Well, a very strange thing

happened about that. It used be over there by the belfry, partly hidden under a seat. One day a gentleman in a carriage called at my house to see the church. I happened to be away from home, and he said to my missis, 'You have no occasion to come down—we are only going to look over the church.' So, being in a carriage, she gave him the keys, and thought no more about it. The next time I went to the church, that *brass was gone!*"

"And I suppose you were pretty well scared?"

"Well, I did not like it at all, but I did not know what to do. I often thought about the stolen brass, but could get no trace of it. At last, one day, a gentleman came here, and he looked down and saw the traces of the brass in the stone—the vacant place, you understand. Said he, 'Why, good gracious, I think I know where that brass is.' 'Do you?' said I, 'where?' 'Why, in my house in London. I bought it not long ago in Soho Square. If you like I will send it to you.' Of course I said I should like it very much, but I thought it was all idle talk. But he really did send it down, and the moment I set eyes on it I knew it again directly, but the inscription was gone. We never got that back. The gentleman said he went to Soho Square to see if he could find it, but it was not there. Very likely some descendant of the family had taken it away. Since then I never let anybody come to the church alone."

"And quite right too," said I. "I wonder whether the gentleman who returned the brass had ever, by any chance, seen or met the gentleman who took it away ?"

The old clerk only shook his head. "How long have you lived here ?" I asked him. He said seventy-five years! Seventy-five years of life in Bletchingley, near that monument. Nothing will kill some people.

As I passed down the town, there were the beagle dogs, and there was the butcher's wife standing at the door, blithe and smiling. I stayed to talk with her a little further in reference to beagle dogs, when the butcher took out a big knife, and began sharpening it on his steel, casting a sheep-killer's eye towards me ; and it occurred to me that I might as well be getting homewards. A very nice sort of place, this Bletching-ley, not in the least dull as I first imagined, and the old clerk is quite right not to give it up just yet. There, however, goes my road to Godstone, and a very pretty road it is, and Godstone is prettier still, with its large and picturesque village-green, its old houses, and its comfortable inn, long, low, and bedecked with flowers. The church, which stands at a little distance from the village, has been restored by Sir Gilbert Scott —and restored in the best sense of the word, not defaced and ruined. If all our churches had been dealt with by a similar hand, we should have done almost as much for ecclesiastical architecture as the Roman Catholics.

After lingering over the ruins of an elm-tree which stands just in front of the inn—the mere rind of one half of the trunk, quite bare and shiny, and yet with a vigorous outgrowth of branches and leaves above—I made the best of my way to Crowhurst. And the best is not good, for the roads soon begin to show a change of "formation"—from gravel and sand one passes to wet, greasy, sticky clay. There had been showers throughout the afternoon, and now the roads were in that condition in which one takes, according to the old saying, "one step forward and two steps backwards." Horace evidently encountered similar roads on his way to Rubi :—

> " Inde Rubos fessi pervenimus, utpote longum
> Carpentes iter, et factum corruptius imbre."

I found my way, after a long and tedious tramp, to Crowhurst church, and soon forgot all about roads and weather. Here is another veritable relic of the old times still left to us—a little piece of the England of our forefathers. Long-past years have left their trace on everything around, on yonder farm-house, called the "Mansion House," with its strangely trimmed yew trees, and its old walls and chimneys, no less than upon this ancient church. Even while yet on the outskirts of the village, the greyness of antiquity made itself *felt* as well as seen—it was in the very air. Generations have come and gone, and seen no change in anything surrounding us here. The yew tree, says Murray's "Guide," "may probably contend with its venerable brother at Crowhurst in Sussex, which, according to Decandolle, is one thousand two hundred years old." The inside of the tree has been " barbarously hollowed out," as the same writer very properly describes the operation, and you open a door and walk inside the tree. There are wooden benches fixed against the trunk, and a little round table in the middle, and according to my calculation, fourteen or fifteen persons could seat themselves at this table. Pic-nic parties still meet here occasionally, drinking and carousing; but a boy from the rectory who showed me the church said that the new rector would not allow this practice to be carried on, and I hope he will be as good as his word. The top of the tree is fresh and green, and in parts it has been strengthened with iron plates. The girth of the trunk is nearly thirty-one feet, about eight feet more than the largest of the yews which I measured at Norbury. Large wens or "bosses" have grown upon it, and yet in spite of all that time and ill-usage can do, it remains a noble tree, worth travelling over many a mile of clayey roads to gaze upon. The boy from the rectory said that the tree was "fourteen thousand years old." I suggested fourteen hundred, but he declined to make any correction in his estimate, and said he knew it was fourteen thousand, for his master had told him so. So fourteen thousand be it.

The church, though small, well repaid me for the time which I had spent in going to it. There are some fragments of the ancient stained glass to be seen here and there; a very old communion table, and a font perhaps still older; an inscription on a tomb near the altar to one of the Gaynesford family (date 1591), which formerly made no inconsiderable figure in these parts, and another memorial to Richard Cholmley, date 1634. A little corner of the church is curtained off, and this, it appears, is the vestry. There is an ancient chest in this inconvenient robing-room, and part of a brass on the floor. The church looks very poor as well as old, and in truth it has been much neglected. The old rector, weighed down perhaps with roads of "bottomless clay," and a somewhat melancholy parish, had allowed the churchyard to get knee-deep in brambles, and I was assured that "the birds had made such a mess in the church that you could scarcely sit down." But all was very neat and tidy when I was there on the 5th of September, 1876, and the new rector's mother had worked a cover for the communion table, and the signs of tender care were everywhere visible. They had somewhat softened the ruggedness of this primitive country church, and thrown around it an air befitting so venerable and sacred a place.

From the church there is a path across fields which affords a "short cut" to the Godstone station on the South Eastern railroad. This path leads out upon the turnpike road, near some tile works, and then the road must be followed till you come to a little public-house and general shop near a railroad bridge. Here you again forsake the road, turning in by a gate at the side of the shop, and pursuing a path on the edge of the fields, with the railroad running on an embankment close to the right hand. It is two miles by this path to the station, and nearly four by the road.

About a mile from the church there is an old moated

house, called Crowhurst Place. The kitchen is of great
size, but apparently lies below the level of the water.
There are great carp in the moat, and the worthy
farmer who lives in the house seldom refuses anyone
permission to fish for them. But, after all, it is the
old yew tree in the churchyard which still brings the
pilgrim to Crowhurst. Surely it was this tree, or its
contemporary in Sussex, which inspired the lines of
Tennyson :—

> "Old yew, which graspest at the stones
>   That name the underlying dead,
>   Thy fibres net the dreamless head,
> Thy roots are wrapt about the bones.
>
> "The seasons bring the flower again,
>   And bring the firstling to the flock ;
>   And in the dusk of thee, the clock
> Beats out the little lives of men.
>
> "O not for thee the glow, the bloom,
>   Who changest not in any gale,
>   Nor branding summer suns avail
> To touch thy thousand years of gloom."

CHAPTER XIX.

EWHURST, ALBURY, AND CHILWORTH.

The Wild Commons and Heaths of Surrey.—A Word of Warning.—
Sutton, Felday, and Joldwyns.—The "Lucky" Leveson-Gowers.
Holmbury Hill.—The Water Carrier.—A Stonebreaker's Recol-
lections.—How Mr. Hull was Buried.—Old Roads and New.—
Ewhurst Church and its Critic.—An English Sleepy-Hollow.—
Moorland and Solitary Roads.—Albury and Chilworth.—Cob-
bett's Curse.

THE road throughout this walk leads on through
woodland and common, by paths bordered with fir
trees, or passing over hills beneath which a great
part of the wealds of Surrey and Sussex lie extended
before the traveller. By far the larger proportion of
the land through which he must pass is uncultivated.
Considering the small size of the county of Surrey, the
extent of it which lies a mere wilderness in these busy
days is simply amazing. The whole county is but
twenty-seven miles in length, and not more than forty
in breadth, yet it contains almost every variety of
scenery, scarcely one mile is like another, and often
the whole character of the country undergoes an utter
change within the space of half a dozen miles. Where,
out of Scotland, can be found such moors and heaths as
those between Thursley and Hindhead, or even between

Albury and Ewhurst? Many of the commons or downs
are familiar to excursionists, but the heaths in the
more distant and neglected parts of the county are
little visited. The cottagers to be met with here and
there will tell you that they scarcely ever see a stranger
from one year's end to another.

The route which I followed between Albury and
Ewhurst, and again from Ewhurst to Chilworth, is not
marked upon any map, and it goes a long way round.
But it has the merits of embracing the best points in
the scenery, and of starting from one railroad station
and returning to another on the same line. The best
way is to begin the journey at the Gomshall station on
the South Eastern railroad, and end it at the Chilworth
station—but particular care should be taken beforehand
to ascertain that a train will touch at Chilworth in the
direction the traveller wishes to go, and at the hour he
expects to arrive there, for Chilworth is a benighted
place, very few trains stop at it in the course of the day,
and there is no other conveyance of any kind to be had.

From Gomshall station the road turns to the left
under the first railroad arch, and then it swerves to the
right soon after passing a blacksmith's forge. Having
got this short distance on the journey, we are apparently
beyond the limits of civilisation. No houses are to be
seen, no farms, no churches. The first village to be
seen, if village it can be called, is Sutton, a very
different place from the comfortable-looking Sutton
known to all Londoners. Here there are but three or
four tumble-down cottages, and a gloomy little public-

12

house under the sounding name of the "Abinger Arms." The road continues through a waste looking region, without any features of great interest, until you reach Felday, another small village not down on the one-inch ordnance map. Except that the houses here are of wood or brick, and not of mud, the place looks very like a Hindoo village in Bengal—a few hovels on each side of the road, and low "jungle" beyond. The country, however, is a little more open than it would be near a similar settlement in Bengal. On the right-hand side of the road is a mean sort of house, which must not be disrespectfully spoken of, for it is " Felday Church"—the only church for some distance round, the nearest to it being the one at Abinger. It is a common private house turned into a place of worship. The parsonage close by looks in a little better condition, but Felday is a wretched, half deserted spot, consisting entirely of the few scattered cottages I have mentioned, a brick field, and a melancholy roadside inn called the " Royal Oak."

From this group of depressing habitations the road took a sudden turn with manifest pleasure, and after a time it plucked up a little spirit, and began to produce its "views." It went rather up-hill till it reached a house called (as near as I could make out) " Jold-wynds," in the grounds of which were to be seen a couple of ladies sketching. If ever you do meet with anybody about here, man or woman, he or she is sure to be sketching, and you dare not ask a question for fear of spoiling the picture and getting most horribly snubbed into the bargain. To ask a stranger a direction in English country places is a serious undertaking. I have sometimes got a civil answer, sometimes none at all, and thus I have been duly impressed with a sense of my own unworthiness, and of the immense superiority of the person whom I had addressed without a proper introduction.

Just above "Joldwynds" the view opens in a very striking manner, with Leith Hill to the left, and a rich and beautiful country lying between. There is now nothing but good in store for the traveller. He may shake the dust of Felday from his feet, and look forward to one pleasant surprise after another. He will soon come to one of the seats belonging to the "lucky" Leveson-Gowers, and assuredly any man would deserve to be called lucky, even if he owned no other place than this. The house stands on an eminence facing the south, and sheltered from the north by Holmbury Hill. Not only are the grounds themselves as fair and beautiful as an exquisite picture, but for miles beyond and around them the whole country looks like a vast park, and one might easily fancy that it was a portion of this estate. Often in passing through such places, after having talked with people by the wayside, the thought passes through the mind, " Will all this last ? Are there not forces at work, and men able and eager to use them, which will make great changes in the face of England ere another century has passed over our heads ? " Who can tell ?

The public road winds round at the back of Mr.

Leveson-Gower's house, but I asked at the lodge gates if I might walk through the park, and was not refused. I saw at a glance that it would cut off a very large corner, and so it did—moreover, the carriage drive opens to the visitor all the manifold beauties of the country. Holmbury Hill at the back of the house is well worth climbing, but on this particular occasion I had my day's work already cut out for me. Through the lodge gates at the other end of the park I passed out to the turnpike road once more, having saved altogether not much less than a mile.

Many good ash trees now fringe the road—the prevailing tree throughout this part of the journey. I noticed a little spring on the road-side, and presently overtook a poor woman walking inside a hoop, with a pail of water in each hand. She looked very thin and miserable, as if it seldom fell to her lot to have enough to eat. The water was splashing all over her patched and worn out gown. I asked her why she did not put a flat piece of wood on the water in each pail, which would prevent any slopping over? She said she had never heard of it. She put down her pails on the road, and we stood and talked. She might have been about twenty-eight or thirty, but a hard life probably made her look older than she really was. As I looked at her and recalled the fine house up above, I thought of Thackeray's stern cry, "Awful, awful poor man's country!" Perhaps there is no one to blame for it, but these contrasts are startling to anyone who has not become so accustomed to them as to cease to notice

them at all. They are all the more startling because
the English people cannot disguise their poverty as the
French and Germans can, or even as the poorer classes
in America manage to do. They make no attempt to
carry it off well. With our countrymen and women
it stands out grim-faced and repulsive, in all its tragic
misery and horror.

This poor woman seemed suspicious at first, but
presently she told me that she had to fetch all the
water that was needed for her family from this spring.
It was full a quarter of a mile from her cottage.
"Have you no water there at all?" I asked. "No,"
she said, "not a drop."

"In the very hot weather we had this summer," she
went on, "this spring was dried up, and so I had to go
all the way to Ewhurst for water. Every drop we
drink or use has to be carried up in these pails. I
has enough to do to get water for 'em all." She took
up her load again and walked on.

"How many of you are there?"

"Three children and a pig." A pig, thought I—
doubtless she means her husband, and not a bad name
for any man who would let his wife drag out her
strength and life in this way. But presently she
mentioned her husband separately, not as a pig.

"Does he ever help you to fetch the water?"
said I.

She gave a dull sort of smile and answered, "Sometimes in the evening—when he can," she added in a
queer tone.

" When he has not been drinking something stronger himself?"

" Yes, sir, that's it. My three children cannot earn anything yet, for they are none of 'em five years old, and that keeps us poor. When they can go out we shall do better." It is the only use of the children of the poor—to be turned adrift to earn something.

" I suppose you find it hard sometimes to get them a dinner?"

" They generally get a good slice of bread, and sometimes a bit of treacle, and it *is* hard to get that."

By this time we had come up to an old man who was breaking a heap of stones by the road side, and who had a great pair of horn spectacles on his nose. We all three fell into a conversation. The stone-breaker evidently knew the woman—her cottage was now in sight. We could also see the tower upon Leith Hill from where we stood.

" When I was a boy," said the stonebreaker, " I heard an old man say that he had seen the funeral of Mr. Hull in that tower. He said he was pitched in head first. The people there were all laughing and playing up tricks, and they just threw the corpse in anyhow."

" Why didn't he want to be buried like a Christian?" asked the woman.

" Because gentlefolks can be buried how they likes." A decisive answer.

" Were the roads hereabouts as good as this when you were a boy?" said I.

" Lor bless you no, sir. They are well enough to look at now, but it is all wet clay underneath the surface. Not many years ago, you would have stuck fast in them in wet weather. You are in a clayey country about here—poor land, poor people."

" How much do you earn a week ? "

" Six or seven shillings—but not always. In the winter I can scarcely earn anything, for you see I'm not very young. Howsomever, grumbling won't help a body, will it ? "

I said I thought not, but was not quite sure, and tried to find out what the old man had been before he took to stone breaking, but he did not seem disposed to tell. A few questions about wages and expenses of living, and the poor will instantly be on their guard, as if they expected a visit from the tax gatherer.

" There's your old man a-calling for you," said the stonebreaker to the woman, and off she went. The old fellow bent down over his heap of stones, and went on hammering away at them, and I walked on thinking of what Cobbett said of these roads. " From Ewhurst the first three miles was the deepest clay that I ever saw to the best of my recollection. I was warned of the difficulty of getting along ; but I was not to be frightened at the sound of clay. It took me a good hour and a half to get along these three miles. Now mind, this is the real Weald, where the clay is bottomless." Such work as that at which I found the poor old stonebreaker has made all the difference.

A sharp walk along a circuitous sort of road soon

landed me in Ewhurst, where I saw very little prospect of getting the simplest kind of refreshment. Yet the day was hot, and the way home long, and even a glass of decent ale would have been acceptable. But the two or three public-houses in the place seemed to be of the most squalid kind.

Ewhurst church rests under the stigma of having been "restored," and indeed it appears to have been almost entirely rebuilt in 1839. It is still pleasant to look upon, in spite of the extremest efforts of the modern plasterer and mason to make it otherwise. A local personage who followed me into the church, and kept a careful watch on all my movements while pretending to look for a book, asked me what I thought of the church. I said that I thought very well of it.

"But, dear me," he continued, looking at both me and the church with the utmost contempt, "don't you see that it is *cruciform?*"

"Bless my soul," said I, starting back apparently much shocked, "so it is. I never noticed that before."

"Certainly," said the stranger, a little relenting towards me. "A perfect barbarism. I *despise* a cruciform church, sir," laying a stress upon the word "despise," which seemed intended to challenge me to take up the cudgels for it if I dared. But I—what could I say for the poor old church? I did not build it, or even restore it. Yet I began to take rather a fancy to it, hearing it thus abused, and admired its old oaken gallery, its carved pulpit black with age, its quaint reading desk, its ancient font. It is not so

pretty as the Rectory hard by, which can show a good
pedigree back to the time of James the First, and
looks rather like the home of some well-to-do squire
than of a country parson. Yet the church is worth
going to see, even with the disadvantage of having
a local critic heaping scorn upon you for liking it.

Then I went forth into the village, which is
sufficiently well described by the Americanism, "a
one-horse place." I met with two or three persons
only in the street, and they seemed to be half asleep.
At the post office a woman and a girl turned out in
some consternation to look at me, thinking perhaps
that I had a letter concealed about me, and was about
to post it, and thus overwhelm them with work. A
waggoner passed by on a load of hay, fast asleep. I
too began to feel drowsy, and hastened away towards
that windmill which makes so prominent a feature in
the landscape in all the southern part of Surrey. The
road leads north, up a steepish hill, with many a backward view over far-reaching heaths and home-like
fields. To the right hand a still higher hill ascends
from the road, covered with deep ferns and heaths. It
is called "Pitch Hill." There is a roadside inn with
the sign of the windmill, and I met with three or four
artists within a mile, and had a strictly "private view"
of several paintings destined to be submitted to public
inspection on the walls of the Academy. No more
delightful scene than this is open to mortal to transfer
to canvas—if only the mortal could be found capable
of doing it.

Drop a man down from a balloon in this part, and ask him where he is, and he will probably guess the North of Derbyshire. There are long stretches of moorland and heather-clad hills, and solitary roads almost swallowed up by the ferns, and disappearing in great fir-woods. For a mile or two you are hemmed in among these woods, and then the whole scene changes as it were in a moment—the heath and firs are left behind, and you come out upon a deep lane bordered with hazel trees and young oaks, and as this lane goes on, you will notice that the sandy soil has been much washed away, leaving the roots of the trees all bare. There is one good-sized beech especially from which the soil has all run away, and which is left like a vagrant, without any visible means of support. Presently we come to a farm-house on our left — the first we have seen since we left Ewhurst, and then a wider sweep of country appears in front, and the Guildford Hills and St. Martha's Chapel. Pass another farm-house, and take the road to the left— this brings us out upon Shere Heath, a noble expanse, the walk across which might make an old man feel young again. Then by a north-westerly course over Albury Common, another wide and breezy heath, where health and good spirits are taken in at every breath. There are neither houses nor land to be had about here for love or money. When you come to a cottage near the palings at your right hand, leave the road, and cut straight across the heath, and go through a wood, down a deep lane, which soon becomes so narrow that it looks little else than a dried up water-course. At the end, take the road to the left, not omitting to notice the double yew tree in front of a cottage, trimmed so as to form an archway. This brings you to Albury, where there lives a being who pretends to let out flys, and never' by any chance has one in—how often have I arrived at his mendacious shop, weary and footsore, in the hope of getting a lift to the station, and been obliged to trudge on amid the ironical remarks of the villagers, upon whom even Mr. Tupper's poems (he lives here, and his books are sold in the chandler's shop) do not seem to have produced that elevating influence which might reasonably have been looked for from them.

Having, then, reached Albury, you must now turn to the left, and keep to the left, for about a mile and a half, till you come to the big pond and the powder mills, and the remainder of Chilworth, which is not much. We are now at the foot of the hill on which stands St. Martin's Church, not far from the place where, according to Manning, was formerly "the mansion-house of the lords of the manor, which it continued to be till the death of the last of the Randylls. After that it was used as a farm-house." And now you may hunt in vain for the smallest trace of the building. If anybody takes an interest in gun-powder mills, there they are at Chilworth—I do not. The roads are bad, the inn is wretched. This is the place so energetically denounced by Cobbett, because in his day bank-notes and gunpowder were manufactured here—"two inventions of the devil." Now only one invention of the devil is left. Although the natural situation of Chilworth is most beautiful, and the hills at the back are glorious, yet the railroad-crossing, and the coal-sheds, and the out-buildings, and the poverty-stricken inn, tend somehow to give the village a depressing look ; and if the visitor should by any adverse chance find himself belated there at night, with the last train gone, he will be sorrowfully inclined to think that in spite of all the charms which Nature has scattered around, old Cobbett's curse still hangs over Chilworth.

CHAPTER XX.

FROM EDENBRIDGE TO PENSHURST.

THIS is a journey of about ten miles, but in some
parts the road is rather hard to find, and if the object
of the visitor be to see both Hever Castle and Penshurst Place, he must devote two days to the undertaking. For Hever Castle is shown only on Wednesdays,
and Penshurst on Mondays and Saturdays. There is
another word of caution which may be usefully given,
and it is this—if you ask at Edenbridge or Hever the
road to Penshurst, be sure that you are not sent on to
the station, unless you are really aiming for that dismal
spot. The station is two miles from the house and
village, and there is only a miserable railroad-inn there,
where the louts of the neighbourhood are always
fuddling themselves over thick beer. All these minor
stations on the South Eastern Railroad are far away

from the towns or villages whose names they bear, and more depressing places in which a man may be doomed to spend an hour or two cannot be imagined.

Edenbridge station is about a mile from the village. The church is small, but it gives that air of dignity and peace to the scene which is so seldom absent in rural England. "The walk to Hever," says the Handbook, "across the fields from Edenbridge, is a pleasant one." This was quite enough to set me hunting diligently for it. Most of the townsfolk declared they had never heard of such a walk, and looked upon me with manifest coldness and suspicion, as if I were a sort of cross between a tramp and a policeman. One man told me to go through the churchyard and then go "straight forrards." I went "forrards" until I found myself brought up at a five-barred gate, without track of any kind leading from it. Then I turned back to get fresh directions. An old woman now appeared, and said you *could* go by the fields to Hever Castle, leastways if the paths were not stopped up, but no stranger could find the way. She told me how to go, but unfortunately her directions were far more hopelessly entangled than those which the clown gives to the foot-sore stranger in the pantomime. I therefore gave up the field path, and took with reluctance to the turnpike road. There is not much to be said for this road, except that it is tolerably short—the distance to the castle being three miles. About half way I met with a brother tramp—a man of foreign appearance, very thin and poor, with something tied up in a torn and dirty pocket-handkerchief, and limping slowly and painfully along. He said nothing, and I passed on, but presently the man's starved look and wan face smote upon me, and I looked back. He was hobbling on at the rate of about half a mile an hour. I leaned over a gate and waited till he came up. "You seem tired," said I, "suppose you take this towards your night's lodging," and I offered him sixpence. "I didn't ask for anything, did I?" replied he, with a frightened look. "No, but take it all the same." "I don't want it—not but what I'm poor enough, God knows." "Well then, why not have this trifle?" "I have just come out of prison for begging a penny on the road, and now you are offering me this to get me another month—I didn't ask you for anything, did I? Keep your money." This, upon the whole, is the most wonderful occurrence that has happened to me in all my walks. My thirsty fellow-tramps have generally taken my small contributions in the most obliging manner.

I soon left this poor fellow far behind, and came to Hever Castle—the castle to which Mr. Froude's hero, Henry the Eighth, went a-courting to Anne Boleyn. I saw the moat, and the pleasant gardens round about it, and the red and white roses which have been trained to grow up each side of the principal entrance—but more than that I was not allowed to see. "Master says as no strangers can come in," said the servant girl. Whereupon I took myself off. But at the church I was more successful, thanks to the school-master who keeps the keys. There are two fine brasses in this poor, neglected, dilapidated church—one to the father of Anne Boleyn, in perfect condition, and dated 1538. The other is to the memory of Margaret Cheyne, dated 1419. " Your church is in a shocking state," said I to the schoolmaster. " Yes, sir," he said, " we have no resident gentry now about here, and no one will do anything for it." The pews are evidently ancient, and there is an old oaken staircase, quite rough, going up the tower to the clock. But the damp is cracking the walls in all directions, and it may be doubted whether the tower itself—a picturesque object for miles around—will last very many years longer if something is not done to strengthen it. "The Rector," remarked the schoolmaster, "thinks of appealing to the public for help—we are all very poor about here. It is a dreadfully poor place." I hope the Rector will succeed, for otherwise the old church will come tumbling about his ears one of these days.

Having ascertained the bearings of Penshurst, I struck across the churchyard into some fields eastward of Hever, and at the distance of a mile and a half came upon Chiddingstone, one of those quaint villages which it is worth making a long day's march to see. The timber houses are very old and pretty, and afford a great contrast to the " Squire's house," which is a large, square, unornamental pile of brick and mortar. From this charming village I got sent on, in spite of all my precautions, to Penshurst Station, with its dismal inn, and had to double back the road to my true destination.

That road may scarcely attract the passing glance of persons who know it well, but the stranger's eye will dwell lovingly upon it, for a deep border of green runs on each side of the carriage way, and numbers of beautiful trees overhang this green margin, and keep it cool and shady. These trees, especially on the right-hand side of the road, evidently form part of an old and fine estate—there are cedars, and ash, and yew, which have not grown up by accident. Just beyond is another pretty property, belonging to Mr. Nasmyth, the engineer. On the left hand, glimpses are occasionally caught of the historic house to which we are going, and long before it is reached a path turns into the park from the road. But the best plan is to keep on the road till the village is reached, for you will then go right past the house, which stands only a few hundred yards back, and has nothing between it and you to obstruct the view. A little further on is the small village of Penshurst, consisting of little more than a dozen cottages and a freshly painted inn called the Leicester Hotel, where the accommodation is plain but comfortable, everything about the house being remarkably neat and clean.

A little below the inn, on the opposite side of the way, is a pollarded oak, and that leads beneath a couple of old cottages into the churchyard, through which there is a path to the great house. The cottages form a sort of archway, and are very fine specimens of the timbered building which was in vogue before lath and plaster played the important part they now do in modern dwellings. From the churchyard their appearance is particularly striking. They form a fit introduction to the old church and "castle," and I was glad to hear that Lord de L'Isle would "not have them taken down for any money." He has, indeed, been at considerable expense to keep them in repair—only a small part of the very heavy drain which this estate must have kept up on his purse. Near the door of one of these cottages I noticed an old-fashioned piece of furniture, and begged to be allowed to look at it. It was of oak, curiously carved, and black with age—a sort of cabinet or sideboard. The woman with the keys said it belonged to her husband's family; that the owner had been offered £5 and even £7 for it by "a person as came from London," but that he would not sell it because it "had been such a long time in the family." I could not help thinking that it was much to the cottager's credit to keep his heir-loom, and resist the temptations of that crafty person as came from London.

The day before my visit (2nd October, 1876), there had been "harvest services" in the church, and the decorations were not yet withered. Round the entrance door was a garland of yellow hops, and the pillars inside were adorned with the bloom of the same plant, intertwined with chrysanthemums and other autumn flowers. There was a wreath of apples near the reading desk, bright rosy-cheeked apples, with a great branch of the "crab" near them, and various specimens of the harvest of the district. This is one of the good old simple

customs which is still preserved in many parts of the
country, and which it is to be hoped will survive
the "march of improvement" yet a little longer.
The church has been wholly "restored," but the work
was done with care, and if the edifice has lost much
of the look of antiquity, it has gained in durability,
and will probably now stand for generations to come.
In the south chancel, or Sidney chapel, are several interesting brasses, among them a small and very plain
one—the plainest and rudest I ever saw—inscribed to
"Thomas Bullayen, the sone of Syr Thomas Bullayen,"
whose tomb is at Hever Church. There is no date.
Close by is a mutilated bust, lying close to the
wall upon the ground, supposed to be of the Thomas
Pencester whose family held the Penshurst estate for
two hundred years after the Conquest. There is a brass
to Margaret Sidney, sister to Dorothy, the Saccharissa
of Waller, the said Margaret having died, as is carefully
set forth, on Easter Day, 1558, aged only one year and
three-quarters. There are also two good figures of
Thomas Yden and Agnes his wife (1558), and a large
monument to Robert Sidney, Earl of Leicester, and his
wife, who "lived thirty happy years together, and had
fifteen children, of whom nine died young." In the
north chancel opposite there is a brass to the memory
of some old parson who seems to have had a touch of
humour in him, and who left for posterity this account
of himself and his belongings :—

> " Here lyeth Wᵐ Darkenoll, P·son of this place
> Endynge his ministeri even this yeare of grace 1596.

His father and mother and wyves two by name
 80 88   50 67
John   Jone   and two Margarets all lyved in good fame .
Their severall ages who lyketh to know
Over each of their names the figures do shewe .
The sonnes and daughters now spronge of this race
Are fyve score and od in every place.
   Deceased July 12th anno supradco."

There follow a scriptural "application" and a death's
head and crossbones. But what is strange is that no
record appears in the parish register of any one named
Darkenoll being "parson of this place," although I was
told there used to be a family of that name living in
an old house somewhere in the neighbourhood. In the
tower wall a coffin lid has been inserted, carved in stone,
with a vivid figure apparently clinging to a cross. The
features are contorted as if in pain. "This is supposed
to be the figure of the guardian of Thomas Pencester,"
said the custodian of the church; but who this guardian
was, or why he was thus depicted, there is no one who
can tell.

Adjoining the Church is the Rectory, a house of the
time of Charles the First, thoroughly home-like in its
appearance, and with that bright ornament, a very
pretty garden, in front. A few yards off is the
great "Kentish shrine" of Penshurst, lying long and
low and covering a great space of ground—partly
ancient, partly modern in its external walls, but wearing over all that indescribable look which speaks of the
long past, and of generations which have flourished and
disappeared while these old bricks and stones were
resisting the winds and rains of five hundred winters,

and owners and builders, and all their descendants, and millions of our kind throughout the world, were being swept quietly into the grave.

Yet time had laid its hand heavily upon this house, and but for great care and prodigal expenditure it would ere now have been merely a picturesque ruin. A few years ago, it was found necessary to shore up many of the old rooms, for they had become absolutely dangerous. The most extensive works were necessary to save the structure. These works have been carried out in a spirit of love and devotion—for surely such sentiments may be kindled by such a house as this—by the present owner, Lord de L'Isle. It is a restoration in name as well as in fact which he has attempted—for example, in one part of the building which it was indispensable to take down, every stone was marked as it was removed, and replaced in its original position, under the personal superintendence of Lord de L'Isle himself and his architect, Mr. Devey. The floors were all sinking in, but instead of removing them, a new flooring was laid down, and over that the original boards were carefully placed. The paint and whitewash of Queen Anne's day, and of some later "restorers," have also been got rid of in a great measure, and the work is still being vigorously pressed forward. The burden of preserving such a house as this, and of meeting inch by inch the destructive inroads of time, is one from which many an owner of a princely income would shrink back alarmed.

You cross the old courtyard, and enter the Baron's

Hall, which the best authorities agree must have been
built in or about the year 1341. So little change has
taken place in it that the imagination can almost
revive the scenes which once took place in this famous
hall—can place before these old tables the groups of
knights and retainers who once made merry here, and
recall the great and joyful festivals of harvest home
and Christmas, celebrated with the broad and generous
hospitality of five hundred years ago. The best table
is still at the upper end on the dais, and on each side
of the hall are the tables for retainers and servants—
just as they stood there when the head of the house,
and his family and dependants, assembled to take their
meals together. Around the walls are pieces of arms
and armour belonging to the Sidneys and Leicesters,
and there in the middle of the floor is the great iron
" dog " on which the fire was built—the open timber
roof above is black with the smoke from it. Huge
faggots and logs are laid upon this dog, and the old
hall is so much unchanged, and everything about it
speaks so eloquently of other days, that one almost
involuntarily begins to think that presently a servant
will come and set alight to that wood, and the knights
and retainers will take their places at the tables,
and the blooming Saccharissa herself will perhaps
appear with other ladies of the family, and the feast
will begin. Standing there alone, in the fading light of
an autumn afternoon, the old scenes seem to come back
and the old actors return—the five hundred years are
as if they had not been, and one thinks in a half doubt-

ful way of the many mighty changes which have happened in this land around us, since the bricks of this
old floor and the heavy timbers of yonder lofty roof
were put together. Is it a dream that these vast events
have happened, or that this old hall was once filled with
gay revellers and lovely women and brave men ? Compared with these slowly changing scenes, what does all
human existence seem but a dream ?

When Mr. William Howitt was here in 1838, he
found, as he tells us in his interesting account of his
visit,* the huge carved corbels of the roof lying in the
music gallery, the roof itself in danger of falling down,
and on the outside some leaden vases and urns and
other "monstrosities" placed there by a Mr. Perry,
who, it seems, had married the heiress to the family.
The "monstrosities" have been carted off into the
lumber yard, the roof has been placed in a fair state
of repair, and the grotesque carvings or corbels have
been replaced. To make such a roof as this watertight
would cost a large sum of money—probably would be
all but impossible ; but the brick floor can take no
hurt from a little wet, and the walls are sound, while
there is now no danger of the timbers of the roof
falling. "There is no such roof to be found out of
England," says an archæologist, and he adds that the
tables "are among the earliest pieces of furniture
remaining in England." Lord de L'Isle has done a
good work in putting this interesting part of the old
house into a condition which will, let us hope, enable

* Visits to Remarkable Places, pp. 1—49.

it to resist wind and weather for the other half of the thousand years.

I cannot attempt to play the part of guide to this house, or to describe the numerous portraits and paintings or curiosities which are treasured up within it. That is a work which has often been undertaken, and for the traveller it cannot be more conveniently performed than it is in Murray's "Handbook" for Kent. The portraits have recently been arranged in chronological order, and have been very carefully cleaned and hung in a good light. No visitor to Penshurst will forget the portraits of the Sidney family, especially those of Algernon and Sir Philip Sidney, and of Waller's "Saccharissa,"—the last appearing in this canvas as a bouncing and buxom lass, such as poets are, notwithstanding their sentiment and romance, very apt to fall in love with. Nor can one forget Kneller's portrait of William "the Deliverer," with his long, grave, dyspeptic face; or Holbein's portrait of Edward the Sixth (who gave Penshurst to the Sidneys), with the tinge of red in his hair, his pale countenance, and small dark eyes; or the portrait of Lady Jane Grey, sweet and amiable, a great contrast to the cross-grained, vixenish features of Mary, whose picture hangs beneath. On the sofa in Queen Elizabeth's room I noticed a broken mandolin, looking as if some one had just injured it and laid it there. I asked the housekeeper about it, and she told me that it had belonged to Sir Philip Sidney's mother. It seemed as if it might have been lying in the same place ever

since that worthy lady finished playing her last tune
upon it. Then we have that curious painting by Lely
of Nell Gwynne, in which ample opportunity is afforded
us of knowing what manner of woman, physically, was
this particular favourite of "merry" King Charles, and
a very singular picture representing Queen Elizabeth
dancing at Kenilworth with the Earl of Leicester. As
for the curiosities, there are the riding boots of
Algernon Sidney in the long gallery, a piece of the
shaving glass of Sir Philip Sidney, some wonderful
cabinets of most elaborate workmanship, locks of the
hair of many Sidneys and Leicesters, all recently
gathered into one large glass case ; a table inlaid with
tortoise-shell on silver, and another table (intended for
whist) with the cover most beautifully executed in
needlework ; a collection of family miniatures, exquisitely painted, and much more that it would take
almost a volume to set forth. Many of these objects
are in the private apartments, which are sometimes
shown to visitors of the more quiet description. The
rooms now used are very tastefully fitted up, the tone
and style of the old house being carefully studied in all
details. The library is essentially a room for use and
comfort, not too large, and with a glorious alcove
window in it, as many other of the rooms have—deep,
snug, offering great facilities to the young for mild
flirtations, and beckoning the elder folk to step aside
and meditate ; overlooking, moreover, portions of the
venerable pile outside and charming vistas of the park.
The best books in the collection once at Penshurst, and

18

the most valuable of the Sidney MSS., were carried off by the active-minded Mr. Ireland, whose Shakespeare forgeries also give him some claim to be remembered. Ireland was on good terms with some member of the family, and had the " run of the house," and improved his opportunities by pillaging it as freely as one of Cromwell's soldiers could have done.

Most visitors to the park have dwelt much upon its neglected appearance, and Walpole's sneer has often been quoted : " The park is forlorn ; instead of Saccharissa's cipher carved on the beeches, I should sooner have expected to have found the milk-woman's score." Mr. Howitt speaks of the " silent park," and of " its grass-grown pleasance and its grey walls." Walpole's remark seems a harsh one, but undoubtedly there is something even now about the park which suggests nearly what must have been in his thoughts. I wandered for some hours over it, and the walk produced a melancholy effect upon the mind, for everything has a deserted and mournful air. The rabbits have made large mounds all over the park, and it is necessary to look carefully to one's steps to avoid falling into their holes, which in some places resemble long tunnels for water-pipes. Moreover, the grass is not grass, if one may so speak, but heavy coarse fern and bramble, which you must go far out of your way to avoid, for in some places it is so thick as to be almost impassable. It does not look like a park, but like a very wild common or some half-forgotten wilderness, and this appearance is heightened by the gloomy

spectre which now and then confronts you of a dead
tree, without bark or leaf upon it, struck perhaps by
lightning or dead of mere old age, and now seeming
pitifully to beseech one to take it away. Are these
utterly dead trees never cut down in this park? Certain it is that they are numerous, and present a most
sorrowful aspect.

But the park is by no means neglected, for the
beautiful avenue of limes leading eastwards from
the house has been continued northwards by the planting of some hundreds of young trees. The original
avenue must be very old, and there are still some
splendid oak and ash trees remaining in it, their
younger brethren, which have been put down at their
side to fill up the gaps, looking as if they meant to do
credit to their training and associations. By following
the limes eastwards from the house, and then turning
through a gate to the left about halfway down, this
northerly avenue is reached, and goes for nearly
two miles to Leigh. I followed it almost to the
end, and then struck off to examine a thick clump of
trees not far off. Was this Gamage's Bower? About
half a mile or so up the avenue is the venerable tree
known as Sidney's Oak, now protected by a railing. It
has evidently suffered much since the sketch of it was
taken for Howitt's "Visits to Remarkable Places" (I.,
13)—its top is almost entirely gone, and large branches
have been battered off or mutilated. But its girth is
still great, and its limbs are gigantic. It is a true
monarch of the woods, grand and majestic even in its

decrepitude, and sturdily opposing itself to the strokes
of lightning and the heavy shocks of winter's gales.   It
recalls the description by Virgil of the oak, so happily
imitated by La Fontaine :—

> " Celui de qui la tête au ciel était voisine,
> Et dont les pieds touchaient à l'empire des morts."

Foliage still covers its trunk and branches, but its
shattered head is crowned only with the " monumental
pomp of age."   Not far northward of this venerable
tree there is a grand Spanish chestnut, with one huge
branch lying prone upon the ground, and its trunk
bearing marks of its great age.   Hard by that is a
yew, growing unusually straight, not particularly large,
but unquestionably very old.   Proceeding still further
northward, and returning to the avenue, some magnificent beeches come in sight—beautiful trees still,
though far advanced in years.   One is a mere wreck,
and others are fast going to decay.   These beeches are
the remains of "Saccharissa's Walk," "lofty beeches"
still, but gradually going the road which Saccharissa
and her love-sick poet travelled long ago.

The visitor who strolls to this part of the park will
find himself well rewarded.   To the eastward he will
obtain a fine view over Tunbridge and the distant
country, and if he looks to the south his eye will rest
upon the weather-beaten roof of the Baron's Hall, the
ivy-clad walls beneath it, the tempest-smitten trees
and lonely park, and the purple slopes of the South
Downs, which form a noble background to the " home
of the Sidneys."

CHAPTER XXI.

THE WYE FROM ROSS TO CHEPSTOW.

The "Lion" of Ross. — The Wye. — Goodrich Castle. — Gilpin's
"Analysis" of the Wye.—From Goodrich to Monmouth.—The
"Kymin" and Buckstone.—The Bachelor of Stanton.—A Re-
turned Indian.—The Railroad.—From Monmouth to Chepstow.
—Encroachments on Tintern.—The Wyndcliffe.—What is good
for Rheumatism?—Our Beautiful Inns.

THERE is nothing much more curious at Ross, not
even excepting its ancient buildings, than the tree, or
double tree, which grows inside the church, on the spot
where of old the pew of the "Man of Ross" was placed.
Formerly a tree grew just outside the church window,
but although it was planted by John Kyrle himself,
the rector sacrilegiously cut it down, and what happened? The tree made itself into two, and grew
inside his church instead of outside—thus a double
visitation of wrath fell upon him. The old pews are
gone, but a couple of elm trees still grow within the
church, close to a window. When I saw them in
August, 1876, they had a wan and sickly appearance—
the foliage on them was very slight, and of a light and
delicate shade of green. "It's the hot weather," said
the woman who had the keys; "they don't look so well

as they generally do. The sun strikes upon them from the window, and the ground is all baked and hard outside." Certainly the poor trees had a languid aspect, reminding one of that saddest of all sad sights, a fair young girl in a decline. They are about four inches in diameter, and the tops are frequently cut to prevent them striking against the roof.

There are more roads than one to Monmouth, but the best is that which goes past the Royal Hotel, and over Wilton Bridge, and enables the traveller to take in Goodrich Castle or Symond's Yat on his way. Of Wilton Castle, which dates back to the year 1141, little but a few shapeless stones remain, but the bridge over the Wye still forms a picturesque feature in the landscape. Beyond the small village, the road to the left must be taken, and very soon the Wye makes its appearance, running amid green meadows, with beautifully wooded hills and soft pastoral scenery beyond. Sometimes it flows nearly to the road, rippling along over the stones with a cool and refreshing sound—at others it wanders far off, or completely disappears from view. Presently the ruins of Goodrich Castle are seen in the distance, with the modern house called Goodrich Court nearly opposite, and the river apparently running between. In reality, they are divided by a dingle. Then the road ascends, and we pass an old farm on the right hand, and just beyond it a private park studded with fine elm trees, and soon we come to a street of cottages, with a meeting house and a blacksmith's forge. This is the village of Pencraig. At the foot of it a road

[Page 278.

ENGLISH RIVER SCENE.

THE RIVER WYE, FROM SYMOND'S YAT.

turns suddenly to the left, and a walk of a mile and a half further will bring the traveller to Goodrich.

The castle is not so beautiful a ruin as Raglan, but it stands on a far more commanding position than the home of the brave old Marquis of Worcester, and consequently it affords an enchanting view of a long stretch of the valley of the Wye. The glimpses of scenery which may be caught through the broken and crumbling windows of the castle surpass all that poet or painter has placed before us. No wonder that Goodrich satisfied even the learned Prebendary of Salisbury, the Rev. William Gilpin, who, although a true lover of nature, was a little too much inclined to measure everything by rule and line. His "Observations on the River Wye" might unfavourably prejudice a reader who had not yet been charmed with the much more genial work on "Forest Scenery." Take, for instance, his "analysis" of the "sylvan Wye":—"The most perfect river-views, thus circumstanced, are composed of four grand parts; the *area*, which is the river itself; the *two side-screens*, which are the opposite banks, and mark the perspective; and the *front-screen*, which points out the winding of the river." He then proceeds with the details of his analysis, thus: "The *ornaments* of the Wye may be ranged under four heads—*ground*—*wood*—*rocks*—and buildings." Perhaps the Wye is not the only river which can boast of the same ornaments. With Goodrich, however, Mr. Gilpin was quite content. "This view," he says, "which is one of the grandest on the river, I should not scruple to call *correctly picturesque;* which is seldom the character of a purely natural scene." He complains elsewhere that Nature is " seldom correct in composition." It must be admitted, however, that the author's own taste was not always faultless, or he would not have preferred those rude and hideously coloured illustrations of his to what he calls the " unpleasant opposition of black and white."

In pursuing the journey to Monmouth, we have to leave Goodrich church on the right, and the wood, called by the folks hereabouts the " coppice " or " coppage " (properly, *copped*), to the left. It is a hard walk from here to Monmouth—six up-hill, tough, and dusty miles. Yet the road has beauties enough to show to reward the man who can truly say that he belongs to the brotherhood of Walkers, even if he cannot quite comply with the exacting conditions laid down by Thoreau : " If you are ready to leave father and mother, and brother and sister, and wife and child and friends, and never see them again ; if you have paid your debts, and made your will, and settled all your affairs, and are a free man, then you are ready for a walk." Soon after you have passed a lodge with a cross over it—which is the entrance to Judge Herbert's house, the " Rocklands "—you will come to a spring by the road-side, Nature's own gift to the tired wayfarer. Pass it not unregarded, O thirsty walker ! Never was there such cool and delicious water ; not all the champagne of France is to be compared with it. Now the " copped " hill is at our back, and the Great and Little

Dowards in front, and all the country has a stern and wild aspect, for we are approaching the border land of Wales. Ere long we reach the secluded village of Whitchurch, with its old-fashioned "Crown" Inn standing all across it. To the traveller approaching it from the other direction, the road seems to be suddenly swallowed up in the inn. A peaceful village, where, if anywhere, a man might spend his days,

> " Free from the sick fatigue, the languid doubt,
> Which much to have tried, in much been baffled, brings."

It was dark before I arrived at Monmouth. Shadows crept gradually over the lovely country ; the trees threw deeper darkness upon the road, the stars were hidden, the very path was difficult to find. Suddenly from a thick wood, a black mass climbing high above the road, a mournful and boding cry fell upon the ear :

> " It was the owl that shrieked, the fatal bellman
> Which gives the stern'st good night."

At last the twinkling lights of the old town came in sight, the town where Henry the Fifth was born, as that thorough Welshman, Captain Fluellen, is careful to remind him : "All the water in Wye cannot wash your Majesty's Welsh blood out of your body, I can tell you that."

And a charming town it is, to my mind, with its ancient bridge over the Monnow, its two or three old churches, its pleasant market place, its civil and homely people,—more Welsh than English in their blood— and the glorious scenery which surrounds it. A dozen

years and more had passed since last I trod its streets,
years of much wandering in distant lands; but I remembered every nook and corner of them, and half
involuntarily looked round for the faces which once
brightened them, now "painted as on the azure of
eternity." In these old inland towns, nothing changes
but human life. Every house, every street remains the
same—it is only when we look for the friends that are
gone that the dread work of Time strikes upon the
heart.

If you go across Wye bridge, and up the narrow path
which runs by the side of the road as you turn to the
left, you will find yourself brought in due season to a
wood. Through that, amidst plentiful green and shade,
the traveller may find his way to the very summit
of the hill called the "Kymin"—following the well-
marked path till he comes to a gate which shuts it off,
and then turning to the right. There is a shorter road,
just outside the wood, but it is full of rough stones and
glare and all manner of evils. The wood is delightful
—full of young birch and elm, and hazel-nut tree and
mountain ash, the last of which keeps its old names
among the Monmouthshire folk of the "quicken" or
"service" tree. There are still many "benighted"
persons in this county and in Wales who regard the
"Rowan" or "Witchen" tree as a potent spell against
the evil-eye. Evelyn assures us that ale and beer made
out of its berries "is an incomparable drink, familiar in
Wales," but it never fell to my lot to be offered a
glass of the wizard-drink, and I think most Welshmen

of the present day would prefer a glass of old-fashioned ale, they being an honest and simple sort of folk.

From the top of the Kymin the eye wanders over the Wye and the town to the Sugarloaf mountain at Abergavenny, and to the Black Mountains of Breconshire, and over the Forest of Dean. There is a mean little shed here, put up in the first year of this century, and then called a "Temple." "The frieze," says *Murray,* "is decorated with medallions of British admirals," and I remember them well—coarse, common, in all respects abominable ; yet the admiration of simple Evan Evans and Morgan Jones and their lasses, who often came up from below with picnic parties. Now frieze and medallions have all but disappeared, and the "Temple" itself is a disreputable-looking ruin. In the south-east, that curious rocking-stone, the "Buckstone," can be discerned, and there is a path from the Kymin to it, chiefly through woods or across fields. You pass a little inn called the "Duke of York" on the way, and then reach the turnpike road, from whence a narrow track runs up the hill-side. Follow this track till you reach a gate, climb over, leave the ruins of a sheep-cote or small cottage to your right, and presently you will emerge upon Stanton Common—a common, take it all in all, without an equal, standing high above the high hills which are near to it, and looking far over the Black Mountains and the Forest of Dean. The home-like village and church of Stanton are just below. The site of the Buckstone is marked by a small flag-staff—a stone weighing hundreds of tons, and yet

poised upon a piece of rock scarcely two feet broad,
like a huge top standing upon its peg. The hill runs
down a thousand feet sheer below it, and the stone
inclines over at an acute angle, and can be rocked by a
strong man. An old fellow, whom I overtook on the
common, told me that the froliesome youth of Stanton
had one night come up here armed with "picks" and
crowbars, but could not move it. "It is considered,"
this old man explained to me, "as it was washed there
when the world was drownded." My friend was scarcely
less worthy of attention than the stone. He was a very
ugly little old man, with staring eyes, and great front
teeth, like a picture of a gnome. He told me that
he kept some "ship" (sheep) out at grass near Monmouth; they had the tick, and he had been to see
them. "There's allus summat wrong!" said he; "if it
aint the tick it's summat else."

"Are you married?" I asked.

"Not I," said this scarecrow, with a hideous smile;
"don't I live as I've a mind to? Could I do that if I
was married? Sometimes I have thought of taking a
missis, but there never was a conweniency without an
ill-conweniency, and so I don't do it."

"But have you ever had a fair chance?"

"Chance!" said he, stopping short in astonishment,
"why lots of women have been after me. They come
in offering to help clean up my cottage, but *I* know
what they're after. They're after *me*. I can't abear
them, but they *will* come. Would you get married if
you were me?" I pondered this question very seriously

in my mind, and replied in the Socratic manner, by
assuring him that whichever course he took he would
be sure eventually to wish he had taken the other. "I
can cook my own food, and clean my own things—what
do I want with a missis?"

"Good-bye," said I; "you are a wiser man than some
people I know; mind you cure your ship of the tick
before you get a missis."

How white are the streets of Stanton, how grey its
houses!—and then there is that charming old church,
with the remains of an ancient cross just outside the
gates, and the old font inside, of which *Murray* says,
that it was "apparently fashioned out of a Roman
altar." All is so clean and calm and venerable in
appearance that one is reluctant to go on any further.
And, in truth, the people whose lot is cast here seem
to be unwilling to change it: there is an old farm
below the church in which the worthy farmer has lived
for upwards of half a century; and in the churchyard—
a friendly churchyard, where the last shelter of our
mother earth ought rather to be called a bed among
violets and roses than a grave—I noticed a tombstone
to the memory of Alexander Gibbon aged 91, his wife
aged 96, a daughter aged 19, another daughter aged 55,
and "Sarah Foster, their faithful servant for sixty-four
years, aged 87." Close by the church there is a vicarage
overlooking a wide and varied landscape, and an easily
discovered path leads to a point called the "Double
View"—a scene which must not be passed unnoticed.
The Wye can scarcely be discovered in more lovely

guise. The return to Monmouth had better be made by the turnpike road until you come to the " Duke of York " Inn, from whence the path through the wood may be taken as before.

This little house is a very good example of the Monmouthshire hostelry—very plain, but not uncomfortable. When I was there last August, I found the innkeeper and his wife, an old and worthy couple, busily engaged in preparing their dinner. The old man asked me to join them: " We can only offer you a piece of bacon, some peas, and new potatoes," said he, " but such as they are you are freely welcome." But who can dine at noon save a true countryman ? I contented myself with my ale and a talk. " I never want to go far from this part again," said the old man ; " there's no place like England."

" Have you ever been far away ? " said I.

" Why, yes, indeed, sir ; I was round the Cape to India and back, and glad enough am I to be here."

" Now don't begin to talk about India," said his wife, " nobody wants to hear about it." Why, thought I, this old fellow is no more allowed to talk about his Indian experiences than the Governor of a Presidency at a London dinner party.

" Do you think it is as hot here as there, sir ? " continued the landlord, when he had recovered his spirits a little, and disregarding the words and gestures of his wife. I told him I was quite sure it was not. " So I tells 'em," he cried out in glee, " so I tells 'em, but they only laugh at me. Yes, indeed. When I tells 'em as I have seen a dozen men die of cholery in one day, they don't believe a word I say."

" Well, I believe you," said I; " you are not saying a word that is not true."

" Why, theer now," said the old man triumphantly to his wife, " when *I* tells 'em about the East Ingies, they go away and say, ' that old Jenkins be a d—— *leear*, so I *drap* it. Yes, sure."

How many burra-sahibs have I seen in England who were treated, much to their surprise, with just as little consideration as poor old Jenkins of the " Duke of York." He had been a soldier in the 32nd Regiment, and showed me several relics of his army days. I hope that if these pages meet the eye of any of his customers they will desist from denouncing him as a " leear " when he spins them a yarn about the Ingies. Englishmen pretend to be very proud of India, and yet never hear its name mentioned without a yawn.

If the pedestrian chooses to go from Monmouth to Raglan Castle or Symonds Yat—and neither ought to be missed—the roads are good and full of interest; or he may pass through Stanton to the still wild and romantic Forest of Dean, with its mining villages, and its foresters, with their ways and manners which have been little affected by the great tide of our wonderful civilisation.

They have made a railroad through the valley of the Wye, even through that lovely part of it which extends from Monmouth to Chepstow. Was this, also, one of the " urgent necessities " of the age ? Already there were three ways of passing from one town to the other, and all good—by boat, carriage, or on foot. Were they not enough? The wise tourist will leave the iron horse to the bagman and his parcels, and will still tramp his way along this gem of a valley on foot, noticing as he goes that the railroad, with all its precious freight, is obliged to plunge into great holes in the earth and rock at intervals, and be swallowed out of sight. And a very good thing too.

From Monmouth to Chepstow it is a walk of sixteen miles. For five miles or so the river flows to the right hand, becoming more beautiful at every movement ere it is lost in the Severn. Then a bridge is crossed, and we arrive at the village of St. Briavel's, which can still boast of its ancient castle. Two miles further on is Llandogo, lying at the foot of richly wooded hills, and with a pretty little church standing close by the river. Cottages are dotted among the woods just as Wordsworth described them :—

> " ———————— Pastoral farms,
> Green to the very doors, and wreaths of smoke
> Sent up, in silence, from among the trees."

The river here begins to assume a yellower hue, like that of the "sandy-bottomed Severn" to which it is fast approaching. It still keeps a very devious course, sometimes running far away from the road, sometimes looking as if at a short distance it went quite across it and cut it off. A few sloops or other light craft also begin to make their appearance—generally stuck high and dry in the mud. It is not impossible that an active trade may yet grow up between this part of the valley and the Severn ports. At Brockweir the people are of a pushing and enterprising character, and have already opened up for themselves a thriving business with Bristol. Some day a large town may grow up here, for the Brockweir hoops are already sought for eagerly in the markets. Nearer still to Tintern there are greater signs of life and activity than there used to be —a new bridge with a tramway, black and smoky works, abundance of soot, blacks, dirt, fuss, and noise. Then come a heap of ugly little cottages, higgledy-piggledy, several public-houses or beer-shops (the ever present curse of all this fair land), one very neat and cosy inn, called the "Royal George," and then Tintern Abbey, desecrated by its surroundings. It has endured great wrongs during the last few years. Tea-gardens, beer-shops, and wretched cabins press close up to it, and a gang of beggars waylay the visitor on the road or besiege the gates. The ruin itself is well cared for, but the neighbourhood does its best to degrade it to the level of a suburban show. The visitors appear to be more numerous than ever; and yet I remember, nearly fifteen years ago, going there one moonlight night to have a quiet look at the Abbey, and finding upwards of eight hundred persons enjoying themselves within the beautiful walls. Bottles were popping off in all directions, and the grass was white with the paper in which what the people called "the grub" had been packed up. It is rare, however, to fall in with such a drove as this, except during the full moon in September—popularly known as the harvest moon—when Swansea, Cardiff, Newport, and Bristol, send thousands to see the venerable Abbey.

Gilpin, whose criticisms upon the Wye it is hard to read with respect, calls Tintern " ill-shaped," and says of it, " a number of gable ends hurt the eye with their regularity, and disgust it by the vulgarity of their shape." He recommends knocking some of them off with a mallet, " particularly those of the cross aisles, which are both disagreeable in themselves, and confound the perspective." Few who look at it from road or river, and mark its exquisite proportions, its glorious east window, its calm and queenly beauty, will feel inclined to receive this criticism with patience. Rather will they think with Whateley that Tintern " suggests every idea which can occur in a seat of devotion, solitude and desolation."

Just before reaching the Abbey, the railroad is fortunately obliged to betake itself to a tunnel, in which it remains for some little distance, so that trains and " tracks " do not litter up the scenery directly in front of the ruin. But it has done much to spoil the banks a little further on—those banks which used to be an unbroken mass of green from the summit to the water's edge, with a strip of meadow below, and the river lapping its sides. Now, about three parts of the way down the cliff, we see an embankment, deep cuttings, fences, telegraph posts, a railroad,—what would Wordsworth say if he could see his beloved Tintern thus invaded ? Soon, however, the excessive steepness of the cliffs has obliged the engineer to take his work out of sight again, and the line makes a sudden plunge round a sharp curve into the solid rock, head foremost. What becomes of it afterwards the happy traveller on foot will probably feel no curiosity to ask.

Through that pretty little toy, the "Moss Cottage," one still makes the ascent of the Wyndcliffe. Rheumatism lords it over this abode, and has seized the poor old woman who lives in it, and tied up her hands into strange knots, and persecuted her bitterly in all her joints. "I have lived here for thirty-five years," she said to me, "but now I can scarcely move. Can you tell me of anything that is good for the rheumatics, sir?"

"The oil of mustard is good, but I am afraid your house is very damp." The wet was trickling down the walls in a small and steady stream.

She shook her head. "My husband died here of the rheumatics, and I suppose I shall have to go too. I live here all the year round, and in the winter it is so damp that you could wring the water out of the clothes." Her knuckles looked like the "bosses" which grow on trees. From this poor old lady's damp cell it is, as everyone who has been here knows, a steep climb up the hill, not to be recommended to ladies, for the steps are often slippery and awkward, and if the air is not very clear, there is less to be seen from the top of the cliff than from the road. From the Chepstow side the ascent is far more easy and can, indeed, be managed the greater part of the distance in a carriage. As for the view when the weather is favourable, it must, like other wondrous things in nature, be left undescribed—although there is a very good account of it in *Murray's* Handbook. Immediately below is the curious farm of Llancaut, in the shape of a horse-shoe, with the Wye running round it like a streak of silver. To the right is Piercefield, those beautiful grounds through which the traveller is free to walk, and which will take him a long way on the road to Chepstow, where, at the "Beaufort Arms," he may find a fair night's lodging.

Can anyone tell why it is that at all these hotels only two or three things fit to be eaten are known to the landlords? For breakfast you are invariably offered "'am an' eggs," while for dinner in this region the *menu* is never altered—"hox-tail, sole, and a cutlet." The waiter has no suggestions—he runs off his old list glibly, fidgets the spoons about, gives his dirty neck-tie a twist, and then stands smiling vacantly. "Steak or chop,"—you *must* want one of those? No?—then try the cold meat; or come now, what do you say to some briled 'am? Not like that either? The waiter, who smells horribly of brandy-and-water, and has a parlous red face, begins to look upon you askance, as a very objectionable person. Evidently a "gent as is hard to please." Will you have some poached heggs? Last week there were some kidneys in the house, but they are all gone. Perhaps it is quite as well that they are. The visitor, feeling rather rueful, mildly suggests salmon,

You might as well ask for the moon. And yet there
are at least two rivers not far off in which the finest
flavoured salmon in the world is caught. But you
stand a much better chance of getting a Severn salmon
in Bond Street than you do at Chepstow or Gloucester.

THE END.

META HOLDENIS.

From the French of VICTOR CHERBULIEZ,

Author of "Samuel Brohl and Company," etc.

Paper, 50 cents.   -   -   -   Cloth, 75 cents.

From the New York Evening Post.

"The story is a good one in itself, wholly unlike the story we expect in a novel. M. Cherbuliez is an artist, a genius, to whom all things are possible; else his success in writing this story in another than his own personality—creating a distinct individual, and then making his creature tell it from his own point of view, with perfect verisimilitude—would have been impossible. It is admirable in itself, and as an example of the high art of narration."

From the New York Express.

"A powerful story, whose characters are clearly portrayed, and whose accessories of landscapes and the like are beautifully painted."

From the New York World.

"Cherbuliez is, after Balzac and George Sand, the first novelist of France. He is more of an artist, and has more insight into human motives and actions, than other contemporary French novelists."

From the New York Sun.

"A companion-piece to 'Samuel Brohl and Company,' and a book which should renew the notable success gained by the English version of the latter novel. In the present volume we trace the fortunes of a winsome and insinuating governess, so happily fashioned by Nature for strategy and wiles as to continually delude herself. As we have previously spoken of Cherbuliez in connection with 'Samuel Brohl and Company,' we need only add that the action of 'Meta Holdenis' is somewhat more fervid and vigorous, and the development of the plot more piquant to curiosity. We commend it to the reader as the most captivating translation from the French which has been printed in a twelvemonth."

From the Philadelphia Item.

"'Meta Holdenis' holds the attention of the reader throughout, as the analysis of character; the dialogue, the descriptions, and the details of the novel, are all in Cherbuliez's most animated and sparkling manner."

From the Hartford Courant.

"Anything more skillfully wrought out than the character of 'Meta Holdenis' we have not met in a long time."

From the Boston Courier.

"The story is artfully contrived and graphically told, with that genius for the dexterous management of details which all Frenchmen seem to possess in some measure, but which M. Cherbuliez has in an eminent degree."

D. APPLETON & CO., 549 & 551 Broadway, New York.

SCHOOLS AND MASTERS OF PAINTING,

With an Appendix on the

PRINCIPAL GALLERIES OF EUROPE.

By A. G. RADCLIFFE.

1 vol., small 8vo.......................Cloth, $3.00.

"The volume is one of great practical utility, and may be used to advantage as an artistic guide-book by persons visiting the collections of Italy, France, and Germany, for the first time. The twelve great pictures of the world, which are familiar by copies and engravings to all who have the slightest tincture of taste for art, are described in a special chapter, which affords a convenient stepping-stone to a just appreciation of the most celebrated masterpieces of painting. An important feature of the work, and one which may save the traveler much time and expense, is the sketch presented in the Appendix, of the galleries of Florence, Rome, Venice, Paris, Dresden, and other European collections."—*N. Y. Tribune.*

"Mrs. Radcliffe is a judicious and an entertaining guide, thoroughly acquainted with her subject, and writing in a style that is happily free from the disgusting cant of pretended connoisseurship. She leads her readers through the great galleries, discoursing in a plain, easily-understood language. She has collected a large amount of useful information, and binds the divisions of her subjects together with a thread of philosophical thought."—*Saturday Evening Gazette.*

"Admirably illustrated throughout, and presenting as it does the different schools in an orderly and methodical manner, it commends itself strongly to the art-student and the artist, its value to them being enhanced by the Appendix, with its catalogue of the noted art-galleries of Europe."—*Detroit Free Press.*

"A work that deserves a wide sale, and one that is especially valuable and suggestive to those who desire a knowledge of the different schools of painting, from the earlier periods to the present time."—*Pittsburg Commercial.*

"'Schools and Masters of Painting, with an Appendix on the Principal Galleries of Europe,' will, we are sure, meet with a flattering welcome from the public. It is at once historical and descriptive, giving the reader a clear though somewhat minute idea of what has been achieved in this department of the fine arts. The author has not omitted to sketch every part of her interesting subject, conveying in the least space consistent with the purpose designed for the work all the material facts with which the public care to interest themselves."—*Troy Times.*

"Mrs. A. G. Radcliffe, the author of this book, has done a useful work in giving, within a moderate compass, a history of the art of painting, from the most ancient times to our day, with brief accounts of the more famous painters and their works. The information which she has here gathered can be found only in a number of tomes, of which the size and cost put them beyond the purse and time of the larger portion of general readers. But, having consulted the best authorities, and made herself mistress of what they have told, she here combines the pith of their works in a clear and interesting manner, with an easy and practiced pen."—*N. Y. Evening Mail.*

NEW YORK: D. APPLETON & CO., PUBLISHERS.